WIRED TRUTH

PARADISE CRIME THRILLERS BOOK 10

TOBY NEAL

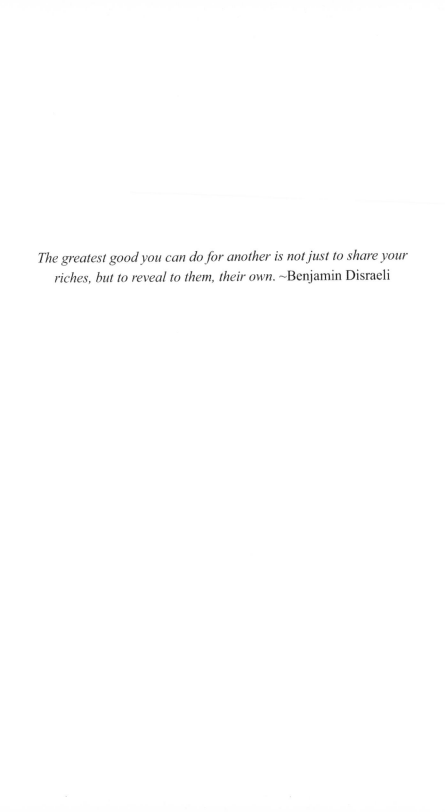

The greatest good you can do for another is not just to share your riches, but to reveal to them, their own. ~Benjamin Disraeli

CHAPTER ONE

Two years after Wired Courage
Sophie: Day One

"DIAMONDS ARE NOT FOREVER." Henry Childer, manager of Finewell's Auction House Honolulu, had a damp handclasp and a plummy British accent. "My diamonds are gone, and I need them found by next week."

Sophie Smithson gestured to the seating area in front of her desk, and wiped her hand on her narrow black pants, out of his view. "Please have a seat, Mr. Childer, and you can tell me all about it. You've come to the right place—Security Solutions specializes in confidential investigations. I have some documents for you to sign that will clarify things. You can review them while I fix us some tea."

Childer looked her over as he took a seat, clearly surprised at her accent. "Delightful to encounter a fellow countryman in this place, and a cup of tea as well, Ms. Smithson." He tugged a handkerchief from his front pocket and mopped his shiny forehead, pale eyes blinking rapidly. "Infernal Hawaii heat. I don't know how you stand it."

Sophie set a computer tablet, already loaded with the company's intake forms and disclosures, at the man's elbow. "Actually, I'm American and Thai, but educated in Europe." She walked over to a glossy wood credenza and pushed a button. A coffee and tea service, along with the equipment for preparation, rose from within. Paula, her assistant, cleaned and stocked it daily, and all Sophie had to do was press a button to begin the water heating. "Do you take lemon or milk in your tea?"

"Milk and two sugars, please. Anything can be endured with a spot of tea, they say, but I'm afraid this is a most distressing situation."

"You said diamonds are missing?" Sophie assembled the tea things on a tray.

"I'm manager of the Honolulu branch of Finewell's Auction House, as I told you. Are you familiar with our company? We're the premier auction house for luxury collectibles in the Western Hemisphere."

That was a big claim to make, but Sophie nodded politely. "Please elaborate on how you came to have the diamonds, and what you know about their disappearance."

"The stones are part of a family-owned set that is being auctioned off next weekend. They arrived at our vault and were authenticated upon arrival—all part of our protocol. We cannot vouch for something that is not truthfully represented."

Once she had their cups prepared, Sophie arranged them on a tray and returned, setting the beverages down on the low table in front of the couch where Childer sat. She took a sleek modern armchair across from him and propped her own computer tablet on her knee, tapping to wake it up. She dosed her dark Thai tea with honey, and began inputting details for his case into a new file.

"This appears to be in order." Childer stashed a pair of reading glasses in his breast pocket, and handed her back the intake information. Sophie scanned the forms as he lifted his teacup. He pursed pink lips and blew upon his tea, then took a sip. "Excellent, my dear.

The set was received, verified as authentic, and stored in our secure vault. All was in order at that time; I watched a video of that process and signed off on it per usual."

Sophie held up a hand. "I see, from this application, that you are hiring Security Solutions yourself. Not as a representative of Finewell's."

"Correct." Childer's cup rattled in its saucer as he set it down.

"I see. Please, go on."

"It's part of my role to oversee preparing the items for sale—photographing them for the publicity catalogs and whatnot. I went to the vault to pull the set for the photographer, and it was gone. I was most perturbed, but had the presence of mind to reschedule the photography shoot. I verified that the other items for that weekend's auction were all accounted for. Only the diamonds had disappeared; the parure included a necklace, earrings, a ring, a bracelet, and even a hair clip. Assessed value was three million dollars."

Sophie blinked at the cost. "Why didn't you notify the police?"

"A theft from our supposedly secure location would be a great scandal. Terrible for the company, and catastrophic for me personally. That's why I'm here on my own dime, as the Americans say." Childer dabbed his mouth with a paper napkin. "I will, of course, disclose the theft if we are not able to reclaim the jewels by next Friday."

"The sale is next Saturday, you said?" Sophie frowned. "Today is Thursday. Eight days is not long to find something like this. That's cutting it close."

"All I can ask is that you try." Childer reached into the inside pocket of his suit jacket and removed a checkbook. "What do you require for a deposit?"

After the contracts were signed and funds exchanged, Childer pointed a plump finger at Sophie. "I researched whom to approach. I want *you* to work on this for me. I can't have this case given to someone who won't treat it with the sensitivity it deserves."

"Mr. Childer." Sophie set her tablet down. "I appreciate your confidence in me, but I'm CEO of Security Solutions. I no longer personally handle cases."

"Please." Childer placed his hands palm-to-palm and bowed a little in her direction. "I looked for the best private investigators and company available, and was delighted to find Security Solutions right here in Honolulu. I was even more impressed with you personally." He ticked off her accomplishments on his fingers. "A trained ex-FBI agent with a background in tech. Inventor of the Data Analysis Victim Information Database crime solving software, and CEO of the top-ranked security company in the United States with a seventy-five percent case closure rate." He gave her a frank once-over. "And a goddess in the flesh who makes a lovely cup of tea."

Sophie smiled at the praise, and ducked her head. "That last part has little actual application to crime solving. I will have to run this by Kendall Bix, our President of Operations. He is in charge of case assignments."

"But you'll consider it? Tell me you will."

"I'll consider it. You've caught me at a vulnerable moment, Mr. Childer. I've been up to my eyebrows in quarterly reports. Who wouldn't rather get into the field, while a clock is ticking, to solve the mystery of a set of missing diamonds?" She stood, smoothing sleek black pants made for movement, and braced herself to shake his damp hand again. "We'll need to come in to review your video footage and see the scene of the crime, as it were. I'll be in touch."

CHAPTER TWO

Connor: Day One

CONNOR SHUT his eyes as he stood on the launch platform, imagining his way through each stage of the challenging obstacle course ahead, breathing deeply to oxygenate himself. In the more than two years since he'd voluntarily joined the ninja training program at the Yām Khûmkạn's fortress, he had spent countless hours in visualization and intense physical practice. He had never been as hard and fit as he was now—but, as the Master had taught him, the real battle was always in the mind.

Today was the culmination of two years of training. He just had to make it through the course and across a gauntlet of hot lava rocks while fighting five opponents, and then he'd be standing in front of the Master . . . a graduate.

The gong sounded.

Connor launched himself into space, reaching for the first of a series of steel rings hanging over the compound's water supply pond.

The rings were all about timing and momentum. Connor let nothing into his mind but the next swinging handhold in front of him as his shirtless body, honed as a blade, reflected back from the glassy surface of the water. He flew unerringly through the challenge, deaf to the yelling and cheering of the watching trainees, three-deep around the edge of the course, a border of dense black *gi* and blurred faces.

He should not have looked at them, because as he flipped off of the last ring, his momentum slipped, just for a moment, and his bare feet barely caught on the wooden landing platform.

Connor threw himself forward, not letting himself lose traction, leaping onto the rolling barrels next.

Each big wooden cask was hand-cranked in a different direction by a ninja, and Connor leaped from one to the next, moving boldly to keep his forward movement. He focused on a single spot on each barrel, imagining they were stationary, propelling himself relentlessly.

He shut out the random bellows of the trainees turning the cranks and even the stinging surprise of bamboo whips held by ninjas lashing his legs as he jumped across the rapidly shifting surfaces. A roar of excitement went up as Connor reached safety on a small platform between two huge, upright wooden logs.

The heavy beating of a *taiko* drum, knocking off the seconds, penetrated his concentration. He didn't just have to make it through the course. *He was being timed, too.*

Connor tilted his head to look up at notches ascending the heavy logs. The "salmon ladder" obstacle was a tough one—for this challenge, he had to heave himself upward, hanging from a crossbar, hefting the bar upward from notch to notch until he reached the top.

The salmon ladder was all about strength, rhythm and accuracy, and he'd practiced this obstacle many a time. Connor spread his arms and leaped up to grasp the staff.

His fingers failed to connect, slithering off the wood—*it was dark with oil!* He hit the platform in a crouch, almost falling to his knees.

Behind him, around him, beyond him, the Yām Khûmkạn acolytes shouted and yelled. The trainees were seldom allowed to give voice—but during the test of one of their peers, they had free rein. They gave tongue like a band of wolves howling for blood.

Connor considered for a precious second how to keep his grip on the bar. He visualized how he would grab the wood, and every swift movement of his lower body to heave himself higher. He took another second to regulate his breathing and heart rate and narrow his focus, even as the noise of the crowd and the sense of time ticking by sawed at his nerves.

Connor shot up from the ground, grasping the pole overhand with one hand, and underhand with the other, guarding against the slippery spin of the oiled pole. He pulled up his lower body using his abs, and then, used the momentum of his swinging legs to heave himself up—*higher and higher and higher.*

The sound of the crowd reached Connor in his distant, focused place as he stepped off the salmon ladder at the top of the logs onto a tiny, unprotected platform. Space and depth yawned around him; the earliest of morning breezes chilled his exposed skin as he assessed the latest challenge.

A cable ran between the peaked roofs of two of the complex's buildings. Dangling from that cable was a rope with one end hooked to his platform.

Connor lifted the rope and gauged the distance from his base to another platform all the way across the courtyard.

He'd never practiced this swing, only seen it attempted by other trainees at their graduations—and most didn't make it, coming up too low to the landing area. Considering that, he grasped the rope well above a handily-placed knot, and jumped higher as he took off so that he caught hold of the rough hemp above where his arms could reach. He launched himself into space, generating power by swinging his legs.

That fickle morning breeze sliced across his bare skin and brought tears to his narrowed eyes as he focused his gaze on the rapidly approaching landing platform. For a second it seemed that his aim had been true—but now he was coming up too high, well above the edge of the platform.

Connor refused to think of the stone courtyard so far below, and with less than a split second to decide, he twisted his body forward, letting go of the rope and falling through the air. He landed on the platform, almost losing his balance, and steadied himself with a hand on the support beam.

He raised his arms in victory, absorbing the cry of the watching crowd, and then scaled down the pole onto the ancient roof.

This section of the obstacle course was his favorite to watch others try to perform, though he'd never been allowed to practice it. Alert for traps, Connor ran on light feet across the spine of the hand-quarried slate, careful never to land more than a fraction of a second in any one spot on the crumbling old tiles, his energy and weight always projected forward . . . and he was making good progress, too, until an entire section of the roof fell away under his flying feet. The large four-foot square must have been rigged to come loose the moment he touched it.

Connor spared a glance toward the ground as the broken section slid downward. The densely packed observers below were already running, scattering to avoid the asteroid plummeting in their direction. He surfed the roof section as it accelerated, and at just the right moment, launched himself off it, landing spread-eagled on the roof's surface, clinging with hands and feet.

The ancient, rough stone tiles cracked and slithered under the impact of his body. Connor pulled himself up with coiled energy from his core and scrabbled forward across the rough surface faster than the tiles could come loose.

He made it across that particular roof, and launched over the five-foot opening to the next building with ease. Avoiding the roofline now, he made his way around the courtyard on the side of the roof, raining loose tiles on those below, and making up the seconds he had lost in earlier challenges.

He slithered down a drain pipe and landed on solid ground, turning to face his final challenge: the gauntlet.

The final course stretched before him: a long path of coals bordered by hot bricks, with opponents holding staffs on either side. His "old" mind screamed that the gauntlet was impossible; that he'd be burned and bruised and never make it the hundred yards distance to stand in front of the Master.

His "new" mind understood that pain was merely a neurological signal, that time and space could be manipulated, and that he could stand in front of the Master's dais without so much as a blister. He was in charge of his body and of the elements around him. He could shape energy into whatever he wanted.

Connor shut his eyes and mentally shaped the smoking coals of the gauntlet into the soft, springy mat of a combat ring, a bouncy and supportive surface that absorbed his every move and amplified his strength as he ran and fought, whirling easily, all the way to the end.

He held that image clearly in his mind, and ran forward onto the hot coals.

There was only now: the *now* of his opponents' eyes, of their movements, of his counter moves, of that moment when he yanked a staff away and turned to battle the next ninja trying to hit him. He moved like a feather, like water, like wind across the coals, warmth and energy carrying him effortlessly along—and then there was the next one, and the next and the next and the next.

His dreamlike state was only broken when he yanked one of his opponents onto the path, and the man rolled, screaming in agony, out of the coals.

Connor almost felt the burning, the bruises through the man's projected agony—but he brushed them aside and faced his last fight, knocking the man back as if he were made of cardboard and stepping off of the gauntlet's path onto the cool stone of the courtyard.

Weirdly, he missed the warmth and power of the coals. They'd strengthened him.

Connor raised the staff he'd ripped away from an opponent high overhead. He walked forward to the Master seated on his dais, the roar of applause ringing in his ears. He bowed, lowering the staff to the ground at the Master's feet. He dropped to kneel before the man with his hands open, palms up and resting on his knees.

At last silence fell. Connor felt the collective straining of the trainees to hear the voice of the Master.

"You have done well in your studies." The Master's voice, that mellifluous instrument of influence, washed over him like a benediction, along with a snow-white robe he draped over Connor's shoulders. Connor looked up into the man's distinctive, dark purple eyes. "You have proved yourself worthy of the number you have been given."

Back when Connor had joined Thailand's clandestine spy agency, the Yām Khûmkạn, he had submitted to his head being shaved and a number inked onto the back of his scalp. Hair was allowed to grow over the tattoo until the time of graduation, and he still didn't know what that number was. Recruits who graduated were renamed by that number and the function that the master assigned them. Recruits who did not graduate never knew what their name might have been—it was branded off of their scalp when they were ejected from the fortress.

Everything Connor had been taught and challenged to do was more intense than what was asked of normal recruits. He had spent more time with the Master in personal training than any other. He was being groomed for the partnership they'd forged, bringing together their unique talents to influence world order.

Connor kept his eyes shut as the Master drew his knife. He did not allow his heart to speed up, his palms prickle with anticipatory sweat, even his scalp to tingle as the Master wetted the knife in a bowl held by one of the ninjas, and slid the blade over the patch of hair covering his scalp tattoo: once, twice, three times. He felt coolness as the hair fell away, and then the Master's hand, fingers spread, upon his head. "You are number One, my successor."

Connor's eyes flew open and he met the Master's gaze. "What?"

Behind him he heard a whisper, a rustle, from the onlookers.

He would not be a popular choice—he was an outsider, a white man, too mature at the time of his recruitment to have been a part of the ancient culture of the Yām Khûmkạn, whose usual recruits were teens.

The favorite to succeed, a man named Pi, was seated on the stairs of the dais. Pi excelled in every physical task and many of the intellectual challenges as well. His graduation the week before had been a course as challenging as Connor's.

"They will not like this," Connor whispered.

"You question me?" The Master's dark brows flew up, then his deep purple eyes narrowed. "Perhaps you would like another opportunity to prove your worth, Number One." He stepped back and gestured to Pi. "Men, choose your weapons. The match is to the death."

CHAPTER THREE

Pim Wat: Day One

P IM W AT TRIED to close her eyes, but someone was holding one of her eyelids open. A light, bright and painful as a lance, pierced her brain. She screamed, a hoarse croak like a carrion bird. She writhed, feeling restraints on her arms and legs. *They'd stripped away the secret, gray place she'd gone to in her mind!* Terror rose in her in a red wave of anguish, and she thrashed harder.

"She's awake," the doctor said above her. "The electroshock treatment seems to be working."

Pim Wat tossed her head from side to side. "No! I want to sleep!"

"We need information," someone else said. Fingers grasped her jaw, forced her face around. "Talk to me. Tell me about the Yām Khûmkạn. What is their priority?"

Warm breath, smelling of American barbecue, fanned Pim Wat's cheeks. She wanted to retch. She clamped her eyes shut, refusing to see whoever her latest interrogator was, refusing to listen to his loud, demanding voice.

"Doctor, make her look at me."

The eyelid retractors took a while to put on because she fought them, biting, snarling, thrashing. All the while, her mind pulsed out a beacon: *Help me, help me, help me, my Master! I need you!*

Why was her beloved Master taking so long? Why was he letting her suffer? Why didn't he come for her?

"You are being punished, Beautiful One, for the evil you've done," the Master's voice said in her mind. She knew exactly why he hadn't come for her. *"Take your punishment, serve your time, give them nothing . . . and when the season is right, I'll come for you."*

Thinking of the Master's hypnotic purple eyes calmed Pim Wat.

They could not keep her here, in the conscious world, if she did not want to be here. There was no technique that could hold her or force her to do their bidding. She had a world within herself to dwell in, where they could not reach her.

Pim Wat relaxed, going completely limp.

They fastened on the eyelid retractors. They shone the light in her eyes. The interrogator's voice pounded at her like a fist . . . but Pim Wat had gone away.

She'd traveled once again to that gray place where she wandered among her memories, waiting for the Master to come for her.

CHAPTER FOUR

Sophie: Day One

KENDALL BIX HAD BEEN the Director of Operations at Security Solutions since Sophie had come to work for the company. The man shook his neatly barbered head and frowned. "No. You can't work this case, Sophie. We've got an entire theft division that hasn't had enough work lately."

"I'm not asking, Kendall." Sophie set the tray of tea things she and Childer had used back on the credenza.

She'd tangled with Bix for control of the company on and off since Sheldon Hamilton had left Sophie his estate, position, and majority shares in Security Solutions. The enigmatic billionaire CEO/owner of the company had disappeared in Thailand, and was in the process of being declared legally dead. Sophie wasn't surprised by Bix's periodic challenges to her authority, nor did she resent them. Bix had been abruptly and mysteriously passed over by Hamilton's appointment of Sophie, who at the time of her promotion was a contract operative, untested in any kind of leadership. She'd relied on Bix to guide her and speak his mind, and she usually went along with his opinions.

Not this time, however.

"I'm in need of a change of pace." Sophie smiled engagingly at Bix. "I'd like you to finish the quarterly reports and give me a week to work this case."

Bix chuckled. "Rank hath its privileges, m'dear. We'll compromise. You can have your case, and the quarterly reports too."

"All right, then. Fair enough. I'll take the reports home with me tonight. Momi is at her father's this month, so I have time in the evenings." Sophie shared custody of her two-year-old daughter with her child's father Alika Wolcott, on a month-on, month-off basis. Alika resided on the island of Kaua`i, and Momi's nanny, Armita, traveled with the toddler back and forth between the islands, providing consistency in her care.

Sophie downloaded and copied the papers that Childer had signed into a fresh case file in her tablet. "I would like a new partner. Do you have anyone from the theft division I could work with? Two pairs of hands and eyes will be better than one with time pressure like we have for this case."

Bix raised his brows. "Funny you should ask. Remember Jake Dunn? He just picked up some of our contract work. He might be available."

Sophie frowned. "Anyone but Dunn."

"Oh, right. I forgot you two were in a relationship." Bix had forgotten no such thing. He just liked to needle her now and again.

Sophie kept her expression neutral with difficulty. "Do you have someone else to suggest?"

"Have you met Pierre Raveaux? We hired him not long ago on a contractor basis. He's a retired detective from the French police, living in Hawaii and France. He's turned out to be quite good with art theft and high-end cases—a perfect fit for this diamond heist."

"Raveaux sounds qualified." Sophie sat down behind her desk. "I'll work on the quarterly reports until you send him up."

"Sounds good, boss." Bix gave an ironic little salute and shut the door of her office behind him.

Sophie waited until his steps had receded down the carpeted hallway, to open her desk drawer. She reached inside and took out a yoga mat. She always wore movement-friendly clothing to the office to accommodate the exercise breaks that were so important to her working life. She rolled out the flexible, brightly colored foam rectangle onto the open space beside her desk.

She pushed in her chair and dropped into a series of memorized *asana*s, moving through them smoothly and automatically.

Just breathe. Feel your body moving. You're okay. Tears welled up as she moved through the structured movements.

She still missed Jake so much.

Sophie stood by what she had told her ex-lover when she sent back his ring more than two years ago: *"I wish you every happiness."*

Yes, she stood by that wish, and Felicia, his new girlfriend, was the one to bring him that. Sophie had never brought him anything but torture and heartbreak.

The yoga wasn't helping. Her old depression flapped its ugly black batwings around her mind, tugging her toward darkness. She rolled up the mat and pulled out a drawer in her desk. A folded, yellow flannel square rested at the bottom of the drawer.

Momi's first blanket.

Sophie's child had been kidnapped when she was only twelve hours old. That blanket had been a comfort during the harrowing time of getting her daughter back. She unfolded the square, sat down, and buried her face in it. The fabric no longer smelled of her infant as it once had, but the softness on her cheeks reminded her of Momi's velvety skin.

She had loved and lost three men. Two of them were with new partners, and one was unreachable.

Sophie let the tears come.

She'd learned the value of unleashing her emotions, of knowing that they couldn't be swept away and ignored, and that expressing them helped her keep them managed.

Eventually done with her "sobfest," as her friend Marcella would've called it, Sophie wiped her face on the precious flannel square. She tucked the blanket in her bag to take home and wash. She splashed water on her face and composed herself in her executive bathroom.

There was nothing to be done but keep going.

Sophie was seated, having a go at the quarterly reports again, when Raveaux knocked lightly on the door frame. Sophie glanced up and gestured for him to come in.

Raveaux was lean and dark, around six feet tall, with a presence that made her sit up and pay attention as intelligent eyes the color of kalamata olives took her measure. "Madame Smithson." He extended a hand. "I am pleased to meet you."

Sophie stood up and shook his hand—*cool and hard, good grip strength.* "Welcome to Security Solutions. I'll be your partner on this recently acquired case."

"I am delighted to have an opportunity to work with you. I have long been a fan."

Sophie quirked a brow in surprise. "A fan?"

"Oh yes. I have studied your career, Madame." Raveaux wore black trousers, Italian loafers without socks, and a white linen shirt, open at the neck, that showed a triangle of bronzed skin. He seated himself in the chair before her desk, crossing an ankle over one knee.

Sophie resented noticing that triangle of skin and ignored his flattery. "We have an interesting situation before us. Bix spoke of your experience with high-end theft; I hope he represented your abilities accurately." She depressed a toggle on her desk. "Paula, can you bring in a printed copy of the newest file?"

"Right away," Paula said through the intercom, her voice cheerful. There was a lot of appeal to having someone respond to her every wish with such prompt positivity. *She didn't blame Jake for falling for Felicia, she really didn't . . .*

Paula, a statuesque Hawaiian woman, carried in the file and set it on Sophie's desk.

"Paula, have you met Mr. Raveaux? He will be working closely with me in the coming weeks," Sophie said.

"I've met him, yes," Paula said. "Hello again, Mr. Raveaux. Glad to have you with us." Her voice was a little too bright.

"Good to see you again," Raveaux murmured.

Sophie smoothed an automatic frown from between her brows. She'd have to question Paula later on what she'd heard about Raveaux—she valued her assistant's opinions on the various staff members they worked with.

Paula removed the used tea tray, still resting on the sideboard, as Sophie spread the file open on the desk between her and Raveaux. "My strength is with computers. We need to pore through every security video involving the diamonds to see if we can identify where the set disappeared between the submission of the parure, and when it was stored. There is bound to be a digital footprint, either in the videos and security footage, or buried somewhere in the company's appraisal process."

Raveaux flipped through the meager pages Childer had submitted. "Agreed. We have several people to follow up on: the manager who takes in the items, the diamond assessor, and of course, the staff on hand at the time. I'd like for both of us to go in and evaluate the premises today, to see if we can develop an angle on how this was done. Once we do that, we may have more leads to follow."

Sophie liked that he was taking the initiative—too often, she'd found that the operatives she worked with waited for her to take the lead. "Your English is excellent." She sat back in her chair and made a little steeple of her fingers, a habit she'd intentionally developed to keep from touching the gunshot scar on her cheekbone. "I would have made the same initial assessment of the case. I think we will work well together."

Raveaux didn't smile, but crinkles appeared beside his dark eyes and they seemed to warm. "Such a compliment, Madame."

"I am no *madame.*" Sophie's words came out more harshly than she intended. "I am not married."

"But you are hardly a naïve young *mademoiselle*." His gaze was unwavering.

"Just call me Sophie, and we will settle the issue once and for all —Raveaux." She didn't want to use his first name; "Pierre" seemed too casual, too intimate, while her own name felt like a declaration of feminism.

Raveaux scooped up the file. "Let us go to the auction house then, Sophie. And on the way, I will tell you about my career investigating stolen artworks, forgeries, and other distressing illegal activities during my time in France's law enforcement."

CHAPTER FIVE

Raveaux: Day One

RAVEAUX SETTLED himself in the passenger side of Sophie's pearl-colored Lexus as she got into the driver's seat.

He hadn't lied—he'd studied her career. Sophie Smithson had an impressive résumé: she was the inventor of the Data Analysis Victim Information Database, a much fought-over crime solving software that searched for trends online, using keywords. She'd had a five-year career with the FBI and an excellent closure rate on cases there—and then she'd joined Security Solutions, taking down criminals and leading the company to further growth and expansion.

What he hadn't counted on was that his boss would be so compelling in person. He'd heard she was beautiful, but he hadn't expected her lithe grace and long-legged height. The hint of sadness in her large, light brown eyes intrigued him, as did the way the line of a scar running down her cheek drew his gaze to her full mouth.

This was a woman with a past; she had a darkness in her that matched his own.

Sophie glanced his way as she turned on the engine. "What do you know about Finewell's? Have you had dealings with them abroad?"

Raveaux scrolled through information on a tablet as they pulled out of the Security Solutions parking garage into traffic. "They rival Christie's auction house for market share. The company's mission, according to their website, is to "bring the best of antiquity into the modern world." Their procedures are time-tested—they have been in business since 1923, and I was able to find no record of any breaches to their security in the past."

"Ha. There's bound to have been something. I will dig deeper." Sophie's smile was a humorous flash.

Raveaux was tempted to smile back—an unfamiliar sensation. "I expect you will use your DAVID software. I'd like to see that, if you don't mind."

"Perhaps," Sophie said neutrally. Hacker types loved their privacy—she wasn't likely to show him anything until she trusted him, and even then, it wouldn't be much. "Tell me more about yourself. Bix says you're retired from the French police?"

"Indeed. I was a member of the *police judiciaire,* and the head of a special task force handling investigations into high-end crime on the Riviera. I specialized in . . . sensitive cases." Raveaux kept his eyes forward, on the road ahead. Blue skies and palm trees passed by his view, but he paid scant attention. He needed to tell her enough to assure her of his expertise—but he really didn't want to tell her anything at all.

She flashed those golden-brown eyes at him. "Tell me more." Not a question—a command. "Why are you here, in Hawaii?"

"Why indeed?" Raveaux lifted his hands in a Gallic shrug. "I wanted a change of scenery."

"From the Riviera?" Sophie snorted. "I can find out anything I want to about you, Raveaux. You might as well tell me what you're hiding."

An icy shiver touched him between the shoulder blades. *She was telling the truth.* "I specialized in high-end cases, as I said. Theft and kidnappings involving the rich and important. Murders of celebrities and billionaires and politicians. Wherever there was a . . . tricky case, I guess you would call it? I was brought in." Raveaux looked down at his hands. Scars puckered his olive skin like melted fabric, twining all the way up his arms. "I angered the wrong person. Someone high up in organized crime. There was a car bomb. It took my wife and daughter."

The heat of the burning car . . . he hadn't even felt it. He'd just tried to get the door open, screaming, his lungs on fire, but there wasn't enough left of his child in the back seat to even fill his hands . . . He couldn't scream anymore, he couldn't breathe, and his arms were burning, burning . . .

"Raveaux." Sophie's touch on his shirt-covered arm startled him. "I'm sorry I made you tell me."

"C'est rien." He tugged his white linen cuffs further down, covering the scars on the backs of his hands and his wrists. "It is nothing. A long time ago. But I resigned following that event, and after a few years of being idle in France, I came here for a change of scenery, as I said. Honolulu is very nice."

"I understand wanting a 'do-over,' as they say in America." Sophie's voice was compassionate. "I've been there myself."

She did not elaborate, as most people would have done.

Raveaux roused himself from the spell of dark memory with an effort—*he needed to establish his expertise.* "I've worked a diamond heist before. There was this time when I partnered with the police in Monaco to capture a notorious burglar who targeted the wealthy guests of a casino . . ."

He was just finishing the story when they pulled into the garage of the building housing Finewell's Auction House. The company's office was located in one of the most historic and elegant buildings in Honolulu, and Raveaux had no doubt that was intentional. Sophie parked the Lexus in an underground parking stall near the entrance.

Sophie got Childer on the phone, her husky, Brit-accented voice authoritative. Soon, she and Raveaux were buzzed into the penthouse elevator of the building. When the doors opened, Childer met them, wiping a shiny forehead with a handkerchief.

"I told my assistant you are insurance investigators, here to check our security protocols," he said. "I ordered up the video and other surveillance you asked for. It will take only a few minutes. If anyone asks, you work for Fidelity Mutual."

"We need to see the actual intake area and the vault," Sophie told him.

"Of course. Back on the elevator, then."

The elevator sank at a rate that made Raveaux's stomach lift uncomfortably. They stepped out on the basement level into a foyer area with a long hallway ahead, lined with closed, locked doors. The temperature was noticeably chilly.

Childer gestured around the immaculate, monochromatic space. "We keep the temperature at a setting that will help preserve artworks and antiquities. We even auction fine collectible wines at times. Our server farm is also down here. All of those things need climate control."

"I'm not at all surprised by that," Sophie said.

Raveaux pointed. "I see you have the storage rooms labeled." Each door on either side of the hall was marked with a plaque and a keypad.

"Yes. We don't have a vault, per se. We have every necessary security on the doors, though, and they are steel reinforced. Inside we have locked cabinetry for the different types of goods."

Sophie put her hands on her hips. "So, by using the word 'vault,' you really just mean a locked storage room?"

Childer's ruddy cheeks went redder. "We consider this entire area to be our vault," he said stiffly.

Raveaux pointed to a camera node aimed at the elevator doors. "As we said before, we will need all of your surveillance footage from the time of the diamonds' transfer, to the time that the jewels were put into storage, and anything after that until you realized the diamonds were gone."

"I told you my girl was already working on it. I explained to her that our insurance investigators needed a week of digital footage to assess our security." Childer dabbed his throat with the cloth. "She will get you anything you need in your guise as agents of the insurance company."

Sophie's nostrils flared—she was clearly growing irritated with Childer's prevarication. "Show us where the diamonds were stored."

Childer led them down the hall to a room at the end, marked *Specialty Items.* "It didn't seem wise to advertise what was inside on the door," he said.

This aperture had both the keypad and a couple of heavy deadbolt locks. Childer fumbled through a massive bunch of keys, muttering as he looked for the right one.

Raveaux elbowed him aside. "Excuse me. I want to try something." He reached into his well-worn leather messenger bag, a personal piece of luggage he'd taken to every crime scene in his past career. He removed a vial of fingerprint powder from an inside pocket, along with a brush stowed in a handy protective flap. He dipped the loose-bristled brush into the powder and whirled the black material over the surface of the door. Fingerprints immediately popped up in black. "We will need to rule out all of the employees who have access to this room. Send us copies of their fingerprints."

"Of course."

Raveaux got out a small Olympus and photographed the prints. Once he'd finished, Childer entered a code into the keypad beside the door.

"Do you have a metric that logs in everyone who accesses the room?" Sophie asked.

"I will have to check with the security company who put in the keypads," Childer said. "But yes." The door beeped, a light above the keypad going from red to green, and Childer inserted a key into the first heavy deadbolt, then the other. "As you can see, we don't rely just on the keypad, or the locks alone." He pushed the door open.

A sensor light came on automatically overhead, and a draft of cold air flushed over them. Raveaux followed Sophie as she stepped in. They scanned the rows of heavy-duty locked metal cabinets that lined the walls inside.

Childer pointed. "That is the cabinet that held the jewels."

The upright, numbered cabinet looked like it was made to hold tools. Brushed steel with a small lock, it was identical to the rest around the room. "How do you keep track of what's stored inside each unit?" Sophie asked.

"On each drawer inside the cabinet is a number. We have a computer inventory that logs the number of the cabinet, with the items stored inside."

"Where are the keys to the doors and units stored?" Raveaux advanced to the unit in question, taking out his fingerprint kit.

"That's a different locked area. I don't carry the keys to the cabinets, nor does anyone in the company. We keep those in a safe," Childer said proudly. "That's why I'm so confused by this burglary. We have several different levels of safeguards in place. I don't know how the thief was able to get any of the keys involved, get past the door pad, or any of the other things that we have set up."

"And that's why you have us." Raveaux spun the fingerprint powder over the locked interior shelving. No prints bloomed under his brush, and he frowned. "No prints inside. Odd."

"This is looking more and more like an inside job to me, Mr. Childer," Sophie said. "It would be very difficult for an individual or individuals to gain access to all of these various safeguards without inside information. I'm going to need an employment history on everyone in the building. Everyone who might have access to this area. We'll look for anyone who might have come to work for you for the purpose of breaking into this vault."

An idea had been brewing in Raveaux's mind. "Perhaps the diamonds were never actually logged in. They never made it into the safe. In which case, our suspect pool is much smaller."

"Oh no, I'm sure that can't be right. I've known Mel Samson, in charge of the intake process, for years," Childer protested.

Raveaux pinned Childer's watery blue eyes with his own. "Never doubt that anyone can be bought with the right incentive. When you give us the information on all the various employees, highlight anyone who is involved in the intake and storage process." He pointed to the shiny metal of the cabinet's interior boxes. "No fingerprints here. Why is it completely clean?"

Childer pointed to a box of latex gloves on a supply shelf. "We recommend that people who handle the gems wear gloves to avoid spoiling the sparkle with hand oils. Perhaps whoever put the diamonds away was wearing protection."

"But what about anyone else who might have had access? Why is it completely clean?" Raveaux turned to Sophie. Her honey-brown eyes were wide, fixed on his face. "Honestly? If I were stealing these gems, I would've had a nice set of fakes put in place to replace them, so that the heist wasn't discovered until well after the auction."

"Maybe the thief didn't have access to the kind of craftsperson he would have needed for such a project, here in Hawaii," Sophie said.

Raveaux flicked his fingers in irritation at Childer. "Go get the keys to these interior storage units. Take Sophie with you to observe where the keys are stored. I want to see how hard it is to break into this rack of shelves." Raveaux took a set of lockpicks out of his bag.

"I'm not leaving you here alone while you pick those locks," Childer exclaimed.

"Oui, vraiment." Raveaux shrugged, his eyes on the keyhole as he inserted the two small flanged rods and wiggled them around inside the lock. "Observe, then. This won't take long."

A minute and a half later, the drawer yielded to his advances. Raveaux pulled the felt-lined, empty drawer out with a flourish. "I hope I have just demonstrated to you, Mr. Childer, how truly unnecessary keys can be."

Childer could form no coherent argument. He led them to the room where the safe with the numbered shelf keys were stored. They observed while he opened the safe—but to Raveaux's mind, the jewels had never made it to that shelf at all.

"Please call your assistant for the employee records and fingerprint records we require," Sophie said, when Childer had re-locked the safe. "We'll be on our way when we have what we need."

They returned to Childer's office, and he directed his assistant to gather the additional information that they requested, with the help of the Human Resources department. Sophie never seemed to waste a moment; she continued to work, using her tablet and phone, as they waited in the lobby.

Raveaux didn't see the point in being a workaholic any longer. What had it gotten him to spend so many years in frantic and obsessive pursuit of his cases? He'd only lost time with Gita and Lucie because of it; time he could never get back.

Now he had nothing but time.

Raveaux sat down on the padded couch and removed a Jo Nesbo novel from his leather messenger bag. It was a twisty mystery, set in an exotic location. He quickly became engrossed in the book. He liked the hopeless emptiness of Nesbo's Harry Hole character, his compulsive drinking and self-destructive death wish—the character's desperation reminded him how much better he felt, having found his own way out of that vortex.

"Raveaux?"

He'd been gone into the book's world for a while, and re-entry was harsh. "Yes?" He folded down the corner of his page. *Gita had hated when he did that; she'd collected bookmarks from all over the world, and loved to drop them into his pages . . .*

Sophie's mouth had a dimple at the corner—not a smile, but as if she were holding one in. "You like reading?"

"I don't like being interrupted when I'm reading," Raveaux said with asperity. "*Merde.* That your only reason for talking to me?"

Sophie's dimple deepened. "I just don't see too many paperbacks these days, let alone men reading them."

"I am certain there are more of us endangered species engaged in this activity in private." Raveaux's neck felt hot—was she teasing him?

"But a paperback. It's so old fashioned." She was definitely smiling.

"I prefer to call it classic." He narrowed his eyes at her. "Is there anything else, *Madame?*" He used the honorific deliberately, his brows raised.

"I have always found the French to be rather touchy," Sophie said, after a moment. "I meant no disrespect."

"And I have always found Americans who don't read to be rather shallow," Raveaux replied. He opened his book again. "And I mean that sincerely."

"I read. Just not paperbacks," Sophie muttered.

Once again, Raveaux almost smiled. How had she done that to him twice in one day? He uncreased the corner of his page and smoothed it carefully.

CHAPTER SIX

Connor: Day One

PI STALKED down the stairs of the dais toward Connor. The man was fresh and rested, his lips curling back from his teeth in a feral grin as he circled Connor, calling for his favorite weapon, the spear staff.

Connor stood up from kneeling, his eyes tracking his opponent. *You've just endured the gauntlet! You're in no shape for a battle to the death!* Connor's "old mind" screamed at him, loud and clear.

His "new mind" simply tracked Pi, unfazed. *All is an illusion, and you can manipulate everything about this scene at will.*

Pi took a moment to shed his black *gi* theatrically. He caught the spear tossed to him by an onlooker, and his muscled torso gleamed— the man had a heavier build than Connor's, but he was just as quick and agile.

Connor's mind scrabbled—*what was his favorite weapon?* He couldn't even remember. He liked them all.

A bloodthirsty roar from the onlookers filled the courtyard as Pi charged, the staff raised over his head.

Connor whirled into action, dodging Pi's swing, spinning in a circle just out of reach. Shame and anger licked along his nerves, weakening him—*he didn't want to take a life this way!* He would never choose to fight to the death as a spectator sport.

He must not have what it took to be the Master's number One.

Connor had tasted the Master's punishments before. He'd done pushups until he collapsed, spent a night in a storm standing on one leg atop a pillar until he fell off, lain on a bed of nails, and been plunged into a vat of ice—but with this test, on top of the obstacle course, he was reeling emotionally. Disequilibrium ate up valuable energy resources as he reacted late, taking a blow to the ribs that knocked out his breath.

A flurry of movement out of the corner of his eye—a blade whirled toward him, end over end, launched by his friend Nine. Connor caught the sword by its handle—the half-length samurai blade was used in Seppuku, and was swift and deadly for close combat.

His distraction in catching the sword caused Connor to take another blow from Pi's staff, this time a raking slash to the back of the leg that buckled his knee.

He inhaled, whirling out of the blow, refusing to feel its pain, and brought the blade up to a ready position as he faced his opponent at last. *No way out but through.*

Connor's eyes locked on Pi's. The wear and tear on his body that he'd never allowed himself to feel during the obstacle course sharpened his focus.

He exhaled gently, and *s l o w e d e v e r y t h i n g d o w n.*

Pi came at him again.

This time, every movement was as meandering as if it were drifting through honey, leisurely and completely avoidable. The man feinted from the left, but planned to strike from the right, a move Connor remembered from previous matches.

Connor stepped deliberately into the space Pi had left unprotected and sliced along Pi's exposed side, laying him open down the ribs.

Pi staggered back, his mouth contorting in a cry of shock that sounded as otherworldly and distant as a foghorn. He made a further mistake in looking down at the blood pouring from the painful but non-fatal wound. Pain contorted his features.

Pi didn't have Connor's ability to block out sensation and distraction, let alone manipulate time.

That was why the Master had chosen Connor.

He understood, now.

Connor gathered energy into a hot ball of power at his core, and leaped high to kick Pi squarely in the chest.

The man flew backward, landing sprawled on the steps of the dais, dropping his staff with a clatter.

Connor walked over to Pi, lazy, easy, still in the time warp he had created. He moved to stand above his opponent and placed the razor-sharp tip of his sword under the man's chin.

The blade nicked Pi's flesh, and his face paled with fear.

Pi was not worthy to lead.

Connor looked up to meet the Master's velvety purple, compelling eyes as the man stood above him on the steps of the dais. "Now I see why you chose me as your One. May I spare this man's life that he may serve you in some other way?"

"Yes. And you will live with the consequences." Those eyes always saw more than Connor wanted them to. "Your first decision as my One."

Connor stepped back and lowered the sword. "I choose mercy."

Normal time dropped over Connor, with its heavy load of tiresome gravity. His ears rang with the roar of approval from the onlookers, spiked by a few catcalls from those who'd wanted more blood and death.

The deep slice on the back of Connor's leg throbbed. His nostrils stung with the coppery tang of blood and sweat. Exhaustion tugged at his body. But he wasn't done yet.

He reached down and tugged Pi to his feet, noting the hatred banked in the man's dark eyes.

He would shame Pi into compliance and harness goodwill from the other trainees. Connor lifted Pi's fist, turning the two of them in a circle before the cheering crowd. "We are brothers! Brothers who serve the Yām Khûmkạn and the Master—together!"

Hundreds of warriors swarmed from their viewing points and engulfed Connor and Pi. Connor was lifted on their shoulders, borne triumphantly around the combat area, and deposited, once again, in front of the Master's chair on top of the dais.

But when Connor opened his eyes, drunk on the energy of the crowd, the Master had disappeared.

The wave of ninjas carried Connor up and sat him bodily in their leader's vacated chair. Hundreds of heads bowed toward him, thousands of hands were extended to him. He spoke the ritual words of blessing over them, as the Master did every day.

"May our hearts be steadfast in service, our bodies strong, our minds our greatest weapon as we serve the Yām Khûmkạn."

CHAPTER SEVEN

Sophie: Day One, Evening

SOPHIE RODE the elevator to her suite in the upscale Pendragon Arches building in downtown Honolulu. She checked both ways when she got off the elevator, the habit of staying alert for threats ingrained, and walked to the door of her apartment.

And then, she paused as she put her key in the lock, leaning her forehead against the door for a moment, steeling herself for the emptiness inside.

The first week is the worst. You'll get through this!

It had only been days since her daughter Momi and nanny Armita went to Alika Wolcott's mansion on Kaua'i for his custody month.

They'd arrived at the unique arrangement after a series of experiments. Armita was the secret to their success; Sophie's loyal, dedicated childhood nanny was able to keep Momi on the same schedule, diet, and routine, so that their daughter's development remained stable and her attachments undisrupted, as Momi spent time with each parent, equally.

And still it was hard. If only they lived on the same island . . .

Anubis's toenails clattered on the square of parquet flooring just inside the door, and roused Sophie from her depressive moment. *She wasn't completely alone.* She still had someone who needed her, who noticed whether or not she came home—even if that someone was a dog.

Sophie opened the door. She smiled at the dignified Doberman as he sat waiting for her in his mannerly way, a slight whine rumbling in his wide chest, his ears pricked and eyes bright with excitement to see her.

"Hey, boy. I'm in need of a run. Looks like you are too. We'll go out, right after our call to Momi and Armita."

Sophie had been given not only Sheldon Hamilton/Connor's business, apartment, and estate; she had inherited his dog. Anubis was a well-trained guard dog, not at all like her boisterous yellow Lab, Ginger, who had gone to live with Jake and his rescue Pitbull, Tank, upon their breakup. Even two years later, Sophie still felt a pang, missing her silly, loving girl.

Better not to dwell. Better just to keep moving.

Sophie changed into running clothes as she contacted Armita via video chat on her tablet.

"Mama!" Sophie's heart felt like it burst into a thousand pieces with love, as her toddler's grinning face appeared on the screen. "Dog!" Momi held up a bright green wad of Play-Doh that could have been anything.

"Darling! That's wonderful. Is it Anubis?" Sophie dropped to the couch, only one shoe on, to focus fully on the call. She tried to contact Armita every day at the same time, part of the stability of Momi's daily routine, and her heart swelled with adoration as she drank in the sight of her daughter's smiling face. Momi really was adorable with her dimpled smile, big brown eyes, and head of thick, curling black ringlets.

"Nubis," Momi confirmed. Hearing his name, Anubis whined beside Sophie, so she held the tablet to let the child and dog see each other.

"Here, Nubis!" Momi impetuously squashed the blob of green

Play-Doh against the surface of the tablet on her side, covering the video camera and blacking the screen out. Anubis gave a startled bark as Sophie laughed.

Armita appeared, laughing, her sharp features softened by her smile as she scraped the malleable clay off the video camera node. "No, my darling. You can't give it to Anubis through the screen." But Momi had already run off, giggling.

Armita pushed a lock of black hair off her forehead as she addressed Sophie. "Momi is a wild girl today, Sophie, and this is after Alika took her canoe paddling! I didn't let her nap. I'm hoping for an early bedtime tonight."

"Great idea," Sophie agreed. Momi was a bright, energetic child, always getting into something. The two caught up on Momi's activities and routine so far that day, and then Armita caught Momi and made her say goodbye to Sophie.

The toddler's attention had moved on to a set of oversized Legos, so it was a perfunctory dismissal. "Bye, Mama." A brief wave, no eye contact.

Sophie stifled sadness as she ended the call. "She's happy and healthy and has no time for me because she is emotionally secure," Sophie muttered aloud. "Anubis, let's get on the road."

Ten minutes later, music blasting in her ears to forestall any thinking, Sophie and Anubis ran down the sidewalk of the busy Honolulu thoroughfare that would dead-end at the beach. Sophie could hardly wait to shed the tension of the day in the mellow ocean off Waikiki. Her friend Marcella liked to joke that no day in Hawaii was complete without a dose of "vitamin sea."

Huge old monkeypod trees spread dappled shade over the still warm city street as they headed downtown, dodging a colorful, multicultural crowd, most of whom were in no hurry as they enjoyed vacation speed.

Sophie jogged in place at the street lights, keeping her heart rate up. She loved running with Momi in her jogging stroller, but during the months she didn't have Momi, she could run hard and long, and even take Anubis on some of the rugged Oahu trails for the run-hikes that had really made her fall in love with this verdant island paradise.

When they reached the long, shallow arc of sand at Ala Moana Beach Park, Sophie tied Anubis to a nearby coconut palm and popped out his foldable water bowl from her fanny pack, filling it halfway from a water bottle. He lapped up his fill and settled in the shade to wait. She'd worn a sleek sports bikini under her running clothes, and when she reached the sand, she kicked off her shoes, peeled off her clothing, and ran down to dive into the warm, gentle ocean.

The crystalline salt water with its mellow, rolling waves seemed to rinse away her stress. Sophie swam forward underwater, releasing a stream of silvery bubbles through her nose. She opened her eyes, braced for the sting of the salt, and was rewarded by seeing a school of brightly striped *manini*, small black-and-green tangs, darting around a submerged coral rock.

Sophie burst up out of the water, grabbing a breath, and turned to parallel the shore, moving into a crawl stroke. She swam laps back and forth, just outside the wave line. Eventually finished, she rolled over onto her back and floated, arms spread, gazing up at the salmon and gold cumulus clouds of sunset.

There really just wasn't anything quite like the sunset in Hawaii: the arch of clear sky, the towering and magnificent clouds floating by as gracefully as galleons, all of it framed by golden beach and graceful palms. If only she had someone to share the beautiful moment with . . .

A recent spate of weddings had exacerbated her loneliness. Marcella had celebrated her nuptials to Marcus Kamuela a year before; Alika, Momi's father, had tied the knot with his physical therapist girlfriend Sandy on Kaua'i around the same time, and now Jake and Felicia were moving to the Mainland together . . . *How had she ended up alone, when she'd had a chance at love with three wonderful men?*

Sophie's gaze feasted on the spectacle of the sunset around her.

She had so much to be grateful for; she had to focus on that. Yes, sometimes she felt incomplete without a partner by her side, or sad about having to share her child with Alika on another island—but whenever she stayed in the moment, there was always something to celebrate and appreciate.

Thinking this way had helped her manage her chronic depression. That, and a little white pill each morning . . . but she wasn't ashamed to take medication to manage her disorder, not when she was a mother whose child, however well cared for, needed her to be present, involved, and functional. Her mother, Pim Wat, had been too ill during much of Sophie's childhood to provide the care and connection her daughter had needed—and now, Pim Wat was imprisoned in Guantánamo, supposedly lapsed into a catatonic state—*and that was Sophie's doing, too.*

Not that she regretted being a part of her homicidal, narcissistic mother's capture!

Sophie rolled over, completing a final lap before she exited the water. She took a quick shower, patted herself dry, and pulled on her running clothes again. She untied Anubis's leash, and headed for home.

The Doberman's sharply pointed ears swiveled even more than usual as they approached Sophie's building, and Sophie heard a familiar, excited bark. As they came around a corner, she spotted her Labrador Ginger immediately. The yellow Lab's whole body wriggled with excitement, and the dog barked loudly, straining toward them on a leash held by Jake Dunn.

Sophie had not seen Jake since their breakup two years before, and he radiated energy and charisma as he strode toward her, laughing at Ginger's antics. His short dark hair, big square shoulders and striking gray eyes still made her knees a little weak.

"Jake! What a surprise!" Sophie kept her voice bright and breezy.

"Hey, Sophie." Jake's voice was also carefully casual. "Ginger's been to obedience school since I saw you last—not that you'd know it by her behavior."

Ginger had reached Anubis. The two dogs greeted each other ecstatically with much whining, jumping, and nuzzling, in marked contrast to Sophie and Jake's stiffness.

"I have some important news," Jake said.

"Let me guess. You and Felicia are getting married." Sophie was surprised that her voice was strong and calm. She noted tiny changes: his waist looked softer, his cheeks fuller, his laugh lines deeper. *This man was contented.* Jake had not been contented the entire time she had known him.

"Ha. No." He cleared his throat. "That's not it." He held out Ginger's leash. "It's sad news, actually. Tank passed away last month, and . . . Felicia and I are taking this opportunity to open a branch of our company in California. We can't take care of a dog right now, and Ginger is a dog who likes company. As you know."

Sophie took Ginger's leash automatically. "Of course, I'll take her. That was always our agreement."

Jake looked down at Ginger with genuine regret in the downward curve of his mouth. "I hope you don't mind how sudden this is. It just didn't seem like something I could call you to talk about on the phone. I knew you still had Anubis, so I was hoping it wouldn't be too much of an imposition for her to come back to you."

"It could never be an imposition to have Ginger in my life," Sophie said with dignity. "Thank you for bringing her to me—and caring for her the last two years."

Their eyes met for the first time. Jake's mouth turned up in the smile she remembered. "You're looking good, Sophie."

"And you as well. It really is good to see you again." She'd never expected that to be so true. Sophie tugged Ginger back; the Lab was excitedly licking Anubis, and the dogs' leashes had become tangled. "I see my girl's still a brat. It turned out to be such a good thing that you had her for those first couple of years; I could never have managed a dog with her behaviors when Momi was an infant."

"Is Little Bean with Alika?" he asked. Sophie felt a pang at his use of the pet name they'd called her baby during her pregnancy.

Jake had hardly seen her child before Momi's kidnapping; had never had a chance to get to know her. *Perhaps that was for the best . . .*

"Yes. Momi's with her father this month. We have a unique custody arrangement that seems to work. She spends a month at her father's, and then a month with me. I miss her, but it's only fair." Sophie shrugged, trying to make light of it.

"Yeah, I keep in touch with Alika. He seems to feel the same way," Jake said. A zing of surprise zipped up Sophie's spine—*they were in contact with each other?*

"I'm surprised to hear you and Alika keep in touch."

"Guy's a good friend. We'd been through a lot together. I've actually seen Momi a few times when I was on Kaua'i." Jake held her gaze. "You've done a great job with her, Sophie. Both of you. She's an incredible kid."

This shouldn't feel like some kind of betrayal, but it did. She'd have wanted to know Jake was visiting her child and Alika. *Though, on second thought, it would have tortured her to know it. . .* "Thank you for bringing Ginger back. And I'm sorry about Tank."

Jake shook his head. "Don't be sorry. That old reprobate had a great life after you and I rescued him. Felicia and I miss him, but we'll get another dog when the time is right."

"Speaking of work, I heard from Bix that you're doing some contract work for Security Solutions."

"Yeah. Mostly training for your operatives. Our company specializes in kidnap rescue."

"I heard that. Smart to keep a tight focus," Sophie said. She couldn't think of what else to talk about, any way to delay his departure.

Jake, apparently, couldn't either. He lifted a hand as he turned away. "Take care of our girl, Sophie. I'm sure our paths will cross again someday."

"Be well, Jake. Say hello to Felicia." She held both dogs close and watched as he walked away, taking long slow breaths and willing herself not to cry.

She was over him. Yes, she was, she really was. Or at least, she needed to be, and she wanted to be . . . which was almost the same thing.

Sophie headed into the building, checking Ginger's leash as the Lab galloped forward. "Oh, *naughty daughter of a two-headed yak,* heel!" Ginger finally fell in line, grinning up at Sophie, her warm brown eyes alight. Anubis pranced happily on her other side.

She took both dogs over to the security desk in the lobby and introduced Ginger to the guard. She had him put the dog on her registered address. The man, a portly gnome with tufts of white hair above his ears, came out from behind his desk and gave each animal a biscuit.

Sophie rode up in the elevator with the dogs a few minutes later, and let herself into the quiet apartment. The animals took care of that silence the moment she took off the leashes, leaping and playing in the living room and making her smile, as she stripped off her clothes and went to the shower.

By the time she'd donned her sleepwear, the dogs had both crowded into Anubis's roomy bed, twined around each other like long-lost lovers. Anubis was clearly delighted to have the company, and Ginger was never a dog who liked to be alone. *This was a good thing.* Her heart swelled with gratitude that Jake had brought Ginger home to her.

Sophie heated a microwaveable glass casserole that Armita had prepared and left for her in the freezer. She carried it next door to her computer lab. She and Raveaux had divided up the Finewell's video footage for review and now, seated in Connor's former secret office, she could begin studying her half of it. She also wanted to dig deeper into the history of theft and fraud that Finewell's might be hiding. For that, she needed to fire up her DAVID software.

Sophie cracked her knuckles and leaned in toward her bank of monitors, eyes intent on the screen and fingers flying.

She might be alone, but she was seldom lonely.

CHAPTER EIGHT

Connor: Day One, Evening

CONNOR SUBMITTED to Healer's hands digging deep into his flesh as he got a massage. The man's weight pressed his body into the rough cotton toweling covering the table. He shut his eyes and let go, allowing his muscles to relax to the point that they felt like they'd drip off his bones. As he imagined them softening like candlewax under the heat of the Healer's hands, he felt the knots and bruises give way even more.

Considering the rigors of what he'd been through that day, he had gotten off lightly as far as injuries go—his mental transcendence had protected him as he'd known it would.

Healer had put several stitches in the slash Pi had landed to the back of Connor's leg and daubed his various cuts and abrasions with salve—but Connor's tissues were already knitting together far more rapidly than he would have believed before he had come to study with the Master.

He could direct his body, at the cell level, to accelerate healing, and he would be back to normal by tomorrow.

The air in the room seem to shift. Connor sensed the Master

nearby. "Come see me when you're done," that hypnotic voice said, and Connor nodded.

CLEAN, fed, and rested, Connor dressed carefully in a new snow-white *gi*. His rank was that signaled by the color of the robe and the black belt he tied around his waist, embellished with a carved jade ornament. He took the stairs to the Master's apartments and knocked lightly on the familiar wooden door.

"Come in."

As he had done hundreds of times before, Connor entered the luxuriously appointed apartment. A fire crackled in the wide hearth, and a table in front of the flames was set up for their usual game of chess.

The Master stood by the cabinet in the corner. He raised a flask of his favorite drink, a liqueur made from dragon fruit juice that was definitely an acquired taste. "I believe a celebratory toast is in order."

"Thank you." Connor took the crystal tumbler of ruby liquid the Master handed him. "And thank you for allowing Pi to live."

The Master laughed, the harsh sound a contrast to his silken voice. "Too soon for you to thank me. Pi is many things, but not forgiving. Pride is his weakness. You handled the situation well. He will look small if he goes against you."

They seated themselves at the chess table. Connor sipped the drink cautiously—it heated his throat going down. "What I can't understand is how you chose me, so long ago, and had my scalp tattooed with that number. How did you know? How do you know with any of the recruits?" That question that had been burning in his mind ever since he'd begun witnessing graduation ceremonies at the compound.

"I don't know what will happen. I only know what I feel led to have marked on a man's skin." The Master smacked his lips in appreciation, and refilled his tumbler. "A gift of discernment. I can see what is in men's and women's hearts, and many times I can influence them. However, I am not omniscient. Many fail. Many fall short of the number they have been given, a number that represents their potential. You did not." The Master lifted his glass. "You have done the work you came to do. I hope you have no regrets."

"No. None." They touched glasses and drank.

The Master set aside his tumbler with an air of getting down to business. He steepled his fingers, studying the board. "We have time for one more game before my flight."

"Where are you headed?" Connor leaned forward, a pleasant sense of anticipation quickening in his veins. The Master had told him early on in his training that they played chess to hone their strategic thinking.

"I will be gone for an indefinite time." The Master studied the pieces, answering but not answering, as he often did. Firelight burnished his golden-brown skin. He picked up a rook with a long-figured hand and made an opening move. "I want you to run the compound, and also our mutual online interests."

Connor's gaze flew up to meet the Master's compelling pansy-purple eyes. "I haven't been near a computer the whole time I've been here. Now you want me to resume the Ghost's activities?"

"I want you to step into the position I have prepared you for. It was always my intention that you could replace me here, bringing with you the additional layer of your computer presence as the Ghost."

"I hoped someday to partner with you, but I had never have dreamed of replacing you." Connor's throat went dry just saying the words. "It's a lot of responsibility, Master." Connor made a counter-move, and his brows lowered in dismay as the Master took his knight. "What has changed?"

"You have graduated. That is what has changed. And you have more talent than I even hoped for. With many gifts, comes much responsibility." The Master made another move. "I suggest you pay attention to the game."

Connor tried to focus, but in three more moves, the Master had taken his queen. "Check."

"You win." Connor tipped his king over. "Now, tell me what you want me to do."

"I must leave the compound for a time, and you will prove your ability to stand in my stead and take care of what I have entrusted to you." The Master rose from the table, graceful as always. "I have left word with the section leaders that you are in charge. After today's events, you will have no trouble from anyone."

Connor's pulse picked up. Running the compound was a lot to take on. The stronghold, and its training program, were only a fraction of what the Master oversaw in his leadership role for Thailand's clandestine spy agency and the last remnant of the Thai royal family's castle guard. The Yām Khûmkạn was the equivalent to the USA's Secret Service and CIA combined, and though he had been briefed, he had not expected to assume command of such a complex organization. "I would prefer if you stayed a little longer, Master. If you took me around, oriented me on all of the aspects . . ."

"Nine will be available to assist you. Do not disappoint me." Coldness in the Master's voice conveyed his displeasure.

Connor's belly tightened. "I will do my best."

A flash of memory, long suppressed, ambushed him: his father's voice. *"You disappoint me." A fall down the stairs into a cold, dark basement . . . the door banging shut overhead. Darkness, for hours.*

"I will communicate when it is safe to do so. Make your acquaintance with the computer lab; I know you have been avoiding it, but that time is over. Nine will serve as your right hand. Good night." The Master walked into his bedroom area, and pulled the door closed behind him.

"Good night, Master," Connor said to the empty room.

He looked down at the abandoned chess game.

He had been obliterated in only a few moves. All this time, the Master had gone easy on him, and allowed Connor to think he could win. *What else had he been outplayed at?*

CHAPTER NINE

Raveaux: Day One, Evening

RAVEAUX WALKED up the colorful tropical walkway to the door of his bottom floor apartment in Waikiki. He'd rented the condominium on the advice of his counselor: "somewhere bright, cheerful, whose location will raise your mood." As he sorted through a bunch of keys for the one to the door, the shrieks and laughter of children playing in the pool that was a part of the complex tested that wisdom.

The setting didn't match his mood—in fact, the presence of happy vacationing families so close to him only served to highlight what he'd lost.

He opened the door and gave it a push. The interior layout was simple: a single bedroom with bath, a kitchenette along the back wall, a living area in front of sliders that gave way to a pretty seating area that looked out between two palms and a mass of plantings, toward the distant beach and ocean.

Raveaux walked to the sliders and unlocked them. His nostrils filled with the smell of the sea as the evening breeze flowed in. He glanced over at the aforementioned crowded pool, visible through clusters of palm plantings. He could sometimes swim laps alone at six a.m. before the kids showed up. A meandering concrete walkway that passed all the major Waikiki resorts wound its way past his unit. And straight ahead, a swath of yellow sand beach radiated leftover warmth from the day's sunshine. Little turquoise waves purled onto the sand, expending themselves again and again like a beating heart.

He turned and headed for the refrigerator, battling through a wave of longing for a drink. *He had beaten that demon two years ago almost to the day.*

Yes, tomorrow was the fourth anniversary of the day his wife and daughter had been blown to bits. The two years following their deaths had been spent in the bottom of a bottle, and, after his sister had staged an "intervention," he'd gotten sober at a high-end facility in Arizona.

Somewhere along the way, between the yoga, the therapy, and the sweat lodge, he'd decided to live. Decided that dying wouldn't bring them back. Decided he might have a little tread left on his tires, after all, though for what purpose remained to be seen.

Close to two more years had passed as he consolidated the remains of his former life, some of which had meant throwing away his own useless possessions and boxing Gita and Lucie's things. He'd sold the flat on the Riviera where they'd lived as a family, with its joyful and terrible memories, and relocated to Hawaii. He was still on a visa that required frequent trips back to France, but his new consulting career had turned out to be surprisingly interesting and fruitful.

The liquor craving temporarily vanquished, Raveaux reached inside the refrigerator for a bottle of seltzer water. He poured the fizzy liquid over ice cubes into an antique cut crystal glass he kept for that purpose. He added a lime wedge and swirled the liquid, enjoying the sound of the cubes and the sight of the bubbles. *Just because the drink didn't have a kick didn't mean it couldn't be pleasant.*

Holding his drink, Raveaux walked through the living area and stepped out onto the lanai. He sat in one of two metal tubing beach recliners, sipping the pleasant bubbles and taking a long moment to watch the palm trees do their hula dance in the evening light, to enjoy the sight of the mynah birds hopping on the smooth grass, chatting in a busy way that reminded him of the common blackbirds of France.

Maybe he would forgo the evening workout.

After all, why bother? It wasn't like anyone saw his body, and it wasn't like he did anything very physical on the job anymore, so he no longer felt a need to be prepared for combat or running. This new case was mostly going to be interviews and computer work, too.

For that reason alone, he probably needed to get his blood moving. He had a lot of surveillance recordings to get through this evening. But right now, he had time for one more chapter of the Nesbo book.

Raveaux got up and retrieved his paperback. He found his page and opened it.

Gita and her bookmarks. He'd enjoyed finding those brightly colored paper scraps to add to her collection from all over the world. He'd boxed them away without looking at them, blind drunk, with a respirator mask on so he wouldn't smell her scent or feel her presence as he touched her clothing and mementos. He'd thrown everything that remotely reminded him of her, along with Lucie's things, into a storage unit to be dealt with someday, when he had the strength for it.

Right now, he couldn't imagine a day when he'd have the strength for it.

A palm frond had fallen to the grass beside him; Raveaux reached down to pull off a single frond. He stripped the brown leaf material from the spine, and slid the woody, springy wand into the book, holding it deep in the pages as he read, sipping his drink. The chapter was absorbing, taking him away—but too quickly, he reached the end.

He set it aside and changed, lacing up his running shoes and picking up a pair of weights. Being efficient at things was a personal value and a trademark of his work. He could do weights and run at the same time, while *"considering the questions of life and the universe too."*

Raveaux heard that last sentence in his mind, spoken in Gita's laughing voice.

He would never forget the first time he met her. She had been involved with one of his cases on the Riviera. As an antiquities assessor, she was often called in to work for the wealthy, giving professional estimates on their possessions for insurance valuation or resale through the different auction houses. He'd met her on a case much like this latest diamond heist one.

Raveaux locked up his place and got out on the sidewalk, hefting his weights as he ran, trying not to think about Gita.

But there was no way to banish her—she'd arisen in memory like a djinn, lush lips framing perfect teeth in a smile that was just a little too large for her face.

Gita had been a small woman with a big personality and the kind of belly laugh that made his toes curl with happiness. She'd always worn her thick onyx hair braided unless he asked her to take it down. He could still see his fingers fanning through it, sorting the long rippling strands, loosening her braid . . .

Raveaux fumbled for his headphones in the pocket of his running shorts. He booted up some German thrash metal on his MP3 player, and that knocked everything out of his mind but the pound of his feet on the pavement, the pump of his arms as he lifted the weights, and the thunder of his heart as he pushed himself past memory.

RAVEAUX'S LAPTOP WAS TOP-OF-THE-LINE, and he had a satellite signal booster and a scrambling program on it to provide him with detection protection and alternate VPN addresses. Showered after his run and the distracting pageantry of the sunset, he settled himself in the small living room with the laptop on his knees, waiting for the

Chinese takeout he had called for. He cued up the recordings from Finewell's.

As he logged in to the encrypted stick drive Sophie had given him containing his half of the footage, his mind wandered.

What was Sophie's personal background? He knew only her professional life.

She seemed so polished, so well put together. He could tell by her accent she had been educated in Europe. The excellent cut of the simple, movement-friendly clothing she wore spoke of sophistication. He'd heard Sophie was a mother, but she wore no ring, and her body was the lithe shape of an athlete.

What did she do in the evenings? Was her lonely routine like his?

Maybe she'd like to share his Chinese food and go over the surveillance together.

Raveaux shook his head abruptly at the intrusive thought, waving his hand as if a fly had buzzed near his ear.

The doorbell rang. Out of long-established caution, Raveaux assessed the deliveryman through the spy hole from behind the door: *Asian teen with jeans hanging off his butt and a gold chain showing on his skinny chest between the panels of an unbuttoned black shirt* —the real thing.

Once he had paid for the takeout, Raveaux set the assortment of small, waxed cardboard containers and a pair of chopsticks on the coffee table.

He eyed the food with distaste.

He loved a good Bordeaux with a nice cut of meat in a red wine truffle reduction sauce; maybe some lightly grilled vegetables on the side garnished with crunchy *pommes frites* for texture, and a fresh baguette to tear apart and dip into the sauce.

What was he doing, ordering Chinese for the third day in a row?

The same thing he'd been doing with a million cruel little choices he made for himself on a daily basis—*punishing himself for being alive, when they were dead.*

Raveaux's therapist had nailed that pattern awhile ago, challenging him to stop his many tiny tortures. He'd been slowly getting better, gradually allowing little pleasures back into his life, beginning with the biggest one—relocating to Waikiki.

What he needed to do was get a good knife and a few pans, and go to the store for something other than coffee and seltzer water. He needed to cook himself some decent food.

Then he might have something to eat worthy of inviting Sophie over to share . . .

"*Merde!*" He had no room in his life for anything but enjoying his supposed Hawaii retirement and the occasional thriller novel. He hadn't had a relationship in four years, and he wasn't about to start now. Once he got sober, he'd decided he was done with that shit. He'd never risk that kind of heartache again.

Raveaux opened the nearest container and ate mechanically, his growling belly overcoming repugnance at the quality of the cuisine. He focused on the footage as it flowed by on his laptop's screen, scanning the boring video as it wound by on fast forward. He had gotten the second half of the video, after the jewels were supposedly in their "vault"—but he didn't think they had ever made it there at all.

Various employees entered and exited the video's capture as they stored and removed different items from the room's shelving, always with a partner. He'd taught himself lip reading, and he amused himself discerning the conversations—mostly useless information about football scores and the weather, along with an occasional off-color joke.

Raveaux made it through three hours of review before succumbing to utter boredom.

He formulated his case notes, provided a quick electronic signature, and logged his hours into the Security Solutions payment database.

And now there was nothing further to do.

Raveaux wasn't ready for sleep, though he brushed his teeth and stripped to his boxers. His mind, once again, ran down the rabbit hole of memory.

Lucie had always had difficulty with bedtime, too. He and Gita had worked hard to get their daughter to bed at a reasonable hour, fighting her many protests and calls for water, and hugs, and having her night light turned on, or off, or the door open or closed. At four, Lucie had been bright, sassy, full of energy. She'd had the incredible vocabulary of her mother, who spoke four languages, and the curiosity and persistence that Gita said were Raveaux's main traits.

Lucie would be eight now, if she had lived . . .

Raveaux threw the bedding aside and got up, once again battling the urge for a drink. Drinking had turned off mind and memory—he hadn't found a substitute that worked as well since he got sober. He would just have to go down to the beach and swim. *Swim until he was too tired for the memories, or the nightmares.*

Swimming was the real reason why he'd chosen this spot; not its over-bright sunlight and infernal crowds during the day.

The ocean took him into its dark embrace, warm and welcoming as a lover's arms. He snapped down his goggles, rolled on the nylon shirt he wore to trap a little body heat from escaping his lean frame, and slid on his swim fins.

He dove into the gentle waves and inky water and began laps, swimming parallel to shore. He focused on his form as his arms slashed through the water; stroke, stroke, turn, breathe, kick, kick, kick. The water was silk fabric he cut with scissoring arms; he was just a machine, mindless, soulless, heartless, as he moved like a sea creature through black water lightly kissed by the reflected lights of skyscrapers that shadowed the beach.

And gradually the soothing metronome of his strokes banished the heartache, at least for a little while.

CHAPTER TEN

Sophie: Day Two

RAVEAUX WAS ALREADY SEATED in a chair in front of her desk when Sophie walked into her office. He sat in his characteristic pose, one ankle cocked on the other knee, and that thriller novel he was reading open before him. As she walked around the desk, a touch of the light cinnamon aftershave he seemed to favor hit her nose. Though nattily dressed in a black button down and trousers over woven leather loafers, Raveaux's dark eyes were bloodshot and circled by purplish skin. "Rough night, Raveaux?"

"Bonjour, Sophie." Raveaux ignored her comment, slipping a piece of coconut fiber between the pages of his book.

"You're in early." Sophie set a thermos of hot, strong Thai tea on her desk and sat down in her chair. "Can you give me a few minutes? I have a routine in the mornings. I'm surprised Paula let you in."

Raveaux shrugged. "Paula was not at her desk when I arrived. Take all the time you need." He opened the book again.

He did not offer to leave and give her privacy.

Sophie suppressed a surge of annoyance. *Jake used to invade her space too.* She didn't like it any better from this man.

55

Sophie turned on her computers with her key fob and opened her tablet, checking the day timer app for her appointments. She answered a few urgent emails and shot Paula some instructions.

She picked up her thermos, unscrewed the cap, and poured some tea into the shiny cup that was a part of the lid. She took a sip of her favorite beverage and realized she'd forgotten Raveaux was even in the room, so completely had he withdrawn his presence.

Unlike Jake's physical restlessness and magnetism, Raveaux seemed to be able to render himself invisible—a handy skill for an investigator.

She sipped her tea and sneaked a glance at her new partner from beneath her lashes.

Raveaux's eyes on the pages of his book were sunken in bruised-looking pouches. His cheeks seemed hollow, as if he hadn't eaten well either. His black long-sleeved shirt was top quality, but wrinkled today, and sand packed the tread of his loafers.

The man obviously had sleep and stress problems—probably PTSD from his wife and daughter's murder. When she'd contacted Paula for the gossip on him last night, Paula had said that several of the other Security Solutions female contractors, and even one of the men, had made romantic overtures toward Raveaux—to no avail. "He's a grieving widower," Paula had said. "About as much fun as a bag of wet cats."

"Well, then we should work well together," Sophie had replied. "Because this particular wet cat is also a mother." That motherly part of her wanted to feed the man seated so quietly and patiently before her, tease a smile out of him. . .

Raveaux was not her problem. Sophie set down her empty cup too hard, and a little tea spilt on her desk. "Paula has a meeting lined up for us with Mel Samson. We're playing the part of insurance investigators, so we have to go over to the Finewell's auction house again," she said, mopping up the tea with a tissue.

"I expected as much." Raveaux set his book aside.

"Did you find anything on your half of the surveillance footage?"

"I did not. I submitted notes and my report through the Security Solutions data portal. I saw nothing out of place. The staff seems to be following a partner protocol whenever they store or remove any items. There was no deviation from that, nor any specific suspicious activity in the footage that I reviewed."

"Well, I did find something." Sophie woke up her tablet with a tap on the surface. She slid it into a holder and turned it towards Raveaux so that he could see the screen. "There's a slight glitch in the tape during the transfer of the gems from the assessor to Mel Samson, who logs them in and puts them away." Sophie swiped through the footage to the exact time stamp that she had identified the night before. "See? The recording jumps. Even though the time stamp proceeds forward without interruption, that segment has been doctored."

Raveaux's level black brows drew together as he viewed the section of video. He fingered a dent in his chin thoughtfully. "Let's watch the fifteen minutes leading up to the break in real time," Raveaux said. "I want to observe the dynamics between Samson and Polat."

Sophie's respect for her new partner shot up a notch—he'd taken time to identify and memorize the names of the players, though his section of video hadn't even contained them.

They watched a large woman with white-gloved hands, her hair a silvery helmet, as she opened a velvet-lined case containing the diamonds.

"I expected a male to be the inventory manager," Sophie confided. "Her name—Mel Samson—had me expecting a man."

Raveaux nodded. "Names can be deceiving. Samson's curriculum vitae is impressive," he said. "She is highly qualified. Multiple degrees in art and history, and a doctorate in nineteenth century antiquities. She's been with Finewell's for twenty years."

The camera recorded the scene from above and at a slight angle.

Sophie's eyes widened in surprise as Raveaux begin interpreting aloud what the diamond assessor, a small, ferret-like man, was saying in the video to Samson.

"An exceptionally fine set. The settings are consistent with the time period of the set's manufacture." Polat adjusted his loupe, handling the main stone at the center of the necklace. "I observe the tiny flaw in the central diamond that is recorded in the previous assessor's report. I will check the stones along the sides randomly, to verify that they are natural."

"You don't have to explain what you're doing, Agrippa. I've heard your spiel before." Samson said.

Sophie tapped Raveaux's arm to get his attention. "I didn't know you could read lips."

He moved away from her touch. "A useful skill in our line of work. Please replay the recording—you distracted me."

"Je regrette, pardon," Sophie said, reversing the feed.

"Parlez-vous français?" Raveaux asked, his brows raised in surprise.

"Une compétence utile dans notre métier, n'est-ce pas?" Sophie smiled, teasing him a little. "A useful skill in our line of work, isn't it?" Raveaux just looked back at the screen. *He was so serious all the time!* Sophie was usually the somber one in her work partnerships.

She re-started the recording.

The assessor was speaking again, and Raveaux continued his interpretation. "These gems are genuine. I can even see dust particles between the stone and the setting. The diamonds have not been disturbed from their mounts." Polat set the necklace down and went on to the earrings, a similar monotone of explanation falling from his lips. Samson sat back in her cushy chair, crossing her arms over ample, caftan-covered breasts.

Sophie reached out a finger and paused the recording as they approached the spot where she had identified an anomaly. "We need to work up a full background on Mel Samson. I did not have time last night to research her using my DAVID software; I was too busy looking at the information on Finewell's. Did you know the auction house has had major breaches at different locations in the last few years?"

A spark of interest lit Raveaux's dark eyes. "I wonder if there's a connection to Mel Samson."

"Exactly." It had been too long since Sophie'd been on a case, felt the thrill of the hunt, and been able to share that with someone. "We have a meeting with Samson in an hour, but after that, I want to take some time to do a deep background workup on her. Why don't you follow up on Agrippa Polat while I do that?"

"Reasonable. Proceed." Raveaux flicked his fingers in a gesture Sophie recognized as habitual. He probably didn't know how arrogant it looked because his face showed nothing but focused interest.

Sophie pressed *play* on the recording again.

Polat finished his assessment, stripped off his rubber gloves, shook Samson's hand, then took his leave.

Mel Samson gazed down at the jewels resting on the black velvet tray for a moment, and then closed the lid over the set.

Sophie stopped the recording and pointed. "There! See that little shimmer? She, or a cohort, cut the video feed and spliced something in. I believe that section contains the part where she removes the gems. See how long the pause is, as she looks down at the closed box? The substitution's done so seamlessly that I almost missed it."

They clicked through the frames one by one until Raveaux caught the tiny jump. Sophie screen-shot the frames and saved the glitched section to their case file.

The action resumed as Samson carried the jewels' container to her assistant. The two of them proceeded down the elevator, and she stowed the box in the storage room's locked shelf per protocol.

"It is as you suspected, Raveaux. The diamonds never made it to that safe."

"We have likely solved the case, as far as who took the gems. But

I'm interested in the bigger picture—how many times has Samson done this? How much has she cost this company? And who is her fence?"

"And why is she doing this, after a stellar career of twenty years with Finewell's?" Sophie rubbed the gunshot scar on her cheekbone. "I think we should call Childer before we interview Samson. The diamonds may be unrecoverable if the fence has broken up the set and sold them already, even supposing we can get his or her name out of Samson. Neither of us is police anymore . . . we have to tell our client what we've found so far, and see what he wants us to do."

"Sometimes I miss the clarity of my former life," Raveaux said darkly.

Sophie ignored his comment and picked up her phone. "Paula, put us through to Mr. Childer at Finewell's on speaker. Don't take no for answer—this is an emergency regarding his case."

"Right away, Sophie."

Sophie put down the handset and turned to her colleague, resuming the thread of their conversation. "Clarity, Raveaux?" She snorted. "Here at Security Solutions, we deal justice to the highest bidder. There are days that priority system really bothers me. This case is not particularly one of them—I don't honestly care about rich people's diamonds and where they end up. I don't mind being paid for finding that out for someone who does care. When I get upset, it's about human trafficking, murder, or kidnapping, the kind of cases where only the rich can get their family members back."

"I could not rest with that," Raveaux agreed.

"And I don't rest with it. I turn information over to the authorities, hoping they can use it, which they sometimes can—and I violate our clients' confidentiality anonymously to do so, not to mention a host of laws we bend in our investigations. I comfort myself with the fact that we've helped some, even if we can't help all. Sometimes we can do more than police, because we are unfettered by due process of law. And that kind of makes up for the inequities."

Raveaux's expression remained cool, neutral—but his eyes held a wealth of sorrow and complex knowledge. "True," was all he said.

The phone rang and Sophie picked it up. "Mr. Childer. Mr. Raveaux is here with me, and we have you on speaker." She pushed the mic button and turned the unit toward Raveaux. "We have some information we think you need, right away."

"I am all ears," Childer said, his voice electronically thin.

Sophie laid out the information they'd uncovered from the video. "There's a good chance Samson is your thief, but with what else I've discovered about your company's situation, Raveaux and I wanted to offer you a chance to go after bigger fish, and uncover, potentially, a network that has targeted Finewell's in the last three years." Sophie detailed the breaches and losses she'd uncovered using DAVID.

Childer sputtered. "I was never told any of this! I'm concerned about what you are telling me, but we must get those diamonds back before the auction event. That is my priority."

Raveaux leaned in to speak past Sophie. "Perhaps, Mr. Childer, we can leverage Ms. Samson to give the diamonds back and help us in a greater investigation by offering her clemency. We will not turn her in, if she helps us."

A long pause. The phone line hissed as Childer thought it over. "Do it. I'll speak to my chain of command about this, once you've recovered the diamonds for me."

Sophie met Raveaux's eyes, frowning. "You're the client, Mr. Childer."

"Yes, and don't forget it," Childer snapped, and banged down the phone.

Sophie frowned. "At least he was clear about what he wants us to do."

"Yes." Raveaux stood up, buttoning his jacket. "This will be a delicate interview. We need to subtly threaten Ms. Samson with legal consequences in exchange for the diamonds—but I think we should go for more. Finewell's will reward your firm for doing so, even if Childer can't see past his own priorities."

Sophie reached for the faux clip-on insurance investigator name tags Paula had made and handed one to Raveaux. "You may take the lead. I have never been very good at delicate interviews."

Raveaux gave a slight bow, and she could swear a hint of a smile hovered around his stern mouth. "I will do my best."

CHAPTER ELEVEN

Connor: Day Two

CONNOR ASCENDED the stone stairs behind Nine, the closest person he had to a friend in the compound. The compound's main building was a step pyramid, and it took a while for the two of them to reach the room at the top.

"You sure you don't want to bathe and change, One?" Nine asked over his shoulder.

"No. I may want to work out more." Connor had just finished an hour of drilling with the recruits, leading them from the front row through participation rather than watching. He'd not only felt the need for a workout himself, he wanted to solidify his influence with the men by bonding with them through shared activity.

Connor didn't need Nine to guide him; he knew perfectly well where the computer lab was. The Yām Khûmkạn computer room was positioned in the highest room of the compound, where the satellite internet hookup would receive the least amount of interference. The remote jungle location of the compound helped protect it, but added to other concerns.

Connor had avoided computers for the past two years—the wired world had been like a seventh sense to him, so early in his training with the Master that they'd decided he should shut that sense off in order to develop others.

Nine worked the combination on a solid steel padlock sealing the door of the computer room, its modern gleam a contrast to the weathered wood and stone surrounding it. "The lock is just to send a signal to any of the men wandering out of bounds that this area is off limits," Nine said. He rattled off the code, and Connor memorized it.

Nine opened the door wide. "Enter. This is your space now."

Connor stepped across the threshold, and the first thing he noticed was his violin.

The valuable vintage instrument was set on a pair of simple wooden brackets bolted to the wall, sealed and safe in its worn leather case.

The sight of that case stole Connor's breath.

How had the Master obtained it? He'd left the violin in a storage unit in Honolulu, registered to his Sheldon Hamilton identity . . .

Connor ignored the computer equipment arrayed on a long table against one wall, and crossed the room to take down the case. His hands trembled as he undid the clasps to gaze at the lustrous wood and gorgeous curves of the most valuable possession he owned.

Small packets of silica gel fell out of the case as Connor lifted out the violin—whoever had transported it was trying to safeguard the instrument from injury from the damp of their jungle setting.

Connor was more than touched that the Master had somehow obtained the violin for him. At one time in his life, music had almost taken over—he'd been that addicted to the singing voice of the instrument, the precision and discipline of practice.

His father's cruelty had shut down his musical passion in high school: "You'll never make anything of yourself with that sissy crap." He'd broken Connor's violin, and almost broken his body, too, when Connor lashed out to get the instrument back.

His father had a course charted out for Connor that had involved a football scholarship and a place in his company—*in his image, in his shadow, and under his thumb.*

Connor had run away and stolen his first identity by stealing a wallet on the street. He'd spent hard years living in a squat, putting every penny he could steal into the stock market and shorting sales on a cheap computer. He'd learned to fight dirty and live rough, and those days were etched on his soul. He'd eventually bested his father and stolen his company from him; he'd read of the man's suicide without emotion.

His first kill as the Ghost had been one of the most satisfying, and grievous, of his life.

He'd slowly, carefully, and craftily built his world, his life, just the way he wanted it—until he and Sophie had discovered each other online. She'd turned his dreams upside down and made them bigger and better.

All of those thoughts whirled through his mind as Connor stroked the satiny wood. Before he'd gone into training with the Yām Khûmkan, he'd regularly spent hours a day in practice and performed with the Honolulu Symphony Orchestra on special occasions.

"What's that?" Nine asked.

Of course, the man would never have seen one of these . . . "A violin." Connor lifted his long-lost instrument to his shoulder. He set the bow to the strings, and coaxed a long, gentle opening note from them, unsure of when the instrument had been tuned.

He need not have worried. The Master must have had the instrument worked on, because the violin sang to him as it always had. He launched into a favorite Mozart piece, starting over when he hit a false note, as was his wont.

This violin, like computers, was an essential part of the life that he'd given up for the last two years. Given up to make room for his training. He didn't regret that choice—but now the music wound around him like smoke, and filled him with a sensation akin to bliss.

The piece finally finished to his satisfaction, Connor lowered the violin. His whole body seemed to glow, reverberating with the remnants of the notes, as if they both surrounded and filled him.

Nine was long gone.

Sunlight slanting through the deep stone window slits, amplified by a beveled bronze plaque that reflected a spot of sun onto the white-painted ceiling, was the cool blue of late afternoon.

Connor set the violin back into its case. His hands and arms were trembling with strain, with tiredness; his fingertips felt blistered by the strings. Though more physically fit than ever in his life, he was badly out of shape for the unique discipline of playing.

Touching that violin had been like drinking deep when he hadn't known he was thirsty.

Connor sat down in the incongruously modern office chair in front of a bank of monitors, configured the way he liked them. The Master had prepared for him here, too.

All of this seemed to point to the Master being gone for a long time.

Nine reappeared in the doorway, carrying a tray set with several covered, steaming bowls, a pot of tea, and utensils. "I thought you might partake of the evening meal up here."

"Thanks." Connor's attention was already diverted by the computers. *Would that intuition that seemed to flow between him and the machines come back to him?*

He cracked his knuckles and eyed the food Nine had brought. He needed a little time—playing had depleted as well as renewed him. "Are you going to eat with me?"

"No, I took my meal with the trainees in the hall." Nine sat down at a computer rig beside Connor's. "You should eat, though. I'll get the Master's email open for you—he wanted you to carry on the compound's business."

Connor uncovered one of the bowls, revealing a delicious-smelling curry over rice. He glanced at Nine. "Do you have any idea where the Master went? Or for how long?"

"He didn't say." Nine's fingers rattled nervously on the keyboard. "But I think his trip might've had something to do with Pim Wat."

Connor's heart jumped like a spooked rabbit. *The Master's disappearance had something to do with Sophie's deadly mother?* He kept outwardly calm, picking up his bowl and stirring the curry with his chopsticks, then scooping it into his mouth.

Pim Wat, Sophie's mother, had stolen Sophie's baby when the infant was less than twelve hours old. That venomous spider of a woman had then executed an entire rescue party sent to recover the child, and only Connor and Jake, Sophie's lover, had been spared. Connor had negotiated Jake's freedom in exchange for staying at the compound as a hostage. Additionally, he'd asked that the Master hold Pim Wat in check, keeping her away from her daughter and granddaughter. That last condition hadn't been necessary once Pim Wat had been captured by the CIA.

"I thought Pim Wat died in Guantánamo," Connor said carefully.

"She is alive, though not in good health, from what I overheard." Nine rubbed at his shiny, shaved skull. "I've had my concerns, and since you are the Master's number One, I think you should know everything I know." Nine swiveled his chair to face Connor. A short, stocky man, Nine was built strong through the chest and midsection. He normally radiated calm and purpose, but worry now tightened the corners of his eyes. "I never thought Pim Wat was a good fit as the Master's lover, but it was not my place to have an opinion."

"The Master can handle Pim Wat." Connor chewed rapidly, considering what more to say. "Since we are speaking frankly—I thought he was using her more than she ever used him. She was an assassin for the Yām Khûmkạn, and he controlled her, at least in part, through their relationship. When she was captured—he showed no interest whatsoever. I was watching for any sign."

"There was much you did not know."

"True. He told me more than most trainees, but he never spoke of her."

"They were lovers. He used her, yes, but he also had an attachment to her. He was distressed when she was captured; I perceived that. Then he seemed to decide something, and put her out of his mind." Nine poured a cup of tea for Connor and set it beside his plate. "I thought she was no longer in the picture, but I was bringing the Master his dinner the other day and I heard him speaking on the phone. He had sent our best team of assassins to free her from the CIA compound in Guantánamo, and was following up. He closed the door before I heard anything more."

This was much more definitive than anything he'd yet said, and Connor dropped a chopstick, scattering rice over the table's surface. "An attack on the U.S. base would endanger the Yām Khûmkan's low profile and put them on the radar. That's not the kind of clever strategy the Master is known for."

"The Master will have done something to obscure who is responsible. I suspect that she has been extracted by now, and that he is meeting her somewhere," Nine said.

"Well. It's none of any of our business what the Master does. We are here to serve him and the Yām Khûmkan. I'm sure he will communicate what he wants us to know," Connor said.

"Yes." Nine stood up. "Do you need anything else?"

"No, thank you."

Nine glided out. The heavy wooden door shut behind him with a *thunk*.

Connor flexed his fingers on the keyboard, collecting himself as he gazed at the blank monitors.

He had to warn Sophie!

If he reached out to her, it would be the first contact Connor'd had with Sophie since he last spoke to her on the phone, severed all ties, and joined the Yām Khûmkan.

Did she ever check the encrypted chat room they had used over the years to communicate secretly?

Connor leaned forward, fingers flying, reaching out to the

woman he loved—the woman he had given up his life for, sacrificing himself to the Master so that she could be a family with Jake and her child. Thinking of them together had brought him comfort on many a lonely night.

Now it was time to ruin that happiness.

CHAPTER TWELVE

Raveaux: Day Two

RAVEAUX ENTERED Mel Samson's office with Sophie close behind, after the woman's receptionist buzzed them in. The visitor badges identifying them as investigators were pinned to their lapels, and Raveaux tapped his as he advanced to the large desk Samson was seated behind. "Bonjour, Madame. Pierre Raveaux with Fidelity Mutual, and this is my associate, Sophie Smithson."

Samson did not rise when they entered. What had looked like a silver helmet of hair in the video turned out to be an artistically draped scarf that wrapped her skull, fastened with a decorative knot in the front. Her face was round and full, with doll-like features and intelligent hazel eyes. She wore a full-length, embroidered caftan, and would have looked like a fortune teller if given a crystal ball. "What can I do for you investigators today?"

Sophie closed the door behind them as Raveaux, uninvited by Samson, drew a couple of chairs close to her desk. They seated themselves, and Raveaux removed a tablet device from his leather satchel. "We are engaged in our annual security audit, and during the course of that, we have come across some anomalies. I have an item in question that we need to draw your attention to."

As the device booted up and Raveaux scrolled, looking for the saved bit of video, Sophie gestured to the paintings on the walls, bright and lively Impressionist seascapes that looked original. "Those are lovely. Are you a collector, as well as an assessor?"

"I am not an assessor. If you have checked my curriculum vitae, I am the manager of inventory, and one of the quality assurance evaluators for intake," Samson said frostily.

"Tell us what brought you to Hawaii," Sophie's tone was still caring and relaxed. "According to the company records, you've only been here a year."

"Why don't you tell me about what brings *you* to Hawaii?" Samson wasn't warming up.

No point in further pleasantries. Raveaux cleared his throat. "We were reviewing video documenting the intake process, and came across a gap in the recording." He set the tablet down on the desk and tipped it toward Samson. He pressed *play*, and the diamond assessment with Agrippa Polat leaped into movement.

Raveaux didn't watch the video. He watched Samson's face instead. The color drained from the woman's already pale cheeks.

"You might find this section of particular interest," Raveaux said, and, with a twist of his fingertips, pulled up the screenshot Sophie had taken of the stitched video clip. "This splice is very well done, but we can see where the video was altered." He laid the tablet down in front of Samson and made a steeple of his fingers on the desk as he addressed her. "Mr. Childer has identified the loss of the diamonds. He has tasked us with recovering them prior to the sale. We know you took them."

"Ridiculous. I've been a good employee of this company for more than twenty years." Samson sat back in her chair, interlacing her fingers across her ample midsection. "If that's your evidence, it's pretty thin."

"We're giving you a chance here," Sophie said softly. "We have discussed the situation with Childer, and he is willing to offer you clemency in the form of not reporting this to the police if you will share the other players in your theft scheme with us—whoever doctors your video. Your fence for the stolen goods. Anyone else involved."

Mel Samson's remarkable eyes flicked between the two of their faces. Raveaux could almost see the woman's prodigious brain ticking through her options.

"You're dying," Raveaux guessed. "You don't have much to lose."

Samson's eyes reminded Raveaux of the heart of a fire: brown, black, gold. "That's exactly right. I don't really care what happens next."

"Why are you still working, then?"

"Working distracts me. Working helps me forget about dying for a few hours."

"You need money," Raveaux said. "For medical expenses, if nothing else."

"And I don't much care whether you believe me or not," Samson said.

Sophie cleared her throat. "I'm so sorry about your health, Ms. Samson. I can see by these paintings, and by the curriculum vitae I reviewed, that you are a woman of sensitivity and refinement. Surely you want to spend your last days in comfort, rather than in a jail cell. You must have someone you are leaving your legacy to, whose opinion you care about, who could be hurt by what happens to you. Please pause to consider the full picture of what you will leave behind."

Samson looked down at her blotter. Tucked in the corner of it was a child's school photo, yellowing with age, its edges curling.

Sophie had hit the right note. There was someone in Samson's life whom she cared about.

They had some leverage, after all.

Raveaux pressed in. "As I said, you probably have medical

expenses. A life insurance policy that will go to your heir. You don't want to endanger your legacy and leave a loved one nothing but a pile of unpaid bills."

"Why do you think I took the stones?" This time, when Samson's eyes met Raveaux's, there was resignation in them. "The diamonds are gone. I can't get them back. I plan to be dead before the auction."

Raveaux grunted, the sound wrenched from his gut by the woman's despair.

"Tell us who your fence is. Tell us where the diamonds went. Tell us who did these other jobs, and we will let you execute whatever end of life plan it is that you already have made, without informing the authorities." Sophie pushed a list over to Samson.

The list denoted a series of three previous breaches in Finewell's security that had resulted in missing merchandise. Insurance had covered the thefts and allowed the auction house to maintain its pristine record—but that record was going to be broken this time. Mr. Childer was going to lose his job, most likely, and Mel Samson would spend her last days in a prison cell, if she wouldn't work with them. Hopefully, that would not be the outcome of this particular drama.

"Tell me again what you will give me in exchange for information," Samson said.

"We aren't really insurance investigators," Raveaux said. "We are private investigators, hired by Mr. Childer, on his own. We've been tasked with recovering the diamonds in advance of the auction. He wants to keep everything quiet, to avoid publicity and any potential impact to his job. He has already been apprised that we've identified you as the likely thief. He just wants the diamonds back."

Sophie picked up the thread. "However, of particular import, if the diamonds are out of your reach, we are interested in the bigger impact of your activities on Finewell's. If you help us capture those who participated in the thefts, we will keep your name private. We suspect Finewell's won't want to go to the police with any of this. The other stolen goods were already paid for with insurance money.

All they care about is that their name is not dragged through the media. Their attitude provides an opportunity for you, Ms. Samson."

Samson's smoldering eyes flicked between them, and then back down at the child's photo, tucked into the blotter. A long moment wound by.

Who was that? A daughter? A little sister? A niece? According to her bio, Samson had never married, nor had any children. But there was someone . . . Raveaux flashed painfully to his own loss. Were he to get sick or die, there would be no one to care, no one to leave anything to.

Samson inclined her head. "All right. I'll tell you what I know. In return, you must keep my name quiet and let me keep my job until I . . . die." Her voice caught on the word, but no expression accompanied it. "I will try to get the diamonds back. I will reach out to my contact and tell him that the loss has been discovered early, that I need the gems returned. Perhaps they aren't gone. But, it's likely I cannot get them back, and things will play out as I first thought they would—the loss will become public. And I will be gone by then."

"Do you have a suicide plan arranged?" Sophie asked softly.

Sophie seemed so matter-of-fact about it. Raveaux could not contemplate suicide without a sense of revulsion—life was too precious, too easily snatched away.

"I do. And though my cancer is incurable, and progressing, my life insurance policy pays out regardless of cause of death." Samson smiled mirthlessly. "It was an expensive policy."

"Now you are asking us to not only cover up your theft, but to participate in insurance fraud," Raveaux said. He tapped the paper before Samson. "Did you perform these thefts?"

"I did not devise them, but I was the one to execute them, yes. I was recruited through an anonymous source on email. This person tells me how and when the theft should be done, and then alters the video and surveillance feeds to hide my actions. I receive detailed instructions, and then my cut of the money is wired into an account in the Caymans. I have been using the money to pay for my medical bills, and for alternative treatments not covered by insurance. But nothing is working. I told my source that I would do one last job." Samson stroked one doughy hand with the other.

Raveaux's eyebrows snapped together. "So, you don't know who is behind the thefts?"

"I figured it was better not to know," Samson said. "I don't know who the fence is, either. I merely place the items, boxed and bagged, in my trash, or in a dumpster where the theft architect tells me to leave them, and they're gone in the morning."

Raveaux glanced over at Sophie, and was encouraged by the alert brightness of her gaze. *Sophie was intrigued by tracking the master thief online.* "Give us what you have. And we will do what we can to find this master thief," she said.

"This is not what we hoped for," Raveaux temporized.

"Ms. Samson will help us all she can, won't you, Ms. Samson? Can I have access to your computer? Perhaps I can track the master thief through his digital footprint."

"That would be fine. I am contacted to do the jobs on a personal email on my own computer. I figured I would wipe the hard drive before . . ."

"Before your suicide," Sophie finished. "Why don't you give me that laptop now."

Samson leaned over and dug into her briefcase. She lifted out a slim, silver HP laptop and handed it to Sophie.

Raveaux was frustrated by the extra challenges to their plan. There was a good chance they wouldn't be able to trace the master thief if he'd hidden his tracks professionally enough. "Open that laptop and give Ms. Smithson all of your passwords. The two of you can compose an email to the thief, asking for the diamonds to be returned. And in the meantime, I will talk to Mr. Childer about this latest development." He stood up and buttoned his jacket. "I can make no promises to protect you, Ms. Samson, with such a minimal amount of information to go on. The company may well insist on a 'fall guy,' as Americans call it."

"It is what it is," Samson said. "I cannot make it something different." She seemed to be speaking a deeper truth.

Sophie inclined her head as she met Raveaux's eyes. *She seemed to be telling him to relax, that she had this under control*—but it was one thing to read of Sophie's expertise with computers, and another to hang their budding case on that premise.

He gave the women a curt nod and exited the office, heading for the elevator. He took the lift to Childer's top floor office, using the moments alone to brush off uncomfortable feelings engendered by Samson's sad situation.

Everyone had a date with death, and sometimes that day just came much sooner than anyone was ready for. He knew that bitter truth more than most.

The portly manager was pacing when Raveaux entered his office, looking decidedly crumpled by stress. Childer patted his cheeks with his kerchief and tugged down his jacket. "Well? What did you discover?"

"It's not good news, Mr. Childer."

Raveaux steered the man by his elbow over to the seating area and settled him on the loveseat. Raveaux took a comfortable armchair across from Childer and sketched out the results of their conversation with Samson. "Samson claims not to know who designed the heists. She will go along with giving us all that she does know, in return for being kept out of a police report."

"This is terrible!" Childer popped up from the loveseat like a jack-in-the-box, pacing again. "Not at all acceptable!"

"Let's get your immediate superior on the telephone, Mr. Childer. It's time to go public with the loss of the diamonds, at least as far as the company is concerned, and appeal to Finewell's desire to stop this master thief. If we play our cards right, you can come out of this smelling like the proverbial rose—you discovered the theft. You took the initiative by hiring Security Solutions, to both retrieve the gems and stanch a bigger leak. If the diamonds cannot be recovered in time for the sale, which seems likely they cannot, then your only hope for saving your job is to bring your bosses a bigger fish."

Childer required more hand-holding and reassurance, but eventually they got the central manager of Finewell's on the line, and with Raveaux's help, Childer explained their case.

An hour later, feeling decidedly sweaty and crumpled himself from all the wrangling, Raveaux left Childer's office with authorization to expand the investigation by going after the supposed master thief through investigating the prior breaches.

Raveaux enjoyed the hum of excitement tingling along his nerves as he got on the elevator. It had been a long time since he'd looked forward to digging deeper into a case.

Was it the familiar world of high-end theft that excited him, or the prospect of working closely with Sophie?

He didn't have to know the answer to that right now.

CHAPTER THIRTEEN

Sophie: Day Two

TRACKING passwords and access codes as Samson input them, Sophie smelled the subtle but deeply unpleasant scent of death rising from Samson's skin and hair.

"I'll compose my email now." Samson opened a private, encrypted email. The sight of the masked interface against a black background screen reminded Sophie of her correspondence with Connor as the Ghost, when she'd first begun tracking his online vigilante activities. They had communicated through an encrypted chat room similar to what Samson pulled up now.

How was Connor doing at the Yām Khûmkạn compound? The surveillance cam looking into the stronghold's dining room that her team had planted had run out of battery power long ago, depriving her of glimpses into his new life.

He'd left a legal folder, containing directions for her regarding his estate and affairs, and one of them was that if he was gone with no word for longer than a year, she was to initiate legal proceedings to have his Sheldon Hamilton identity declared dead. She'd begun that process, using the information from the jungle massacre to accelerate the seven-year timeline.

Not that she believed for a minute that he was really dead . . .

Sophie shook her head to return to the present moment, and devote her attention to the woman who was composing a difficult email beside her.

Mel Samson read the email out loud to Sophie. *"The diamonds have been discovered missing. My boss found a glitch in the surveillance video, and is threatening me with exposure if the stones are not returned in time for the auction. He's desperate to cover his ass and has promised that if they are returned, I can keep my job. He does not want any publicity, or for this to be discovered and made public. Please get the diamonds back, and we can return them to the vault prior to the auction. I will be able to keep my job and be in a position to help you in the future. I will wait to hear back with next steps."*

"Do you think I sound suitably desperate?" Samson turned Sophie's way. Even the woman's breath was tinged with decay.

Compassion softened Sophie's heart as she took in Samson's pallor. "Give me a moment to embed a tracker in the email." She swiveled the laptop toward herself, and in a few keystrokes, downloaded one of her favorite spy programs from the Cloud. She embedded the tracker in a bit of code at the end of the woman's email, hidden as a bit of punctuation. "I'll take the computer with me, and monitor this. This email source is likely masked, but we might get lucky. In any case I will try to lure the thief out of hiding and get him to interact with me."

Samson nodded. They closed up the laptop and Sophie slid it into her own bag, a backpack she used in lieu of a purse.

"Do you want to tell me about your suicide plan?" Suicide was a dark devil that had sat on Sophie's own shoulder many a time; there was relief in sharing that uneasy burden. Perhaps she could help Samson out of her own painful experience.

"No. You are responsible for more than enough. I don't want to make you responsible for that knowledge, too." Samson gestured to the paintings. "I was going to leave these paintings to a museum, but since you admired them . . . which would you like?"

Sophie stared at the beautiful impressionistic land-and seascapes, each of them an original work likely to appreciate. Giving away one's possessions was evidence of intention to die by suicide; but nothing Sophie said would talk Samson out of it at this point. The woman was dying, and perhaps it would comfort her to know that something of her collection was appreciated.

Sophie pointed. "That one." Turquoise waves splashed over black volcanic rocks as an oncoming Hawaiian storm lashed palm trees edging the rocks. Sophie could almost feel the spray and the wind, hear the waves. Energy and passion suffused the painting, and Sophie responded to its visceral power with a feeling of excitement.

"A favorite of mine by an up-and-comer named Michael Clements." Samson smiled, a brief expression that left Sophie wishing she could see more of it. "Take it with you. And if you talk to Childer, tell him that I will try to resolve this mess before I go."

"I will tell him. Thank you for helping us. And thank you for the painting. I will treasure it, and remember you when I look at it." Sophie took the art down off the wall. She wrapped the painting in her jacket and tucked it under her arm as Samson dismissed her assistant on a makeshift errand. When Sophie peeked out into the reception area, the room was empty.

She turned back to the woman behind the desk, feeling a profound sorrow. "It's going to be okay, Ms. Samson."

That sad smile switched the woman's pale lips. "Whatever that means," she said. "Goodbye."

"I prefer 'aloha.'" Sophie returned to the desk and leaned down, offering a hug. Samson awkwardly accepted it. Sophie shut her eyes, accepting the smell and touch of oncoming death as part of touching another, however briefly. *Death was what made life so sweet . . .*

"Aloha, then," Samson said, and her smile lingered this time as Sophie exited and pulled the door shut behind her.

She headed down to the car to wait for Raveaux, sending him a text about where she would be. Once in the garage, she stowed the painting in the doggy-smelling back of the vehicle under a blanket she used when she took Momi and Anubis to the beach.

She was sitting in the driver's seat, working her phone, when Raveaux reappeared.

"Childer's superiors gave us a go for the bigger op," Raveaux said. "It's all on you, Sophie, to lure the master thief into the open."

CHAPTER FOURTEEN

Sophie: Day Two, Evening

GINGER AND ANUBIS were feisty and ready to run when Sophie got home, so it was a brisk and energizing trip down to the beach and back before she did her evening check-in with Momi and Armita on Skype, showered, and took another of her reheated casseroles next door to the computer lab to follow up on the email situation with the master thief.

Sophie settled herself in front of one of the racks of monitors set up on a long table in Connor's former office. The cool, orderly space with its two computer stations and workout area in the corner was unchanged from the days when he had set it up and they had worked there together. She was a little superstitious about changing anything about it, as if to do so would ensure that he'd never return.

The only thing she'd done to alter the space was blow up the arty black and white photo Connor had sent her, early in their relationship, of his perfect, naked body doing a pullup at the bar of the workout area. She enjoyed looking at the photo while she did her own workout breaks.

She was just keeping his chair warm for him. She'd tell herself that as many times as she needed to.

Sophie hooked up Samson's laptop to a write blocker, beginning the process of duplicating the woman's entire hard drive and online record. She had routinely copied and worked with mirror constructs of computers at her former job as an FBI tech agent, but it had been a while since she had a rig to tear apart personally. Her fingers itched with eagerness to start digging into Samson's records—but first, she had to see if the master thief had responded to the email lure they'd sent from Samson's office.

She was logging into the encrypted email address Samson used when her private phone rang. The highly confidential phone was kept plugged in and stored in this locked office, and only a few people in the world had her number. Sophie's brows drew together as she picked up the slim silver device off the charger—she didn't recognize the digits on the caller ID.

"This is Sophie Smithson."

"Sophie. It's Connor."

"Connor!" She sagged backward into the office chair. She would've recognized that voice anywhere—though she had first gotten to know him speaking with an Australian accent. "I can't believe it's you!"

"Yes, it is I. The rumors of my demise are greatly exaggerated." The subtle mockery that he often employed on himself filled his voice.

"Well, the paperwork associated with having you declared dead is *not* greatly exaggerated," Sophie quipped back. "Where *are* you?"

"Still at the Yām Khûmkạn stronghold. It's good to hear your voice."

Sophie's heart pounded, and she couldn't tell if the feeling was apprehension or joy. "I have kept everything going for you. The company is doing better than ever."

"I never had a doubt. And I trust you are enjoying the CEO's chair?" Connor sounded teasing.

The company and the CEO job were no laughing matter to her, and irritation replaced Sophie's initial excitement at hearing from him. "Not enjoying it much, no." She'd been so overwhelmed at first, trying to fill his considerable shoes at the same time as she got used to being a mother. "I've taken an actual case for the first time in two years, and I'm enjoying leaving the office and getting out in the field." She rubbed the old gunshot scar on her cheek with a trembling hand. "Why are you calling me? Why now, and not . . . so much sooner?" Emotion clogged her throat. "I can hardly believe I'm hearing your voice right now."

"I love you too, Sophie," Connor said.

She didn't like his light tone. Anger flushed her, and Sophie shot to her feet, shoving the office chair back. "You left me here to deal with everything, and now, two years later, you call me out of the blue to make fun of me?"

"I'm sorry. We're getting off on the wrong foot." He sounded serious now, contrite. "I do have a reason I'm calling now, and not before this."

"Speak. I have work to do." Sophie was riding the steepest emotional roller coaster that she remembered in a long time, and she was pretty sure it wasn't over yet. She flattened a hand over her thumping pulse. "Tell me what you called to tell me."

Connor cleared his throat. "I graduated from my study under the Master. That's one thing. Until now I haven't had any access to communication equipment, but he named me his successor."

"I don't know how to respond to that." Sophie grabbed the chair for support. "His successor? What does that mean?"

"I'm not sure yet, but he's left me in charge while he went on a mission for an undisclosed amount of time." He blew out a breath. "The Master has left the compound, and I have reason to believe he means to rescue your mother from Guantánamo."

A rush of emotions had brought Sophie to her feet; now, with this shock, her legs gave out. She dropped like a sack of rice into her office chair. "I always thought he would," she whispered. "I'm surprised it didn't happen sooner. And why hasn't that CIA agent Devin McDonald called me to let me know?"

"I don't know. Actually, I don't know much of anything. I have spent the last two years in intensive study and training for eight to ten hours a day. No days off, no weekends. I graduated yesterday, and today he's gone. The only reason I have any idea where he is at all, is that one of his closest men overheard him talking about sending a team to extract Pim Wat." Connor gusted out a sigh. "I called to warn you."

Sophie's last sight of her mother had been of Pim Wat's broken, bloodied body being loaded onto a door in lieu of a gurney, and that crude support being settled onto the floor of a CIA helicopter. The chopper had taken Pim Wat from her sister's house in Thailand to the infamous internment camp. Later, Sophie had learned that she had been treated for severe injuries incurred during her fall down some steep stairs. She had been kept in isolation at the outpost. McDonald, Sophie's CIA contact regarding her mother and other operations, had been disappointed over the years by Pim Wat's lack of useful intel. She had gone catatonic soon after her arrival at the camp, unresponsive to any attempt to rouse her for information. Photos Sophie had seen showed Pim Wat shrunken, her silky black hair streaked with white, her face misshapen from the fall.

Sophie had felt nothing when she saw the photos.

She'd felt nothing when she heard her mother was on a feeding tube.

She'd felt nothing until now.

And now, fear and anger warred for supremacy in Sophie, making her chest tight. She breathed in short pants. "Pim Wat cannot be allowed out of that place. She's dangerous," Sophie said. "I don't care if McDonald says she's been catatonic and looks a hundred years old. I know her. I know what she's capable of."

"Agreed. But what's done is done. The Master's gone, and so is Pim Wat, unless you hear otherwise from McDonald. I'd get in touch with him right away."

"What else do you know?" Sophie's fingers flew as she pulled up McDonald's email.

"Like I said, not much, just what I could get out of the Master's manservant—which is that he overheard the Master assigning one of his assassin teams to break her out. I don't know why the CIA hasn't called you. Haven't you been working with them?"

"Hardly. I've been rather busy running a multi-million-dollar security company," Sophie snapped. "But we've boosted intel we've picked up on our various jobs to the CIA on topics they have asked for us to monitor. My debt to the CIA for their help in getting Jake out is discharged, from my perspective at least, though I have no doubt they'd have a different take on it."

Connor's voice was thoughtful. "You and I are each sitting on some of the world's most powerful online search tools, and yet we have very little information to go on at this point. Until today I didn't have access to the computer lab at all—but, now the Master's left me in charge of the compound, and that includes communications. I'll dig in with the Ghost software and see what I can find."

"In charge of the stronghold?" Sophie had taken a moment to really process what he'd said. She reeled at this disclosure. "You mean like . . . you're the leader of the Yām Khûmkạn?"

"Not specifically, no, but he did name me his successor, and I'm in charge here." Connor's voice was tight with something: satisfaction? Regret? Pride? Sophie couldn't tell. "I can't leave."

"Oh. Kind of like how I can't leave Security Solutions since you left me in charge." *Had she meant to sound so bitter?*

A long beat went by. Connor cleared his throat again. "How are you and Jake?"

"I am fine. Jake is even better. He just moved to California with Felicia," Sophie said. Yes, bitter was how she sounded.

"Wait. What? Jake is . . . with Felicia?" Connor's voice sounded hollow with shock. Dimly, Sophie remembered he'd believed she and Jake were still together during that last, fateful phone call, when he told her he was staying at the Yām Khûmkạn. She hadn't had the strength back then to explain.

"Jake broke up with me almost as soon as he escaped the compound," Sophie said, her voice crisp and matter of fact. "He felt betrayed by discovering that you weren't who you said you were. He —accused me of divided loyalties, of keeping secrets from him. And of course, he was right." *Connor had not only broken her heart once, but again by causing her breakup with Jake.* "Thanks for the warning about my mother. I will see what I can find out about Pim Wat from McDonald. I assume this number is a good one to reach you at; I'll be in touch if necessary."

Sophie ended the call with a push of a button, and turned off the phone in case he tried to call back. She set the device back on its charger and stared blankly at the wall of monitors.

Pim Wat had been set free by the Master, and Connor was in charge of the Yām Khûmkạn. "What fresh hell is next?" Sophie heard her friend Marcella's voice in her head.

Marcella. It had been too long since she called her FBI agent friend—they were both so busy. They sparred on occasion at the gym Alika owned in downtown Honolulu; perhaps her friend was available for a workout—and a catch up. Unfortunately, she still couldn't talk with anyone but Dr. Wilson, her therapist, about the fact that Connor was still alive and well.

Sophie used her regular phone this time. "Marcella. Want to meet me at Fight Club?"

CHAPTER FIFTEEN

Connor: Day Two

SOPHIE HAD HUNG up on him.

Connor stared at the phone in his hand. He couldn't decide if he wanted to get up and punch a wall, drop to the ground and do push-ups, or try to master his rioting feelings through meditation.

He was in control of his mind, body, will, and emotions.

He had just made his body endure unspeakable things in the last days; he could control the pain of this emotional blow, too—but the shock of adrenaline surging through him right now was too powerful to be suppressed.

Connor dropped the phone onto the desk and threw himself to the ground, his fingers spread on the cold stone floor. He powered through push-ups, his arms pistoning like a machine, his body taut as a bowstring.

Down, exhale, up, inhale, down, exhale, up, inhale, down, exhale . . . the rhythm became a meditation that calmed and centered him.

A long time later, angst discharged, Connor stood back up.

His body was telling him it was hungry and tired, and that he was pushing the limits of his ability to master himself by letting things get too far out of balance.

He hadn't submitted to the Master for two years to lose so easily what he'd learned.

Connor sat back down at the desk and picked up the latest bowl of food, long gone cold, that Nine had brought in. Closing his eyes, he infused the contents of the bowl with warmth, and allowed his senses to open up and smell the flavors, taste the textures. He scooped the curry and vegetables over rice into his mouth deftly, using chopsticks. "Life is all we have. Time is all we have. How is it of any benefit if we are living in the past, or projecting into the future? If we squander these precious moments with bitterness, judgment, or regret?" The Master's voice rang in his mind.

Slowly, Connor regained his equilibrium. The food steadied him. Being grounded in the moment centered him.

But every time he thought of the illusion he had lived for, the sacrifice he had made for nothing . . . his belly tightened, threatening to reject the food.

No. It was time for him to admit to himself that he had been drawn to this journey; that he had wanted an excuse to join the Yām Khûmkan, to study under the Master, and to change his life completely.

Talking to Sophie and feeling guilty about burdening her with the leadership of his company . . . All of that had reminded him that he'd felt trapped when he came to the compound. He had been surrounded by enemies of all kinds, the FBI watching his every move, and he'd been strained by continually living a lie—boxed in by the false identity of Sheldon Hamilton, that fake hipster CEO with his brown contact lenses, immaculate suits, and dyed hair.

The Master had provided him a way out, and had even allowed him to hold onto the illusion that he was a hostage, that he was a *hero,* giving up his liberty so Sophie and Jake could be together. The Master had known that Connor needed that illusion to justify his selfishness.

Connor's stomach tightened again. Bile tickled the back of his throat as the urge to vomit rose in him.

"To truly master yourself you must first see yourself clearly, and then completely and totally accept yourself as you are. There is no other true baseline for growth." The Master's voice was burned into memory; Connor could still see the firelight reflected in the man's violet eyes as he delivered this nugget of truth.

Connor had just suffered a hard day on the training field, landing on his ass again and again. He'd been battered and bruised, sure he was too old, in his thirties, for the rigors of training that had defeated men who joined when they were much younger.

At the time, Connor had believed that nugget of wisdom pertained to his body—but it turned out the Master was talking about *character.* The Master had carefully doled out each idea when Connor was most able to hear it; and now, in the man's absence, he had a new level of insight.

He had lied to himself on a number of levels. One of them was that he had used Sophie to keep his interests in the United States going. The Master's sources in the CIA had confirmed that Jake had turned his Sheldon Hamilton identity in as the Ghost vigilante. Those sources confirmed that there was a case being built against Sheldon Hamilton by both the FBI and CIA. Hence, Connor's direction to Sophie to have that persona declared legally dead after a year of no contact.

Sophie was the only person he trusted implicitly. When he made his will, he'd known he was leaving her both a burden and an opportunity. He'd also counted on her to "keep his seat warm," as she said, so that he could return to it.

He'd manipulated her . . . but he'd also sensed her potential for leadership; maybe there were parts of the job she enjoyed. He could hope so, couldn't he?

And Jake? During the hardship of their attempt to get Sophie's baby back, he'd come to love the man like a brother, but he hadn't trusted him with the knowledge of his dual identity.

Why? Because he'd known that knowledge had the potential to drive a wedge between Jake and Sophie. He loved Sophie—enough to want her to be happy with the lover she'd chosen, a man who'd wanted to be her one and only.

Jake had reacted in anger in turning Connor in to the agencies, but he bore Jake no ill will. The man had been betrayed, even if there was no malicious intent behind it.

What would have happened if Connor had told Jake the truth while they were naked and shackled together, between bouts of being tortured? Would Jake have been able to accept and believe that Connor meant no harm to him and Sophie? That Connor had given up on trying to win Sophie back, that he just wanted Jake, Sophie and Momi to be a happy family?

Sadly, he hadn't told Jake his secret when he had that chance. There might have been a possibility the man would have believed him, when they literally couldn't escape from each other and Connor had no reason to lie . . .

"Life is a series of forking roads," the Master had said once. "You take the one that seems best to you. If you're a thoughtful person, you consider before you choose. But only in hindsight are we able to see how the turns we've chosen have led to now. And still, we have to accept all we've done and been, to reach our fullest potential."

Connor shut his eyes, surrendering to regret, to sorrow . . . and then a flicker of that most elusive feeling, acceptance.

It was what it was.

Each of them had been a free agent. Jake could have worked through his issue about being lied to. Sophie could have tried harder to win Jake back. And Connor? If he'd known they'd broken up, would he have been able to get through the rigors of the last two years?

No. He would not have stayed the course.

Knowing Sophie was single would have pulled him away from

his training. He'd have found a way to return to her, to Anubis, to his island, Phi Ni, to his company . . .

That flame of hope that Sophie might love him again someday flared up bright and hot. He'd ruthlessly crushed it to set her free, but now it scorched him with joyful possibility. *Maybe they could be together again* . . .

She was single. She was running his company, taking care of his dog. Maybe even living in his house. Waiting for him to come back. "Keeping it warm for you," she'd said.

His heart gave a squeeze of pain. He thumped his left pec and coughed. "Freakin' hell. Love actually hurts," he muttered aloud.

But how could he return, even if Sophie would entertain the idea of a relationship?

The Yām Khûmkạn compound had become destiny, refuge, and prison. He could conduct his life as the Ghost from here, unfettered by any government, and he'd added to his skills exponentially as he'd set out to do. But the minute he left the compound, he'd be the target of the FBI and CIA and probably Interpol, too.

An answer would come to him eventually; a door would open.

He would use what the Master had taught him to stay the course and focus on the outcomes he wanted.

And he wanted it all: the power and reach of the Yām Khûmkạn, his role as the Ghost vigilante, and the woman he loved.

CHAPTER SIXTEEN

Sophie: Day Three

THE NEXT MORNING, Sophie circled her friend Marcella in the mixed martial arts practice ring, her arms cocked and ready, her knees bent, looking for an opening.

Marcella stood upright, her lush figure packed into a pair of tight spandex shorts and an exercise bra, her chocolate hair drawn back into a ponytail. Her friend had always been more of a kicker than a striker, and that was evident in her stance. "Come on, Sophie!" Marcella taunted. "You're the one who wanted a workout!"

"That was last night. But you were too busy sleeping to get out of your warm bed."

"Who says I was sleeping?" Marcella grinned. "Marcus gave me a fine workout of another kind. You're just jealous, you and your battery-operated boyfriend. Ha!"

"Foul-breathed cow!" Sophie charged, dodging Marcella's kicks. She grabbed her friend around the midsection and tossed her to the ground. Only minutes later, she had Marcella on the mat, thumping for mercy.

"Sexually frustrated, anyone?" Marcella panted as Sophie let her up. "Sorry I teased you about B.O.B."

"That wasn't nice," Sophie growled. "I *am* a little lonely when Momi's at Alika's. I'm woman enough to admit it." The blown-up picture of Connor's naked body doing a pull-up flashed into Sophie's mind. *She should probably take that picture down.* If he ever returned and saw it there . . . "I'm just . . . oh, *cursed seed of conjoined twins.* Jake and Felicia returned Ginger to me. They moved to California together."

"Oh, damn!" Marcella's eyes widened and she covered her mouth with a hand. "I'd hoped you were over him. I'm so sorry."

"It's okay. He brought me back Ginger. That's something." Sophie wished she could tell Marcella about Connor's call, but her friend had been part of the FBI investigation into the Ghost; Connor's ongoing presence in her life had to remain a secret from everyone but Dr. Wilson, who was bound by confidentiality.

They walked around the ring as Sophie described her encounter with Jake the other evening. "It just seems like everyone around me is happy and settled. Jake and Felicia. Alika and Sandy. You and Marcus. Lei and Stevens. I'm just . . . unlucky in love, I guess."

Marcella shook her head. "Oh, girlfriend. I'm sorry I was so insensitive with that crack about you not getting any, but it's your fault too. You've hidden yourself in that CEO office and are using Momi as a chastity belt. Not much can get going while you're locked in motherhood mode."

"But it's not just me now. I can't risk Momi getting attached to anyone who doesn't work out." And she just didn't feel ready; didn't feel over Jake, or Connor either, for that matter.

"But how can you get to know anyone if you don't give them a chance? Men falling in love with you is still your crazy superpower," Marcella said. "Waxman is still carrying a torch for you after all this time."

Sophie's brows lifted. "Carrying a torch. What a strange phrase that is." Her boss at the FBI had declared his feelings the day she quit, and she'd done her best to forget that little episode.

"Yep. He was just asking if you were still single, if I thought you'd go out with him for a cuppa coffee." Marcella brushed down her exercise gear with gloved hands, getting rid of dust from her takedown. "I told him hell would freeze over first."

"That's not actually true, Marcella." Perversely, her friend's words made Sophie want to see her former boss again. Ben Waxman had been more than a mentor to her; though she hadn't reciprocated his feelings at the time, thinking of him now, she felt a surge of affection. "I would have a cup of coffee with him. Maybe more, if the conversation was good."

"I'll pass that on. Apparently global warming has cooled down hell."

Sophie punched her friend lightly on the shoulder. "I have time for one more round before I meet with my new partner Raveaux. I've left the CEO office to work a case that's pretty interesting—a diamond heist. There's some kind of master thief operating behind the scenes, manipulating thefts from a major auction house."

"Ooh!" Marcella's eyes widened. "Diamond heist? Perhaps you need some FBI assistance?"

"We're off the books," Sophie said. "I will let you know, as well as the good people at Interpol, as soon as we have someone to bring to justice. The interesting thing about doing private work is that . . . many times, the client wants things to stay private."

Marcella snapped her fingers in disappointment. "Dang it. Just say the word if you want company. Other than the new guy, of course." Marcella quirked a brow. "Tell me about him."

"Raveaux is older," Sophie said. *Let Marcella think Raveaux was a doddering old senior citizen*—he probably wasn't more than forty, but she didn't want to encourage the matchmaking gleam in her friend's eye. "A retired French detective with international connections. I'm hoping to track the architect of the thefts online and have some kind of dialogue. But we don't know how far we'll get beyond the immediate problem of the current batch of diamonds missing—the auction house we're working for doesn't want word getting out that they've been breached. They just want the thefts to stop."

She still didn't know enough about the master thief, his network, or anything really. She had to lure him out, get him to respond to an email with an embedded tracker . . . *The best way to deal with the thief was to get some kind of leverage on him!* Blackmailing the mastermind into giving up his activities, at least as far as their client, Finewell's, went, was likely a better strategy than trying to gather enough evidence for an arrest . . . And how better to get the dirt on him than her DAVID software? And then, to set him up, she could use the Ghost program—its unique tracking and overwriting capabilities could be used to break in and send messages from almost any source to manipulate a mark.

Marcella snapped her fingers. "Earth to Sophie!"

"Sorry, I was just having an idea about my case."

"Since you seem distracted, maybe I can take you on the next round."

They circled again. This time, Marcella's roundhouse kick sent Sophie into the ropes. She came back with a grappling hold, but her friend seemed to have dug deep to some core of inner power, because Marcella took her down next, crowing and flashing victory signs to scattered applause from the rest of the gym after she finally let Sophie up. "You're getting soft, my friend, as well as distracted."

"I know," Sophie wiped her face with a thin gym towel. "I have a lot on my mind."

"Want to come have dinner at our place? You could bring those rowdy dogs." Marcella and her husband lived in a little plantation-style cottage on the edge of Honolulu, and Sophie, Momi, and Armita enjoyed dinner with them at least once a month.

"Let me get through today and see if I can get away from the computer long enough," Sophie said. The women parted ways with a hug, and Sophie headed to the showers before her meeting with Raveaux.

CHAPTER SEVENTEEN

Connor: Day Three

CONNOR WAS STILL UP and hard at work on the computer when someone knocked on the door of the lab. "Enter."

Nine's voice came from over his shoulder. "It is time for morning drills, One."

Connor glanced up at the narrow, slit-like window. Sure enough, the faint gray of dawn showed. Connor paused, lifting his fingers off the keyboard, stretching back fully.

"I am still working. Have Pi run the men through their routine."

He had lost track of his body in the hours immersed into the Ghost software, connecting neglected threads of situations his computer had tracked in the two years he'd been gone.

He had also gone looking for the Master and Pim Wat.

Locating the general area of their likely location had not been too difficult. He had simply used the satellite he'd hacked to track the helicopter the Master had left the compound in, followed the helicopter to where it landed, a private airport where the Master had then boarded a small aircraft. Connor had been able to pick up its company and number and tracked its trajectory. The small craft had landed on an unidentified island off the coast of Japan.

Connor suspected that it was the Master's hideaway, and that Pim Wat was already there.

He wasn't the only one to enjoy a private island . . .

"Can I bring you some tea? Breakfast?"

Connor looked around, surprised that Nine was still there. "My apologies. I was up all night. I should get some rest instead of food right now, though."

"As you wish, master."

"Don't call me that!" The objection burst out of him forcefully. He held Nine's gaze with his own. "The Master will be back, and I doubt he would appreciate losing his title."

"I merely meant to honor your position," Nine said with dignity. "But I will do as you say." He cleared the tray from the previous evening and left the room.

Connor stood up. Stretched. He really did need to get some rest, but he felt satisfied with not only cycling through the Master's business correspondence, but getting back into his own vigilante role, so long neglected.

Now he just needed to figure out how to integrate his leadership with the day-to-day running of the compound. He could not absent himself regularly from the drills—his headship was too tenuous at this point. But perhaps letting Pi take charge on occasion could solidify the man's loyalty, and satisfy his need for power.

Connor powered down the computers and touched the wood of his violin lovingly, stroking it as it rested in its case. The violin reminded him of the other things he loved: *Anubis. His island. Sophie . . .*

How was her child growing? How was motherhood treating her? Temptation to pull up some surveillance rose in him—but he had already decided not to disrespect her that way.

Connor locked the computer lab door and took himself to bed for a nap, satisfied.

He had located the Master geographically. Now he would have an excuse to contact Sophie again, to tell her where he thought Pim Wat was, and ask her what she thought they should do.

All in all, a good night's work.

CHAPTER EIGHTEEN

Sophie: Day Three

SOPHIE'S PHONE rang as she pulled out of the parking lot at Fight Club. She already had her Bluetooth in her ear, in case of any work calls. "Sophie Smithson."

"Sophie? It's Agent McDonald." The portly CIA man sounded tense—but then, he usually did. Sophie pictured his florid face, watery blue eyes, and blondish combover. McDonald looked like an aging golfer, not a deadly operative, part of his dangerousness. Sophie navigated the Lexus into another stall to take the call. She definitely didn't want to be caught in traffic for what he was likely about to tell her.

"It's been a while since I've heard from you, Agent McDonald." Sophie kept her voice carefully neutral.

"That's because there hasn't been any useful intel from your end," McDonald snapped.

Sophie's hackles rose. The man always put her on the defensive —no matter what she provided the CIA, it never seemed to be enough.

"I wasn't aware we were working on any further projects together," Sophie said. "I consider my debt to the CIA discharged."

"I decide when your debt is discharged, not you. And with what's been going on with your mother, that might be a while."

"I am not accountable for my mother's actions. You cannot judge me by them." Sophie struggled to keep her voice crisp and calm.

"Yes, yes, I know all of that." McDonald cleared his throat. "I called with a purpose, and that is to let you know that there was a raid on the facility last week, and your mother . . . she was extracted."

Even though she was prepared for this, Sophie sucked in a breath. "Extracted? Was anyone hurt?"

"No casualties. Some injuries. Must've been a crack team, because nobody saw or heard anything. The guards were rendered unconscious with blow darts, and when they came to, Pim Wat was gone." McDonald crunched loudly on the mints he chewed when anxious.

"I hope you're making every effort to find her." Sophie's chest hurt with anxiety and old trauma. "Pim Wat is dangerous."

"So you keep saying. But quite frankly, the woman has been nothing but a limp dishrag the last two years. We haven't gotten two words out of her, in spite of numerous attempts at interrogation. She seemed to have gone into a catatonic state, according to our doctor on site. She refused to eat, so she weighed less than ninety pounds at the time of her kidnapping. Pim Wat's about as dangerous as a starved kitten right now." He crunched a few more of the mints. "Of course, we're trying to track the kidnappers. They got out by helicopter, but where they went—all that is still under investigation. I just thought you should know, as her next of kin."

"Calling it a kidnapping—that's nice, considering she was a prisoner," Sophie said.

"She was removed by persons unknown for a purpose unknown," McDonald said. "What else would you call it?"

Best not to prolong the conversation; McDonald was irritable enough. "Thank you for the call. Keep me apprised." Sophie hung up with a punch of a button. She drove on auto pilot, her thoughts whirling, to the Security Solutions building, rode the elevator to her office on the top floor, and greeted Paula at her desk.

Her assistant held up a finger, stopping Sophie. "Check your email and your messages. And Raveaux is already in your office."

"Can you tell him to wait out here in the future?" Sophie's brows snapped together in annoyance. "I like to have a little space to do my routine before I go into meetings."

"I can tell him," Paula said. "But that doesn't mean he would listen. Raveaux's like oil pouring downhill: smooth, slippery, and hard to stop."

Sophie paused; might as well get a temperature check on what Paula thought of Raveaux. "At least he's prompt. And smart. Also, he dresses well."

"Don't forget easy on the eyes." Paula handed Sophie an insulated mug of strong Thai tea. "And that *accent*!" She fanned herself.

"I suppose." Since she grew up internationally, the accent didn't do much for her, but she did like Raveaux's conversational strength and good vocabulary. "Back to work, Paula, and put your fan on if you need it."

Paula laughed. "I'm a little young for hot flashes, but that man . . ."

Sophie rolled her eyes. She pushed down the lever opening her heavy teak door with her elbow since both hands were occupied with her backpack and the mug.

Raveaux was seated in the chair in front of her desk in his characteristic pose: ankle on knee, paperback open. Midnight blue shirt and black pants, comb tracks in his curling brown hair, a slight scent of cinnamon as she passed. Setting down her items on her desk, Sophie put her hands on her hips. "Raveaux. You're here already! Coming into my office is becoming a habit."

"Bonjour, Sophie."

"I see you finished that other book you were reading." She hit the encoded fob that turned on her computers.

Raveaux held up a worn copy of the first of the Jack Reacher novels. "I found a used bookstore near my place and picked up this Lee Child first in series. Vigilante justice explains so much about American culture."

Vigilante justice. She felt a quiver in her belly. The last thing Sophie needed was for Raveaux to get some whiff of the Ghost. "I'm not a fan of vigilante justice, though I concede its usefulness."

Raveaux narrowed his eyes. "Seems like you've given this some thought."

"You're early for our meeting. Read your book, Raveaux. And don't come into my office again without being invited."

Raveaux went still at her snappishness. "As you wish, Madame," he murmured, and re-opened his novel.

Sophie studied him from under her lashes as the computer booted up. His skin wasn't so pale, the darkness under his eyes less pronounced. *Perhaps he had slept better.*

She dealt with her email—no small amount, but she hacked through it with the triage system she used. She had a message from Bix, and a meeting scheduled with him later in the day to go over employee performance records. She made sure the meeting was logged into her phone and set a reminder alarm.

"Ugh." *She hated those employee performance reviews.* Sophie leaned back and ran her fingers into her short, thick hair, closing her eyes for a moment to massage her scalp deeply, sighing out that tension. She carried a lot of stress in her neck and jaw.

Raveaux cleared his throat. *Once again, she'd forgotten he was there!* The man was a ninja that way.

"It is ten-thirty, time for our meeting," he said. "Are you ready to discuss our case?"

"Our meeting. Of course." Sophie refocused, rummaging in the backpack that doubled as a purse. She extracted the silver laptop

Samson had given her. "Let me see if the thief has responded." She got Samson's computer booting up. "What did you uncover about the diamond assessor?"

"I do not have access to a deep dive program for background checking, but I was able to track Agrippa Polat's bona fides. He is part of a family-owned diamond dealing consortium, and is one of the main buyers, so he's certainly seen a few stones in his time. The company has a good reputation. At first glance, he seems to be legitimate. There are no outstanding complaints or legal actions of any kind against him or his company."

"Good. I didn't expect that there would be." Sophie kept her eyes on her screen as she typed rapidly, inputting the security code and pulling up the encrypted email site. A smile tugged at her lips. "The thief did not reply to the email, but it was opened. The tracker was engaged."

Raveaux leaned forward to look as Sophie pushed the laptop toward him. Her nostrils flared, picking up his scent. Not cinnamon —*cloves*. And soap. *Very pleasant.* "See this? It's a geo positioning algorithm connected to the IP address of the computer receiving the message." The software worked, a globe spinning in the corner of the screen.

"Ah. Why wasn't the thief using a VPN to mask his IP?" Raveaux's black brows had drawn together. "Seems very careless."

"I agree, and I don't know. Should we look a gift horse in the mouth?" Sophie smiled. "Sometimes, it's best not to."

"Gift horse," Raveaux muttered. "I don't know that one."

"Google it." Sophie enjoyed throwing out colloquialisms now and again after so many years of struggling with them. "Look at that. The IP is here on Oahu."

Raveaux straightened up. "Seems very odd. Out of all the world . . ."

"It's probably someone Samson knows. Or who works for the company. Just because this architect is hiding behind a computer doesn't mean he isn't local," Sophie said, though she too was surprised. "Let's go check out this address. The software can only track the nearest coordinates, not an address, so I need a few more minutes to cross-reference and come up with an actionable location." Her fingers flew. A moment later, she looked up to meet Raveaux's deep brown eyes. "Ready for a field trip?"

CHAPTER NINETEEN

Raveaux: Day Three

RAVEAUX DROVE the generic-looking white Security Solutions Ford Escape SUV along the steep elevations of winding, scenic Route 61, more commonly known as the Pali Highway, an important artery connecting Honolulu with the town of Kaneohe on the other side of the Koolau Mountains. He drove more slowly than was strictly necessary, craning his neck to take in stunning views of velvety, crenellated mountains scored from a thousand downpours, mounded cumulus clouds caught on their majestic tops. Huge trees trailed vines from the umbrella of branches overhanging tumbling streams in the valleys on either side of the highway. And off in the distance, the ever-present backdrop of the ocean gleamed, crinkled cobalt satin . . .

"So poetic," Gita would have said, teasing him if he'd described such a scene to her aloud, but she would have loved it. Many of the plants of Hawaii, and the ubiquitous mynahs, would have been familiar to her from her native India.

Sophie, seated beside him, had her tablet propped up on her

knees. A video chat with her daughter was open on the screen. "Sing me the ABC song, darling," she cooed.

He'd never heard that warmth in her tone before. Raveaux, curious about Sophie's child, flicked a glance away from the road at the screen. The open video chat showed a cherubic little girl whose rosy cheeks were framed by silky black curls.

"A, B, C, D, E, F, G . . ." the toddler chanted, then stopped suddenly, popping a finger into her mouth.

"H, I, J, K . . ." prompted another feminine voice from behind the little girl.

"It's okay, Armita," Sophie said. "I don't want to force this." She switched languages, speaking Thai. The women spoke rapidly back and forth over the child's shoulder. Momi leaned her head back against her nanny's shoulder and closed her eyes, still sucking her forefinger.

Raveaux kept his gaze on the road—the route was smooth and beautiful, but commuters were in a hurry and didn't appreciate his deliberate speed and divided attention. They entered a long tunnel that went through the mountain, and Sophie muttered a foreign curse as the screen went black.

"That's an unusual custody arrangement you have," Raveaux said. "I don't know if I could have done without my child for a month at a time—I'd have missed her too much."

And now he had to do without her forever. His mouth tasted bitter at the memory of all he'd lost.

"I don't like it, quite frankly," Sophie said. They emerged from the tunnel and she stabbed at the tablet with her finger, trying to get the connection back. "But I don't believe in gender-based parental role stereotyping, and neither does Momi's father. We share responsibilities and access to Momi equally, because we think that's best for her. Armita is an exceptional caregiver and provides consistency as Momi goes back and forth between the islands. Her involvement and support makes the arrangement possible."

"You and her father aren't a couple?"

"No. Momi was a surprise to both of us—but a wonderful one." Sophie couldn't get the connection going again. She slid the tablet back into her bag. "What about your daughter? How did you and your wife handle being working parents?" She switched to French, and Raveaux's pulse picked up. *Speaking his native tongue was such a pleasure.*

"We were more traditional, I suppose, in how we handled parenting," he said. "Gita had her own business assessing antiquities, and she went to a part-time schedule after Lucie was born. My investigations always demanded as much as I could give; we had a parenting leave of several months available, which I took when Lucie was born, but time off meant time away from my cases, and that never sat well with me. Gita and I fought over it; she always said my work was 'the other woman.'"

He caught Sophie's eye, and she smiled. "I certainly understand that from my FBI days. The private sector is easier to regulate."

Raveaux nodded. "It got easier when Lucie began school."

"I hear France supports working families through quality care and education programs."

"We have high taxes to pay for that," Raveaux said. "Always a trade-off there. We'd planned to have a bigger family, but it didn't happen. Perhaps it was for the best because Gita was always after me about my schedule. At the time my cases seemed so urgent. Matters of life and death, when going home to play at the park or read a story with my daughter . . ."

Just that suddenly, his throat closed. His eyes filled. He clenched his hands on the wheel.

"I'm sorry I asked. I thought it might ease you to speak of them a little," Sophie said softly. "I can't imagine your loss."

Raveaux coughed, trying to clear his throat. Sophie touched his arm, just a stroke on his sleeve, but like the other time she'd touched him, it burned. He pulled his arm in, close against his side.

"I thought I would have more time. I took my beautiful life for granted." He glanced at Sophie, his eyes hot with emotion. "Don't make my mistake. Nothing about your work will ever give you back the times you could have been with family."

Sophie's eyes widened. "I know that."

Raveaux refocused on the road.

They were descending the mountain range now, curving back and forth toward Kaneohe. He had never been to the utilitarian coastal town before. He tapped his phone, pre-programmed with the IP address, and woke up the GPS. A mechanical female tone, butchering the Hawaiian words, directed them beneath spreading trees to the entrance of Kaneohe.

They angled down into the grid of a planned community, winding along narrow residential streets bordered by sidewalk. Cars parked in driveways indicated a middle-class demographic. Sophie frowned. "I didn't expect this location for the master thief."

"What did you expect?" Raveaux was relieved to be back on neutral ground.

"I don't know. But not this." Sophie pointed at a couple of children on the sidewalk, the older one pushing the younger on a wheeled toy. The only indication that this generic neighborhood was located in Hawaii was a plethora of decorative palms at every corner.

"Your destination is on the left," the navigation voice declared.

Raveaux continued past the house, maintaining the same speed. He turned his head to case the dwelling, a nondescript ranch in shades of beige. A short concrete driveway ended in a two-car garage, and the door was down. A short, well-maintained lawn—*he could never understand Americans' obsession with their lawns*. Blinds covered the windows.

"Very impersonal," Sophie said.

"Nothing about that house to draw attention. It could be low profile on purpose. Let's go take a look." Raveaux checked the rearview mirror; no one was behind them on the quiet suburban street. He turned right at the next block and found a spot to park, directly across from a well-marked community center where their vehicle wouldn't stand out.

Raveaux only wore an ankle piece here on Oahu; he was mildly surprised to see Sophie check her weapon, a Glock 19. She rammed the magazine back into the grip after checking the number of rounds, and glanced up to meet his gaze. "Never know what you'll find on a home visit. Let's go." She got out of the SUV, holstering the gun in a shoulder rig concealed by her linen jacket.

Raveaux beeped the SUV locked, and followed as Sophie walked in front of him, her head up and eyes moving. "Let's explore the exterior of the house, check the premises, before we ring the doorbell," Sophie said. "We're insurance investigators, right?" She reached into her pocket and held up a business card and the ID badges they'd already used.

"Reasonable. We could be verifying the value of the place for some kind of claim," Raveaux said. He clipped the badge onto the pocket of his shirt as Sophie did the same. The streets were empty, to his relief, as they headed for the address. He welcomed the uptick of his pulse for the second time that day.

CHAPTER TWENTY

Sophie: Day Three

SHE GLANCED up and down the deserted street. This was the kind of neighborhood where everyone was gone by eight-thirty in the morning, destined for purposeful places like worksites and school. Once they got to the target house, Raveaux walked with casual grace ahead of her across the lawn toward the side of the house.

Sophie followed, moving up the driveway and circling around the enclosed, attached garage. She peeked in the windows, spotting a dark SUV, make and license plate number hidden by the angle of the aperture. She continued on, reaching a metal rack holding trash cans.

She lifted the lid on one of them. A waft of ripe refuse hit her nostrils: *someone was living here, and putting the garbage out on a regular basis.*

The kitchen window above the cans jutted out from the back of the house, the only uncovered one she'd seen. Sophie rose on her toes and peeked in across the sink.

A lamp shone over an immaculate little dinette set directly across from the bay of the kitchen area. She scanned the room, taking in a sideboard with antique dishes, a watercolor of Kaneohe Bay, and a collection of poi pounders. *Whoever lived here knew something about Hawaii art . . .*

Sophie moved further to the corner to get a different angle of view into the room.

She sucked in a breath.

Through the doorway into the living room she could see a pair of dangling feet. Anything more was hidden by the angle of the window and the low archway between the rooms. Sophie looked around for Raveaux, and sure enough, he was circling the corner of the house, headed in her direction.

"I think we have a body." Sophie pointed. "Maybe you can see a little more than I. The toenails are painted, so I'm guessing it's a woman."

Raveaux fitted himself tightly against the window, pressed against her body as he craned to see. His mouth tightened grimly, his eyes narrowing. "Yes. I can only see from the knee down, but it's a woman hanging."

Sophie pulled away from the window, turning her back to the scene. She took her phone out and worked with her thumbs, cross-referencing their address with the employee database at Finewell's Auction House. "I probably should have done this before . . . Oh my God. This is Mel Samson's house."

The jolt of adrenaline generated by their discovery seemed to have sharpened all of Sophie's senses. She met Raveaux's intense gaze. She breathed in his clove smell, activated by the heat of exertion and emotion.

Raveaux stepped back. "Do you want to call it in?"

"Let's take a look first. Once we call it in, we won't have access to the body or the case."

"Someone could see us. We might leave trace, and that would be very hard to explain." Did he ever relax that severe mouth of his and smile? He had a few silver hairs at his temples; he was one of those men that would only get better looking with age.

"We can call it in anonymously, afterwards. I want to see the body, check for foul play." She turned to look back inside. Those pale feet were so pathetic. "I think it's Samson."

In fact, she was sure it was Samson. The mushroom-pale of the woman's skin, the puffiness of her calves and feet—all of that matched the woman they'd met. Whatever note Samson might have left was information that they would not be privy to in the future without disclosing their client's investigation. Her mind buzzed with the repercussions, and she spoke them aloud. "If the tracker led us to Samson's address, there was no master thief."

"True. The master thief was likely a stratagem employed by Samson to buy time," Raveaux agreed.

"On the other hand, how convenient this all is! The case wrapped up nice and tidy, with the criminal's body a suicide to seal the deal." Sophie firmed her jaw and turned to Raveaux. "We need to go in and try to determine if this is a homicide. Once the police get the case, we will have no further access to anything here."

Raveaux reached into his back pocket and pulled out a handful of latex, holding the rubber gloves out to her. "Let's do what we can to minimize trace."

"You come prepared." Sophie tugged on the stretchy rubber gloves.

"I've been around the block a time or two." He snapped on his gloves with a flourish. He pulled a black knit cap out of his pocket and put it on, tucking his hair inside. Sophie wrapped the scarf tied around her neck up over her own curls, containing them. They brushed down their clothing for any loose hairs or fibers, then approached the back door, which opened into the kitchen. Sophie stood back, scanning for any interference, letting Raveaux do the honors with his lockpicks.

Once Raveaux had the door open, he slid out of his shoes, proceeding on stocking feet into the house. Sophie did the same, looking for any disruption, such as a pet or burglar alarm. She tiptoed across the kitchen's immaculate linoleum, one hand on her weapon.

That strange scent that Sophie had smelled on Samson's hair and clothing filled the house, a perfume of death now in full bloom. The woman had lost control of her bowels, and that ripe stench overlaid the rest. Raveaux walked a perimeter of the kitchen and dining room, as Sophie approached the body directly.

Samson hung from a decorative beam in the center of the living room. The rope was utilitarian hemp; a slipknot rather than the traditional hangman's noose. A chair lay on its side on the carpeted floor. Her caftan was rucked up on one side, exposing her legs from the knee down.

Raveaux entered, but continued to roam the perimeter, presumably looking for a note. Sophie took out her phone to take photos, scanning the body, looking closely for any sign of foul play. She stepped up close, breathing shallowly through her mouth.

Yellow and green bruising dotted Samson's pale, puffy arms in the nook of her elbows and at her wrists—likely the site of injections or blood draws. Sophie touched the woman's arm gently. There was no give to the flesh—*stiff with rigor.*

She walked around the body, examining it from all angles. Samson's face was dusky purple, her eyes bulging and fixed with petechial hemorrhaging—she'd strangled without enough of a drop from the chair to break her neck. She hadn't put on her head wrap. A few pitiful hairs decorated her mottled scalp. Sophie wished she could cut the woman down, close her eyes, give her some dignity, but that was impossible. "I'm so sorry, Mel," she whispered.

Raveaux called from the bedroom. "I found the suicide note."

Sophie turned and walked back through the dining room and turned left down a short hall into a bedroom that was as pristine as a nun's cell: white comforter, white walls, and even a painting done in white, thick with *impasto,* was mounted where it could be viewed from the bed. Leaning against a framed photo was an envelope with *Elisa* written on it in bold cursive. Sophie leaned close to examine the photo: it was a candid of the same young girl on Samson's desk, only grown, wearing a cap, gown, and college graduation tassels.

Raveaux picked up the note. Very carefully, holding it by the edges, he turned it over. The envelope was not sealed, and he worked the paper out gently.

"*Dear Elisa,*" he read aloud. "*I have decided to end my suffering ahead of my natural expiration date. It is the final gift I can give you, along with everything I have. Be happy. Grow old. Enjoy your life, and remember our good times. Your loving Mel.*"

Raveaux refolded the note and slid it back into the envelope. They both scanned in the room, hands on hips. Nothing was disturbed, nothing out of place.

"I see no sign of struggle," Raveaux said.

"So far, everything is consistent with suicide," Sophie said. "I know she was planning this. I'm just surprised it was so close to our meeting. I can't help but think our meeting prompted her action."

"Agreed. It's a shame."

Sophie met Raveaux's gaze. His eyes were liquid and soft; she was surprised by that and felt an answering upwelling of emotion. Her eyes prickled. "I'm sorry we pushed her over the edge."

"Me too. But discovery of her theft only pushed up her timetable. The outcome would have been the same."

They retraced their steps, passing by Mel Samson's body. Sophie was glad she'd accepted the gift of Samson's painting. She would choose to remember this woman's keen eye for art and love of beauty, rather than the terrible scene of her death.

She followed Raveaux out through the kitchen. They re-locked the door, donned their shoes, shucked off their gloves and headwear, checked that the coast was clear, and walked rapidly across the lawn and down the street.

Sophie ticked over their options aloud as they walked. "We could call this discovery in on our cell phones, and just make it quick, but that would leave a trace on our phones if we were ever questioned. Or, we could call it in from a pay phone, say that we were walking by and saw the body. Another option is that I could call my contact in the HPD, and report that we came out on a home visit and spotted the body. Disclose that we have a case that possibly relates to the death, that we might have pertinent information. That would embed us in any investigation."

Raveaux cocked his head thoughtfully as they reached the Security Solutions SUV. "If this were a homicide, I would recommend that you make the call directly to your HPD contact and we give them all we have. But since we're in agreement that it's suicide, nothing is gained by disclosing anything about our investigation and violating our client's confidentiality."

"Pay phone it is," Sophie agreed.

Raveaux pointed to a metal half-booth attached to the community center. "There's one right there. You or me?"

Sophie thought of Raveaux's accent. Perhaps he could disguise it, but Sophie felt responsible for having discovered the body. "I will make the call."

Raveaux nodded and beeped open the SUV, getting in. Sophie waited for a car to pass, then crossed the street.

She stepped up to the shiny rectangular phone unit which was sheltered by a plastic and metal hood and picked up the handset. A dial tone met her ear, and *"Deposit coins or enter card number"* tracked across the LED display below the square, numbered digits meant for dialing. She patted her pockets. She had no change and had left her backpack in the car—*not that she'd want to enter a card number and identify herself . . .*

Staring at the phone, Sophie smiled ruefully. She'd never actually used a pay phone in the United States to make a call—but perhaps a 911 call would go through without payment.

She decided to give it a try.

The call connected. Sophie suppressed her accent, channeling Southern California. "Oh my gosh! I'm calling to report . . . I was going through a yard and . . . I think I saw a body!" She gave the address and street number, but hung up before the operator could collect anything more.

She hurried back across the street and got into the SUV. Raveaux had already started the vehicle, and they pulled out. He glanced over at her. "Hungry?"

Sophie barked a laugh. "Hardly. But I haven't had breakfast. We should eat and discuss what's next for the investigation."

The GPS guided them to a nearby Zippy's, a local chain restaurant. Sophie took extra time in the bathroom to wash her face and arms to the elbows, trying to slough off the pall of their discovery. Later, over a hearty vegetable omelet, she felt her equilibrium coming back. Raveaux had ordered French toast and eggs, and she smiled at the sourness of his puckered mouth as he ate with mechanical precision.

"Not to your taste?" Sophie asked.

"No." But he kept eating, cutting the thick, soggy white bread into squares, swirling them in a puddle of syrup, and forking them into his mouth efficiently. His eggs were already gone.

"Are you a—what does Marcella call it—a foodie?"

"Foodie?" Raveaux's brows lifted in an incredulous arch. "Is that like a selfie? Some bastardization of the word *gourmet*?"

"I'll take that as a yes." Sophie hid her smile in her teacup. "Please, refresh me on the meaning of the word."

"A gourmet is a connoisseur of fine comestibles. You will notice that both *gourmet* and *connoisseur* are French words." Raveaux pushed his empty plate away. "This country, however, favors large portions of mediocrity."

Sophie inclined her head toward his empty plate and tipped up her own. "Americans want speed of service, basic quality, and value for money. We got all of the above, today."

Raveaux snorted. "The body has needs . . . but the palate should be better appeased." His dark eyes gleamed as they met hers. "I will cook for you and show you what I mean."

A quiver of heat zipped up Sophie's spine. *Was he asking her over to his place?* Admittedly, she was curious about him. Where did he live? What did he do in his free time besides read thriller paperbacks? *But she couldn't let him get the wrong idea* . . . "Let's talk about the case," she said. "What do you think of our discovery?"

Raveaux pushed his plate even further away and leaned back. He laced his fingers over his flat belly and tipped his head back, shutting his eyes. Light fell through the window, highlighting the silver in his hair and on the planes of his stubbled cheeks. "I thought we settled that. Mel Samson committed suicide. Sad, but not unexpected given her health. She must have decided not to chance a scandal, or being brought in on charges, once she knew we were on to the theft." He did not open his eyes.

Sophie poured a little more tea from a utilitarian steel pot into her thick china cup. "Something does bother me about Samson's death. Two things, actually. Firstly: the method. Hanging. She strangled. It's an awful way to go. Why not just overdose on medication? I'm sure she had plenty of pain pills, or could get them. And secondly: why the ruse about the master thief?" Sophie sipped. "It all seems . . . both too neat, and messy."

A long moment passed. Raveaux still didn't open his eyes.

Sophie's phone dinged. She looked down. Her heart rate spiked —Connor had sent her a text on their secure chat room.

Need to speak to you ASAP.

It had to be about Pim Wat . . . She did a quick mental calculation, considering the time difference. *I won't have time until tomorrow.* She texted him back.

His reply dinged. *I'll expect you at the usual place. Evening your time.*

The "usual place" was their encoded video chat. Despite the way their last video call had gone, she couldn't wait to see him again —*would he have changed?* Probably. They both had. Sophie fingered the wild riot of curls brushing her shoulders. She was softer, too, and had put on some weight. Motherhood had changed her body. Changed her priorities.

Raveaux spoke, startling her out of her reverie.

"There could be something to what you say."

"What?" Sophie had completely lost the thread of their conversation.

"The fact that the suicide was both too neat, and messy."

"The question is, where do we go from here?"

"That's not really up to us." Raveaux sat forward, placing his elbows on the table, and making eye contact. "We're in the private sector now. The client dictates. We have to contact Childer and let him know that reclaiming the diamonds appears to be a dead end. I don't know what he will consider a priority at this point, or what his superiors will want now that we're going for a bigger picture. Samson was our best lead . . . but perhaps they will want us to keep digging, looking for traces of a master thief."

"Let's start by calling Childer in the car, where we can get some privacy."

They paid the bill and exited the restaurant. Sophie's phone alarm went off for her meeting with Bix. "*Son of a two headed goat!* I have a business meeting for Security Solutions, and have to get back to the office for it. I would call Childer on the drive back over the Pali, but we already know how bad the reception is on that highway. We will have to do the call here."

Raveaux nodded. Sophie took out her phone and set it in the holder attached to the dashboard. She called Childer on video chat.

Childer looked ruddy with high blood pressure, and overdressed in a tuxedo. "Is that an ascot?" Sophie asked, peering at the screen.

"I'm about to attend an auction and assist the auctioneer," Childer said stiffly. "Keep this short, please."

"I regret to inform you that Finewell's employee, Melanie Samson, is dead of an apparent suicide in her home. We found her when we followed a lead that ended there," Raveaux said.

"Oh no." Childer clenched his fist, biting a knuckle. "I thought you said she was just sick!"

"She was," Raveaux said. "Terminal cancer. That was why she got involved with stealing—to pay her medical bills. Sophie followed a lead embedded in the email address she gave us to the supposed master thief, and the IP address turned out to be her own house. We checked the body and the premises before anonymously tipping off the police. Everything appeared consistent with suicide."

"But what about the diamonds?" Childer wailed.

"At this point, it appears that our only witness and best lead is dead. We can continue to look for this master thief, but there is a good chance that everything Samson said was a ploy to gain time and avoid being questioned," Sophie said. "The trail led back to her. And now it's a dead end, pardon the expression."

"That's it? The diamonds cannot be recovered?" Childer yanked at his ascot, spoiling the knot.

"I told you that yesterday," Raveaux said. "Your superiors authorized a deeper investigation . . ."

"But I was still hoping you'd get something from Samson, or maybe the master thief . . ."

"That was unlikely," Sophie said. "Mr. Childer." Sophie made sure she had eye contact with the frazzled manager. "It's our professional opinion that the diamonds cannot be recovered. You need to begin your procedure, now, for reporting them missing. As for the other aspects of the case, there are things that we can continue to investigate, in case Samson was not the only thief."

Raveaux leaned into the screen to address Childer. "For instance, we can travel out to the other Finewell's locations where disappearances were reported and interview the players there, looking for what they might have discovered about their burglaries. Perhaps they have some leads. In other words, we can dig further for any accomplices. Sophie and I are not convinced that we have turned over every stone in this case."

"What about her computer?" Childer asked. "Have you sifted through all of her contacts?"

"I did a preliminary scan of Samson's laptop. It's true, I can dig deeper, and we have the computer in our possession," Sophie said. "But it is unlikely to give us anything that we can track to the fence that received the diamonds. They've been gone long enough for the set to be broken up and sold. Samson said she left them in the garbage can to be picked up at her house. I checked those garbage cans, and there was nothing in them but rubbish, and rather ripe rubbish at that. The diamonds are long gone. Deal with it, Mr. Childer, and let us know further instructions when you have checked with your superiors."

"But if Samson did the job herself, they weren't left in the rubbish bin," Childer argued. "She has a fence. In fact, she has a whole network if she is the master thief!"

Sophie glanced at Raveaux—*the man wasn't taking no for an answer.*

Raveaux shook his head. "I guess we can keep working your case all the way to the end, Mr. Childer. I have some contacts in the gem world I can reach out to, see if they know anything about a fence that works in Hawaii. I could also contact the other branches of Finewell's that experienced breaches, see if they have any information, as I mentioned before. And Ms. Smithson can dig deeper online looking for the actual master thief, if it's not Samson. It's your company's money."

"Those diamonds may be gone, but I'm not satisfied. Don't stop working on it until I tell you to." The man's double chin wobbled with the force of his emotion. "I will contact my superiors." Childer ended the call with a stab of his finger.

Sophie sighed. "I guess we both know what we have to do. Now get me back to the Honolulu office. I have a performance review meeting to attend in forty-five minutes."

CHAPTER TWENTY-ONE

Connor: Day Four

CONNOR HAD CAUGHT up on sleep, then spent a productive afternoon drilling with the men and working on the Master's business of running the compound. He ended the day meditating, sitting cross-legged atop a six-foot column of tiger's-eye in the Master's garden in front of the reflecting pool with its koi and lily pads.

He'd never forget seeing the Master seated in this same spot, completely still and mostly naked, morning light turning the exotic one-foot-diameter stone pillar to fire. The man's means of getting atop it had been a total mystery to Connor at the time.

There was no mystery now. The means was simple: mastery of timing, matter, and space. The achievement of those things continued to be a challenge for Connor, especially today.

He needed to calm and center himself; nervous at the prospect of seeing Sophie again, even on video. He had to contain all of that energy and focus it on the outcome he wanted: *forging a new connection to her.*

Connor opened his eyes, checking the angle of the sun. *Yes, she would be calling soon.* He concentrated, and, riding the wave of *chi* that rose within him, stood up to set both feet side by side within the narrow diameter of the column. He drew a deep breath, focusing the energy that flowed through his mind and body, standing tall. He visualized his movement through the air and the landing, then flipped his body off the pillar, flexing his knees as his bare feet hit the ground.

He'd done this dismount three times now, a good imitation of that perfect move the Master had seduced him with two years ago. Triumph made him smile. "Next time, a double flip," he murmured.

Nine approached from the table under the orchid tree and handed Connor his *gi*. "Shall I bring your evening meal up to the computer room, One?"

"That would be fine, but I have an important phone call. Don't come until I summon you."

"As you wish."

They ascended the stone steps out of the walled garden and parted ways at the entrance to the main pyramid.

Once out of Nine's sight, Connor bounded quickly up the steep stone staircase to the computer lab in the compound's highest room. *He didn't want to miss Sophie's call . . .*

Inside the lab, Connor turned on the computer rigs and locked the door by lowering a crude wooden bar into a cradle.

He gazed longingly at his violin in its mount—perhaps he had time for just one piece?

Connor was deep into a Mozart concerto when the monitor dinged with the incoming signal from Sophie.

He exhaled, releasing a held breath, and lowered the violin. He set the instrument in its case, sat down in front of the monitor, and hit the Accept Call button.

Sophie's face bloomed into focus on the screen. Huge brown eyes, full lips, sculptured cheekbones, that long neck—*she was Nefertiti come to life*. His heart actually stuttered at the sight of her. "Your hair is longer."

Sophie touched the mass of ringlets framing her face self-consciously. "And yours is shorter."

As a Yām Khûmkạn graduate, Connor no longer had to shave his head, but his blond hair hardly covered his scalp at this point. He rubbed the back of his neck, wishing he could see more of her than just the slope of her shoulders and the tops of her breasts, showcased in a simple scoop-necked shirt. "You look beautiful. Softer."

"And you look harder. Older."

Hopefully she didn't mind that his new life had sharpened him to nothing but hard muscle and tough bone, deeply tanned from hours of outdoor practice. There were wrinkles beside his eyes from squinting into the sun. Yes, he looked both older and harder.

"Two years is a long time, Connor. Are you . . . all right?" Her well-marked brows arched in question.

"I am more than all right. The Master has named me his number One, his successor. It is a great honor." His words sounded pompous and self-important; speaking English felt stilted and awkward now. Connor switched to Thai. "I have learned so much. As I told you, the Master left me in charge."

Those expressive brows drew together as she replied in the same language. "That's what you said. What does that mean, exactly?"

"I am running the compound, keeping our enterprises going. So far, that's all it means."

"For how long?"

"I don't know."

"McDonald called me and confirmed that Pim Wat was broken out of Guantánamo." Sophie's mouth tightened.

"Yes. She and the Master are likely together. I think I know where they are."

A long pause. He expected Sophie to ask where the two were hiding, but instead, she ducked her head, breaking eye contact. "I've missed you. You were . . . my good friend." Her lips trembled.

Connor sucked in a breath as his heart took off at a gallop. "I tried to be your friend, but it was always more than that for me." He shook his head, regret suffusing him. "I thought I left you with Jake.

I believed you were together. Making a life. I thought I gave you that."

Sophie still wouldn't look up. Her thick curly hair provided a screen to hide behind. He wished she'd cut it again, to reveal that perfect profile that hid nothing of her from his hungry gaze. "I know that's what you believed. It was too hard to tell you that he'd broken up with me during that one phone call we had." She rubbed the scar on her cheek, now so faded that it scarcely marred her beauty. "I am too busy to be involved with anyone, anyway. I have my daughter, and your company to run."

His heart jumped again—*she wasn't involved with anyone!* "I'm sorry if it's been a burden."

"No. It's been good for me." Sophie looked up and met his eyes at last, straightening her shoulders proudly. "I have learned what I needed to run the business. Strategic planning and budgeting; people skills. The company has grown by eighteen percent in revenue since I took over. I prepared some profit-and-loss reports for you to review."

Connor laughed. "I don't need to see them—I never doubted you'd be great in the CEO's chair."

Her eyes narrowed. "So. When are you coming back? Because I am working a case right now, and enjoying getting out from behind the desk. I miss investigations."

"I don't know. I can't leave until the Master returns, and he left no word when that would be."

"And now, we circle back to that. What are your thoughts about approaching the Master? About . . . my mother?" Sophie knit her slim fingers together as she leaned forward into the frame. Connor felt like he could reach out and touch her, so vibrant was her image. "McDonald fed me reports over the years. The CIA never got any useful intel from Pim Wat. She did not recover well from her injuries, and she was in a catatonic state for most of her time in that prison. Honestly, I thought she would die there."

"I was too busy training to know any of that, and until the Master left, I had no access to the online world." Connor rubbed the velvety fuzz of his skull in agitation. "I assumed Pim Wat was safely incarcerated and the Master never mentioned her. I don't know why he waited so long to break her out, or if he still had any feelings for her. I never could read him unless he wanted me to."

"That's why he was the Master. I met the man, and he was . . . extraordinary." Sophie's voice dropped, husky and intimate. "As are you."

A flush burned Connor's chest. *Was she flirting with him?* He could only hope. "I am who I am," he said. "And you are extraordinary, too."

They gazed at each other a long moment.

"I want to see you," Connor's tone was harsher, more abrupt, than he'd meant it to be. "Can you come to Phi Ni? I think I can go that far without being detected or losing my authority at the compound. But I can't leave my position here for any length of time until the Master returns. I've got responsibilities."

"I have those, too." Sophie's brows snapped together. Clearly, he'd hit a sore spot. "And none of *my* responsibilities allow me to take off to Thailand at a moment's notice."

"Bring Momi with you to the island. I want to meet her," Connor urged. "I never even got to see her, and it's been a sorrow I've had to carry ever since she was born."

Sophie's mouth tightened. "I don't think so."

A stab of hurt—*did she not want Momi to know him at all?* "Just consider it. We can discuss what to do about your mother and the Master so much more easily in person."

He felt her physical and emotional withdrawal like a slap as Sophie sat back in her chair, folding her arms over her chest. "Let me know when you're returning to take over your company, even if it's under another identity. I'm getting tired of keeping all of this going."

Connor leaned forward. *He had to tell her what he'd come to in so many restless nights of pondering.* "Sophie, please. This is important."

He waited until she met his gaze reluctantly, resistance in every line of her body. "I am not coming back. I've had a lot of time to think, free from distraction, and I'm no longer willing to live a lie. Disguise myself. My Todd Remarkian identity is dead, but the FBI, CIA and Interpol are all still looking for Sheldon Hamilton."

"I'm in the process of having you declared legally dead! I mean, the Sheldon Hamilton identity . . . I've done all you asked." Her voice cracked. "Come back, Connor. Please. I don't want to do this alone."

"By 'this,' I assume you mean running my company. I thank you for that, but I'm so sorry. I can't live a lie anymore," Connor repeated. "Here at the compound, I am simply number One. My first name is irrelevant, my last name doesn't matter, and my appearance?" He turned his head so she could see the Thai number inked on his scalp. "Completely authentic. What you see is what I am, all I am. I'm done with make-believe."

"What are you saying, exactly?" Her voice had risen; she sounded panicky.

"I'm saying that when I deeded the company over to you, I meant it. When I left you my estate, I meant it. I didn't know then that I wouldn't want to return to my former life, but I know it now. It's all yours, Sophie. Yours to keep."

"You bastard! *Son of a diseased yak!*" And Sophie hit the disconnect button, and cut him off.

CHAPTER TWENTY-TWO

Sophie: Day Four

"FOUL BREATH OF A TWO-HEADED DOG!" Sophie pushed away from the computer with a curse as the adrenaline of hurt and rage flushed her system.

She hadn't realized until this moment how much she had been counting on Connor's return.

Sophie had set up a workout area in the corner of her office for just such moments as this. Rubber padding covered the floor, a rack of weights was propped up on one wall, and a treadmill set at a steep incline occupied the other. Sophie stood up and hurried to the office suite door. She locked it, and walked to the bathroom area. In a few efficient gestures. she shucked off her business wear and donned her workout clothing, stored in a locker beside the shower.

Sophie took a weighted jump rope from her gym bag and got on the rope, jumping as fast as she could, spinning the rope until her pulse zoomed to max capacity. Then, she got on the treadmill and ran.

Sophie ran until that point of peace dropped her thoughts into calm and her heart rate settled into a rhythm that was no longer panicky. The metronome of her feet beating against the flexible belt of the treadmill settled her gradually into her body.

What was she so afraid of?

Was it being trapped in this office, behind this desk, carrying this load of responsibility?

With the Sheldon Hamilton identity in the process of being declared dead and his will clear, she was heir to the company. There was nothing stopping her from selling it, farming it out, or even willing it to her daughter. She could promote Bix to CEO and take whatever role she wanted to.

Sophie looked the real source of her stress in the eye.

She hadn't just been waiting for "Sheldon Hamilton" to return from the dead and relieve her of a duty. Responsibility sat easily on her shoulders.

No.

She had been waiting for Connor to return to *her*.

She'd alleviated some of her heartbreak over the breakup with Jake by waiting for Connor. She had been able to suppress her sexuality and her loneliness with the hope that he would return and step into the place she had held open for him, both in her heart and in the business.

But he wasn't coming back.

In fact, he couldn't—Connor was a wanted man, hunted by the CIA, Interpol, and the FBI—and now, he wasn't willing to live a lie any longer.

She respected that. She understood it, and in fact, she liked him more for it. But what options did that leave?

Connor had to continue to stay under the protective umbrella of the Yām Khûmkạn. Perhaps he could go as far as Phi Ni, the private island he owned off the coast of Thailand, but without the cloak of a false identity, he couldn't return to the United States.

And where did that leave Sophie? Still raising her daughter alone, one month on, one month off, tied to the US by her custody arrangement with Momi's father, Alika.

Connor had proposed that she go to Phi Ni to meet with him. Would that be enough? Could she have a relationship with him every other month on their private island, and continue to keep his existence secret from her closest friends, Lei and Marcella, since both of them were affiliated with law enforcement?

That idea turned her stomach. Unless her friends were willing to turn a blind eye to Connor's identity as the Ghost, they'd always be living a secret life, a constricted existence hidden in shadow and bounded by geography.

Her computer monitor buzzed with an incoming call. Gradually the tone penetrated the dark world of her thoughts. Sophie slowed down the treadmill to a walking pace, sweat streaming down her body. She hopped off and walked over her desk, depressing the intercom button on her keyboard as she wiped her face on a gym towel. "Yes?"

Paula's businesslike tone came through the speaker. "Sophie, Mr. Raveaux has been trying to reach you. He says it's urgent."

"Put him through."

A video conference window opened on the monitor as Sophie swiped the towel over her sweat-soaked breasts and midriff. She belatedly remembered she was wearing nothing but a sports bra and a pair of tight Lycra shorts. "What's so urgent, Raveaux?"

Raveaux blinked at her outfit, but his gaze stayed carefully on her face. "I thought I should let you know that the manager of Finewell's in San Francisco was willing to meet with me and talk about their breach. I have a flight reservation for tomorrow morning. Want to come to the city with me?"

Sophie glanced up at the clock on the wall. "I don't think so. It's already six p.m., and I planned to dig into the copy I made of Samson's hard drive. I want to see if I can find any hidden files; anywhere she might have stashed her network's information. I haven't had a chance to get into it, what with the meetings I had at the office today."

"I see you've been busy." Sophie couldn't be sure, but Raveaux might have been checking out her body. "I've been busy, too. I've been cooking. Why don't you come over? The food will be ready at seven, with or without you."

What the hell. She was hungry, and the man she'd been saving herself for wasn't returning. Maybe it was time for her to "to get back on the horse," as Marcella would say—*though sleeping with a partner had ended up breaking her heart . . .*

Sophie didn't have to know exactly where things were going. She just had to decide whether or not she wanted a home-cooked meal, and her stomach, growling loudly, cast its vote. "What's your address?"

CHAPTER TWENTY-THREE

Raveaux: Day Four, Evening

RAVEAUX BUSTLED AROUND HIS APARTMENT, running the vacuum over the already immaculate floor, straightening the one bright pillow that softened his Danish modern couch, wiping down every surface so that it shone. Smoky jazz played from his phone app through an excellent pair of speakers.

He was a minimalist, so all of that preparation took five minutes.

He'd bought Sophie a bottle of the best wine they had at the nearby liquor store, and now that barely adequate Cabernet sat breathing. Perhaps it was psychological, but he imagined he could smell it from across the room, its tantalizing fume teasing his nostrils.

He wouldn't drink for anyone. He could have alcohol in the same room, uncork it, even pour it, without having a drink himself. He no longer needed that crutch, no matter how nerve- wracking it felt to be inviting a woman into his personal space, no matter how his belly churned that he was even acknowledging his attraction.

"It's well past time, Pierre." Gita's gentle voice spoke in his mind.

They had talked about whether or not they would ever want each other to date again should one of them die. He remembered that conversation distinctly.

They'd been in bed after a bout of vigorous lovemaking early in their marriage, before Lucie had joined them. A light wind, smelling of salt, stirred the long white curtains at the sliding glass window, cooling their bodies. Their apartment had been sandwiched between a couple of hotels in a crumbling old building, but the ocean was still visible.

Gita's slim leg slid up and down his rougher one. Her hand smoothed circles on his chest. His eyes at half-mast, most of the way asleep, he caught her fingers. He could feel her thoughts swirling around him, an inchoate flood—she was a thinker, his Gita. "What is it, G?"

"Are you happy, Pierre?" Her voice was husky and small.

He kissed her fingertips. "You know I am."

"I am too. And if I'm ever gone from your life . . . I want you to have someone, and be happy again."

That would never happen. There would never be anyone but her. To please her, he'd kissed her fingers again. "And you as well. I love you more than my life, G."

They'd said those words. *But had they ever thought it would come to this?*

Raveaux shook his head to clear it, turning back to the stove where a reduction sauce bubbled gently. He gave it a stir, tasted it with a clean spoon. "*Très bien.*"

He set out plates, glasses, and silverware on the small, round glass table on his lanai. The tinkle of laughter and conversation from the nearby hotel carried to his unit as it usually did, but this time it didn't remind him of his isolation. *He was going to have company.*

Raveaux let himself dwell, just a moment, on the memory of Sophie as she answered his video call: slick with sweat, wearing nothing but an exercise bra and a pair of spandex shorts, her cheeks flushed, a towel clutched in her fist. He'd almost fallen off his chair at the sight.

He picked up his glass of seltzer and ice. He swallowed a deep draft to cool down, then settled into chopping a pile of mushrooms, tossing them into the sauce.

The doorbell rang, a chime so unfamiliar that it took him a moment to process. Raveaux left the stove and checked the peephole, standing to the side out of long habit. Sophie's face and neck were visible through the distorted fisheye lens.

He opened the door. "Welcome to my humble abode."

"Thank you." Sophie's curvaceous mouth was cherry red, but she wore no other makeup. Her bronze skin gleamed in a simple black tank dress made of some slinky fabric that skimmed the edges of her body, hinting at its perfection. A slim silver laptop was tucked under her arm against her side, as other women would hold a handbag. "I am very hungry for the cooking you've been talking about." She walked past Raveaux into his apartment, trailing the scent of floral-infused coconut oil. "I didn't expect you to live in a ground floor apartment right in the heart of Waikiki."

"My therapist suggested this location." Raveaux shut the door and put the bar on behind her. "She said being around other people might help with my grief."

She turned to face him. "And has it?"

"No. But I am moving on as best I can." The words felt as bold as if he were propositioning her. His neck felt hot.

"That is all anyone can do." She walked through his sparsely furnished living area to look out the sliders. "Great spot, Raveaux."

"I like it for running and swimming at night."

"Perfect." She smiled as she turned back to face him. Pearls like drops of moonlight swung on tiny chains at her ears.

"Now that you're here, I will put on the steaks. Wine is on the counter." He gestured to the deep green bottle and the single goblet he had purchased for her.

Returning to the kitchen, he turned the gas on high, superheating the already warm iron grilling skillet. He turned on the overhead fan and submerged the mushrooms in the sauce.

"Where's your glass?" Sophie asked from behind him.

"I don't drink. Alcohol became a problem for me after my family died." *He would be brutally honest with her, always.* And now that he had told her this, he could never take a drink in front of her without being accountable for the words he'd uttered.

It felt like relief. It felt like freedom. And it was a little frightening, just like having her in his space in a purely social context.

Raveaux rolled his shoulders back, straightened his spine, and tossed the seasoned ribeyes onto the raised metal grill in the center of the pan. The meat crackled.

"That smells incredible," Sophie said. "I've never felt so hungry."

Raveaux turned to face her and picked up his glass. He lifted it toward her. "To new partnerships."

"Yes." Sophie's expressive brown eyes held his, and there was something new in them: a bruised quality, defiant anger. *Something had happened since they'd talked last.* Her gaze held something hot and dark that he'd never seen before. She slid off the raised stool at the bar and stalked over to him, standing a little too close. The bowl of her goblet rang forcefully against his glass. "To new partnerships. May they be deeply fulfilling."

They drank. He turned back to the grill; she returned to the bar that separated the kitchen from the living area. He breathed easier with more space between them. "How do you like your steak?"

"Medium rare."

"Oui. Moi aussi." He flipped the steaks, tossed the Caesar, pulled a baguette out of the oven and sliced it.

"You move like a matador in the kitchen." Sophie's voice was warm.

"A pretty compliment. I hope the food holds up to it." He checked the steaks, and gestured with his head. "Can you bring me the plates?"

She fetched the china and stood holding the plates. Even with the smell of rich sauce filling Raveaux's nostrils as he served, her tropical scent tantalized him.

They carried their food out onto his small lanai.

"Oh, this is lovely." Sophie settled herself in her chair. She gestured to the expanse of beach, palms waving as the last of sunset's hues faded from cloud-galleons sailing the horizon. "I can see how hard it could be to stay depressed in a place like this."

From the nearby pool complex, a burst of children's laughter drowned out the jazz drifting from the apartment. Raveaux smiled wryly as he tipped his head toward the sound. "But then, there's that. A double-edged sword, always reminding me of what I no longer have."

Sophie nodded. "I understand. Only a little—but I am childless for a month at a time. I cannot imagine your loss, nor do I want to." She held her glass out toward him. "To moving on, as best we can."

"*Oui.*" He clinked his glass against hers, and they drank their second toast.

Raveaux watched out of the corner of his eye as Sophie picked up her knife and fork, and attacked her steak with vigor. She cut a large, juicy segment of meat and soaked it liberally in sauce, making sure a couple of mushrooms were speared on the tines. She forked the large bite into her mouth.

She moaned as she chewed. Her eyes fell shut. Her head tipped back. Finally, she spoke. "I think this is the best steak I've ever had."

Raveaux felt his lips tug upward, an unfamiliar sensation. He addressed his plate. "The sauce takes a while, but some things are worth waiting for."

They ate in silence. The only sounds were the wailing sax from the music playing inside the apartment, the fading of the children's voices as they were herded out of the pool by some adult, and the clinking of their silverware. Overhead, the palms soughed, and the waves washed gently on the beach. Raveaux enjoyed the feeling of every one of his senses being stimulated; it was a beautiful half hour of time, and that they didn't converse made it somehow profound.

Sophie finished first, sitting back at last with a sigh. She lifted her wineglass. "Sublime. I need a refill. Do you?"

"Oui, merci."

She picked up his empty glass along with hers, and walked back into the apartment.

The sight of Sophie's clean, empty plate, the last of the sauce mopped up with bread, gave Raveaux a warm, full feeling that went perfectly with his own satisfied belly. He pushed his plate aside as she returned. "The moon is full tonight. Should be some antics starting soon down here on the beach."

"Antics?" Sophie's teeth shone like pearls in the dim light as she handed him his drink.

His neck flushed for the second time that evening. "Am I saying it wrong in English? The wolf howling at the night sky. Craziness. The tourists throw their clothes off and run into the ocean at the full moon."

She was still smiling, all shadow and fluid edges, as she sat down. Her arm brushed his. "*Je comprends.* Perhaps that's what we need. A little craziness."

Raveaux squeezed his drink glass—*was she saying what he thought she might be?* Was he ready for that? The way his dinner congealed suddenly into a cold, hard ball in his belly told him *no.* "I have an early flight tomorrow."

"Ah. Then I'd better show you what I found on Samson's computer and be on my way." Her voice had gone businesslike. *She got the hint.* "Shall we go inside? I need a little more light on the laptop than is available out here."

Inside the apartment, Raveaux felt his jangled nerves settle. They'd flirted a bit. Nothing inappropriate, nothing that couldn't be backed away from. He closed the glass slider on moonlight and gentle waves. "You must have worked fast since we talked on the phone earlier."

"It didn't take long because I'd already made a copy of Samson's hard drive." Sophie had the laptop open on the coffee table already, her long golden fingers flying as she leaned forward and typed. "I am storing both editions on her machine for simplicity's sake. There wasn't much on here, just a basic office program. I ran my search keyword DAVID program and did not come up with anything of interest. But when I ran a spyware diagnostic program, I found this."

Raveaux switched on the bamboo standing lamp and circled around the table to sit beside her on the couch, leaving plenty of distance between them. "Show me."

Sophie turned the laptop toward him. "See? It's a keylogger. Someone was spying on Samson."

Raveaux was familiar with keyloggers, spyware that could record every stroke of a keyboard and redirect it elsewhere. "Wireless broadcast tracking, or email?"

"Email. Whoever was spying on Samson wasn't close by." Sophie pointed at the screen. "Results were sent weekly to this IP address."

"Think it's masked?"

"I don't know. Ran a global positioning diagnostic on it, and it's in San Francisco."

Raveaux met Sophie's eyes, startled. "That's where I'm going tomorrow—to the Finewell's office in downtown San Francisco."

"I know. And that's why I'm coming with you after all. We can track this location after the meeting. See what we see." Sophie closed the laptop and stood, all in one fluid motion. "I've moved the meeting up to twelve thirty, to give us some time for that. We'll be taking the corporate jet, because there's no commercial flight that will get us there in time. Thanks for a great meal. Get some sleep. Meet me at the airport at four o'clock in the morning."

CHAPTER TWENTY-FOUR

Sophie: Day Five, Early Afternoon

SOPHIE SMOOTHED stretchy black dress pants down her thighs, her hands prickling. She wasn't nervous, she was *alert* as she faced the gleaming mahogany double doors of Finewell's, San Francisco.

She glanced over at Raveaux standing beside her. Her partner tugged at a lustrous tobacco-brown tie, straightening and smoothing it in a gesture that imitated hers with her pants. The rich color of the tie exactly matched his eyes as he glanced her way. *His dead wife probably picked it out for him.*

"You forgot your name tag." Sophie tapped her jacket's lapel, where she'd already fastened her faux insurance investigator ID.

Raveaux's mouth tightened. She could have sworn he'd almost smiled last night, when she took that first bite of his fabulous cooking. He took the ID out of his pocket and clipped it onto his lapel.

Sophie grasped one side of a pair of ornate brass door handles, and tugged it outward.

The lobby of the sixth-floor suite in downtown San Francisco's swanky business district was as elaborate as one might expect for a multi-million-dollar auction company specializing in estate sales:

elaborate Turkish carpets, shining brass, glossy wood, and original oils lit by a crystal chandelier all communicated an atmosphere of money and class.

Sophie hefted the calfskin briefcase she carried and strode up to the receptionist's curving teak desk. "We're here to meet Fred Matthews." Sophie held up the ID badge on its extendable clip. "We're from Fidelity Mutual Insurance Company, and we have an appointment."

"Yes, indeed. Mr. Matthews is expecting you." The receptionist had bright white-blond hair in a tailored bob that reminded Sophie of platinum and diamonds—she was a decorative note, just like the crystal overhead.

"I hope your office has gathered all the video records we asked for," Raveaux said.

"Of course. They were delivered to Mr. Matthews' office." The woman depressed a button on her console with a scarlet-tipped finger. "Mr. Matthews? Your appointment is here."

"Send them in." The manager's voice sounded as clear as if he were standing before them.

Sophie led the way, uncomfortably aware of Raveaux at her elbow. It was hard to admit, in the cold hard light of day, that she'd considered sleeping with him last night.

Not that he wasn't attractive.

Dapper in an elegant suit with that gorgeous tie, Raveaux had been turning female heads their whole trip. No, it wasn't that he didn't intrigue her on a number of levels—she even liked the man, let alone his cooking! But she must have been having some kind of reaction to Connor's devastating news to even consider getting involved with a colleague again.

Matthews, an imposing older black man, stood up from behind an expanse of burled walnut desk topped in glass. "Welcome to Finewell's, San Francisco. You must be Mr. Raveaux. I'll admit, you've got me mighty curious about the security breaches. And who is this lovely lady?"

"Sophie Smithson." Sophie stepped forward to shake the older man's strong, dry hand. "Thank you for seeing us on such short notice."

Raveaux gestured elegantly, indicating the office. "Do we need to be concerned about . . . confidentiality?"

Matthews snorted. "This is my private office."

"Any amount of time as a policeman will make one a bit paranoid," Raveaux said. "And I was a detective for many years. Would you mind if we give your office a quick security sweep?"

"You never know who might be listening," Sophie chimed in. "We discovered breaches in the Honolulu office video system and on computer." She set her briefcase down on the edge of Matthews's desk, popped the brass clasps, and removed a surveillance detection instrument.

"Well, since you came prepared—wand away." The man fell silent as Sophie scouted the office, searching for bugs. Raveaux utilized a different device, checking for video.

They finished at the same time, returning the equipment to the briefcase. "Your office is clean. We can speak freely," Raveaux said, as Sophie closed the case with a snap.

Matthews sat down abruptly. "Well. That's a relief. You had me going there, for a moment."

"Tell us more about the burglary your branch experienced last December," Raveaux said.

"As I told you on the phone, we lost an important heritage jewelry collection." Matthews took a file out of the side drawer and opened it. Sophie leaned forward, along with Raveaux, to peer at glossy promotional photos of a set of what appeared to be blue diamonds. "These are the Nelson family jewels. The patriarch was an investor in South African diamond mines, and kept some of the best of them for his wife."

The sparkling stones shone like bits of deep blue sky surrounded by clear white diamonds. Like the other set, this parure included a necklace, drop earrings, a hair clip, and a bracelet.

"Tell us about your security intake procedures," Raveaux said. "We are familiar with the way the Honolulu firm handles its intake and security, but we need to know how your team does things."

"Virtually identical to the way the Honolulu office handles their intake," Matthews said. "In fact, Ms. Samson, who's affiliated with the Honolulu office, was the one to do the assessment coordination of this set."

Sophie resisted the urge to make eye contact with Raveaux. It was important that they were able to get their own impressions of this man, his office, and how things were done before they gave him any more information about Samson or their case. They had not discussed when to share the news that Mel Samson might have been involved with the theft, and of her subsequent suicide.

"This is why we need to review your data recordings of any times that the diamonds were in the firm's custody," Raveaux said. "We may be able to see something others could not."

"Of course, that's why my assistant processed the video for you." Matthews opened a drawer, and slid a stick drive across his desk.

Sophie picked up the drive and slipped it into her briefcase. "Thank you. I'm sure your security team already reviewed all of the footage."

"They did. However, they found nothing to report. We had to report the missing diamonds to the police in order to activate our insurance claim, but they have pretty much washed their hands of it. They had no leads, either."

Sophie was not surprised. Local law enforcement in San Francisco was likely swamped with much more pressing crime than the recovery of expensive gems whose loss would be covered by insurance. "Is there a detective whose information you could share with us so that we can interview him or her?" Raveaux asked.

Sophie didn't have much hope anything would come of that, but it was always good to "leave no stone unturned" as her friend Marcella would say. She liked Raveaux's initiative.

"Yes." Matthews handed over a file. "Here are all the reports, including the contact people with the insurance company. They also sent out their own investigator."

Sophie slid the file into her briefcase. "If there is nothing further that you can give us, do you have a couple of confidential computers where we can review this footage on site? Otherwise, we will have to take it with us to review it privately."

Matthews raised his hands. "Unfortunately, we don't have a computer lab or anywhere for you to work, unless you want to use a conference room. We do have a copy of this footage, already stored. You are welcome to take that flash drive. The usual agreements hold about confidentiality of our procedures, yada yada."

They said their goodbyes. "We will be in touch in the next day or two," Raveaux said. "Please keep our work confidential as well. We don't know who in the company might be involved with this scheme."

"Absolutely." Matthews showed them out.

As they got on the elevator, Sophie's belly grumbled—it was well after lunchtime, and the light meal they had on the plane had been a long time ago. Unfortunately, with the short notice about the flight, there hadn't been time to get the galley properly stocked. "Would it be all right if we get something to eat before we go to check out the IP address?"

"I was hoping you would say that," Raveaux said with a quick flash of teeth—but still, no smile. "Let me pick the place. I have a favorite spot for crab on Fisherman's Wharf."

Sophie's stomach growled in agreement with this plan. "Lead on, partner. I've been to the Wharf with my father, many years ago. We're both fans of Dungeness crab. Hopefully, it's as good as I remember."

CHAPTER TWENTY-FIVE

Pim Wat: Day Unknown

PIM WAT WAS FLOATING SOMEWHERE warm. The dull pulse of pain she was so used to, a backbeat to the gray place she lived in, was gone. Pleasant sensations washed over her like gentle waves lapping on a warm beach.

Something was different.

Fear seized her. This was some new trick. They'd found her, deep inside herself. They were trying to root out her soul . . .

"Beautiful One."

His voice. The Master was calling her.

But was it a trick? Some new mind game McDonald and his henchmen had come up with? Pim Wat struggled to cling to the gray, to run deeper into it.

"Beautiful One. Come back to me. You've been punished enough. It's over now."

No one could speak like he did. No one, human or instrument, had a voice like his, a Stradivarius of a voice that could bend time, move mountains, orchestrate the rise and fall of nations.

At least, she'd always believed so.

But she was still afraid.

"Beautiful One. I'm losing patience. Enough of this. You are not this fearful creature, hiding in its shell. You are my deadly viper, my fierce queen. Come back to me." His voice was a crack of thunder now, and she felt pressure, squeezing.

She always obeyed when he used that tone . . .

A heartbeat against hers. Warmth. The strength of arms holding her, rocking her. Light against her closed eyes, a red-orange brightness.

Some kind of sharp, penetrating aromatic smell burnt her nose, made her gasp.

Consciousness dragged her eyes open at last.

She saw only shapes and colors: something white, a woven cloth that her cheek rested on. A column of golden-tanned flesh, so close she could see the pulse beating against the skin.

Her eyes hurt. Her ears hurt. Everything hurt. Her body was not a place she knew anymore.

She tried to move her arms but they were held down.

Pressure.

She opened her mouth and tried to speak, but her throat was sore and her lips cracked.

She felt a warm, wet drop hit her face. *A tear?*

"She's awake, Master. She's returned." A different voice. She didn't know this voice. She shut her eyes, afraid again, but now she felt a damp sponge at her lips.

Moisture.

She sucked at the sponge eagerly, desperate for liquid, for water, for wetness.

"Beautiful One. I knew you'd come back to me." His voice in her ear, his warm breath against her neck, his arms holding her, hugging her, rocking her. "My poor darling, my Beautiful One. Your suffering is over. Drink."

A straw at her lips now. She sucked, and moaned as warm water, flavored with herbs and honey, flowed across her tongue and down her throat. She drank in great, healing gulps.

"She's in bad shape, Master. We should keep her on the feeding tube . . ."

"No. She will recover now. She was waiting for me, and now I'm here. She'll be fine." His voice shivered with something. Fear? *Was he worried for her?*

It was true. She'd been waiting for him, and now she could come back, if only this husk of a body would let her. She rubbed her face up and down against the warmth of the Master's chest, nodding. She forced her throat to work, and a hoarse whisper emerged: "Yes."

"Yes. My darling says 'yes.'" He rocked her, and she felt his kisses along her hairline like the gentle touch of summer rain on parched soil.

CHAPTER TWENTY-SIX

Raveaux: Day Five, Late Afternoon

APPROACHING sunset began to cast long, pewter-colored shadows over San Francisco as Sophie and Raveaux exited the restaurant. Sophie's mouth was shiny, and Raveaux suppressed a sudden flash of desire to lean over and kiss that leftover butter right off. Instead, he cleared his throat and handed her an extra paper napkin he'd slid into his coat pocket. "You missed a bit."

Sophie rolled her eyes and dabbed at her mouth with the napkin.

"I'll call for our rideshare." Raveaux pulled out his phone, activated the app, and typed in the address that matched the IP location of the computer that had been receiving the keystrokes harvested from Samson's confidential laptop.

He glanced up at Sophie. "The moment of truth is upon us."

Sophie shrugged. "Not necessarily." She shivered a little in a black silk tank top worn with a light gabardine blazer over those clingy black pants that tortured his imagination. "The tracker can get only the street address location, which could turn out to be an apartment building, business complex, something with multiple offices or dwellings. We will only be able to find out where the computer actually is through old-fashioned detective work. This could even be a dead end. I didn't find more masking software, but that doesn't mean this address is the pot of gold at the end of the rainbow."

Raveaux lifted his brows in question just as a Toyota Prius pulled up at their curbside. "Another Americanism I'm not familiar with."

She grinned. "Never mind. Not worth explaining."

They greeted the driver. Rap music vibrated the vehicle and their driver nodded to the beat, bouncing an impressive set of dreads. Raveaux tried to keep his eyes off Sophie's butt while she slid into the seat ahead of him, but failed. The interior of the car smelled strongly of Lysol disinfectant, warring with a pine tree deodorizer hanging from the rearview mirror.

Raveaux moved as far from Sophie as he could, belted himself in, and stared out the window as the Prius navigated away from the pier area toward the center of San Francisco. He had already looked up the street name and knew the location was near the major thoroughfare of Van Ness Avenue, an artery that connected to Highway 101, which traversed the entire length of the state.

Fifteen minutes later, the Prius disgorged them in front of a tall, gleaming high-rise building. Sophie frowned, gesturing to it as Raveaux waved the driver off. "The computer could be anywhere inside of here. What we need to look for now is some connection to Samson, or Finewell's. But frankly, that might still not be enough to give us an exact location within the building."

Raveaux's eyes traveled skyward. The last of the daylight twinkled against the skyscraper's mirrored windows like fool's gold. "Is it even worth trying to get in?"

Sophie approached the double glass doors, tugged at one of the handles, and shook her head. "This is a locked building. We are going to have to find some legitimate reason to be admitted. I suggest we go back to the airport hotel, load that video footage onto our computers, and search for some connection to this building related to Samson or the Finewell's investigation." She turned back to him, frowning in concern. "At least, we know that this is a real address with some possibility of having a connection to the case." A draft of chilly wind, smelling of the sea and San Francisco fog, billowed up the hill, blasting them. Sophie hunched in her thin jacket, her arms wrapped around herself.

Raveaux shrugged out of his sensible wool coat and draped it over her shoulders. "I agree that we need to regroup somewhere more comfortable. But I think we should reach out to the police. See if that detective assigned to the case found any leads. Perhaps he knows of some connection to this building. At the very least, if we get him on our side, he can gain us admittance."

"Needle in a haystack, as my friend Marcella would say." Sophie slid her blazer-clad arms into his coat, and buttoned it. "Thank you. I was freezing."

Raveaux watched her button the coat all the way to the top. The feeling of satisfaction he had was the same he'd experienced looking at her empty plate.

He had fed her. He had warmed her.

Sophie took out her phone. "It seems unlikely that the detective will know anything that will get us any closer to that computer. But, if you want to work that angle while I review the surveillance recordings, that's fine with me. My turn to call a rideshare."

THEY HAD DECIDED to work in Sophie's hotel room because she had paid extra for high-speed Internet and a suite with a wet bar, fridge, and work area.

Raveaux rang her door, irritated that his heart rate was elevated. *He wasn't coming in for a nightcap in any form.* They were working. He would keep it all business.

Sophie must've decided the same because her scarlet lipstick had been wiped off and she now wore a large, concealing sweatshirt that came to mid-thigh over black yoga pants. She handed him his over-coat. "Thanks for the loan. I'm happy to see that you brought your own laptop." She gestured to the MacBook tucked under his arm. "An Apple acolyte?"

"I never claimed to be a techie." Raveaux entered, ignoring the way the hair rose on his arms as he passed her. "I just like everything to work efficiently and not be bothered by viruses. You can't say the same, using that." He pointed to the silver case of Samson's laptop where it rested on the coffee table. "I'll take the desk. I'll be using the hotel phone for calls, since the numbers I'll be calling are mostly local numbers."

"Sounds good. I would offer you a drink, but you don't partake, and we both need to stay sharp. How about coffee?" Sophie headed for the beverage station set up on top of the room's mini-refrigerator.

"Perfect."

The little coffee maker rumbled in the corner of the room as they settled into their work areas. Raveaux focused his attention on the telephone and a list of numbers from the case file that Sophie handed him from her briefcase. She put on a pair of headphones and plugged them into Samson's laptop, booting it up.

Raveaux called Detective Deke Pellman's direct number, provided by Matthews. He introduced himself as a private investigator who was doing a "probe into a pattern of high-end thefts that the Finewell's Auction House has experienced."

Raveaux had compiled a rough figure of the known losses to date, and the detective sucked in a breath when he heard the amount. Detective Pellman had a loose rattle behind his voice when he spoke. "I didn't get very far with that case. Interviewed all the staff, no one knew anything. Looked at all the video, didn't see anything. The insurance was covering it, anyway. If I had known it was part of a bigger picture, I would've taken it more seriously, at least boosted it to the Feds for the interstate aspect . . . but Finewell's didn't see fit to let me know that."

"When I worked for the French police, we often faced corporate subterfuge. Even when they wanted their criminals caught, they didn't want anyone looking too far up their ass," Raveaux said, infusing his voice with camaraderie.

"Wish I had something more to give you." Pellman coughed, an ugly sound.

"Do you know anything about this address?" Raveaux told Pellman the address of the building. "We've uncovered a link to a possible computer at this site. That computer collects information harvested by spyware related to one of the thefts in Honolulu. It doesn't seem like a coincidence that Finewell's San Francisco was also hit, when that building is only a few blocks away." Raveaux gave Sophie a grateful nod as she deposited a paper cup of coffee at his elbow. He sipped the dark brew and refocused. "We have been able to dig deeper into the background of someone we know is affiliated with the robberies, and we're still looking for more connections. We need to get into that building, and look for the computer that was collecting results from the spyware. I know it's a stretch, but do you have any cases or information related to this address?"

The detective cleared his throat with an ugly rattle. "I'm not at my office. I would need to get into my own computer files. I was just Googling that address and it goes to the Lambert Building . . . which sounds familiar, but not from this case. It might be related to a different investigation, but who knows, maybe the two will cross." The wet sound of his cough drew Raveaux's brows together in concern. "It's six p.m., in case you haven't noticed, and I'm at home. Give me a number where I can reach you tomorrow."

Raveaux gave Pellman his contact information and said goodbye. He looked around at Sophie. She sat on the couch, laptop on her knees, her fingers flying, her headphones on and her eyes never straying from the screen.

He was free to stare at her as long as he wanted.

Raveaux indulged in a long moment of doing so, then reluctantly re-opened the file. He still had a few more phone calls he could make.

CHAPTER TWENTY-SEVEN

Sophie: Day Five, Evening

SOPHIE LOOKED UP AT RAVEAUX. He had his back to her at the desk and even through her headphones, she could hear the low rumble of his voice as he talked on the phone.

An unapologetic aesthete, Sophie enjoyed beauty in all its forms. Raveaux's lean, hard build, his debonair dress, even the silver at his temples and the chiseled sternness of his mouth—all of it pleased her eye.

And everything about him was so different from the other men who'd stolen her heart . . .

Sophie tightened her lips. "Focus on the job, chica," Marcella's voice said in her mind. She bracketed the clip of video that she was pretty sure was doctored to hide where Samson had stolen the San Francisco set of diamonds. She isolated the clip and shunted it to their case file in the Cloud, inviting Raveaux to view it via text.

She glanced up again.

He was still on the phone, leaning back in the chair, gesturing with his hands in that Gallic way he had. Hopefully he was getting somewhere with gaining them access to the building.

Now that she had the spliced clip of the video, she dug into the copy of Samson's hard drive, sifting through the woman's contacts on email. She wanted more on Samson's contacts, friends, colleagues.

Most of all, she wanted more on Samson's heir. Who was this mysterious young woman Samson cared about so much?

Sophie set up a deep dive search into Samson's cloned hard drive using the DAVID program, her patented software designed to penetrate firewalls and find keywords. Using the right keywords, the program had soon located a copy of Samson's will, hidden in an encrypted file. A few decryption software minutes later, Sophie pulled up the will.

"Elisa Bell. Got you," Sophie murmured. Samson didn't identify what their relationship was in the will. An address was included on the document—and Sophie's spine tingled as she read it. *Elisa Bell lived in the Lambert Building!*

Now, she had an apartment number to investigate. Bell must have been spying on Samson for some reason.

Sophie ran a quick background on Bell, and soon pulled up a good deal of basic personal information. Counting from the woman's birthdate, Bell was thirty-seven years old. She was single, a professional freelance graphic designer, and in Sophie's estimation, her work was quite good.

Bell's social media presence was limited. She couldn't be a niece —Samson had no siblings. She wasn't a direct offspring, either, because Samson had never been married, nor were there any children listed anywhere in Samson's background. *Perhaps she was a student Samson had mentored?*

Sophie began a new keyword search on the two women, looking for university or college connections, club or other associations.

Raveaux wrapped up his call. He set the hotel's phone back in its cradle, turning to glance her way.

Sophie pushed her headphones down around her neck as she caught his eye. "I found some good stuff."

His brows arched and his mouth curled up just the faintest bit —*still not a smile, damn it.* "And?"

"The segment of video that was doctored to hide Samson's theft of the gems—same MO here as Honolulu. I sent you an invite to view the clip. And then, I found us an address we need to recon inside the Lambert Building." She cracked her knuckles with excitement, and rippled them across her keyboard. "Elisa Bell, Samson's heir, lives there. She was likely spying on Samson's computer—but why? We have a couple of real leads, here."

"Excellent." Raveaux stood and stretched, raising his arms high overhead, his fingers locked. His turtleneck rode up, baring a couple of inches of ripped abs and olive skin. He bent over to touch the floor, laying his palms flat on the floor. The shirt rode up again, showing his supple, well-defined back. He straightened to face her, and his eyes sparkled with an excitement that matched hers. "I too found some good stuff. I talked to one of my old contacts. He knows a San Francisco fence who had a batch of blue diamonds pass through his hands."

"They broke up the set. What a shame." Sophie had wanted to see those magnificent, unusual stones in their original settings.

"Those blue diamonds were way too distinctive as a collection. But with any luck at all, the fence can positively identify them as part of that set, maybe give us some information on who brought them to him. I have an appointment to meet my contact tomorrow, and we'll pay the fence a surprise visit. Tomorrow, we'll know more from Detective Pellman about getting into the Lambert Building. He said he might have some information related to it, but needed to get back to the office first."

"Sounds good." Sophie closed her laptop and stood up. "I'd like to call it a night, if you don't mind."

"Not at all." Raveaux picked up the wool coat she'd returned to him and shrugged it on. "I'm going to grab a bite to eat. Want to come?"

"No, thank you. Room service for one this evening." Sophie needed to get some distance. "I'll see you in the morning."

"I'll let you know what I hear from Pellman. Hopefully we can all go to the Lambert Building together. Get some rest." He shut the door quietly behind him, and was gone.

Sophie walked over to the door and put the bar on. She turned and checked the clock radio—*Momi would just be getting up from her nap on Kaua`i.* She perused the room service menu, ordered a large pasta salad and a glass of Pinot Grigio to go with it, and then took out her tablet.

Armita answered the video chat right away. Her nanny's long black hair was snarled and mussed, and her brown eyes were ringed with dark circles. "I finally got her down for a nap," she said in Thai. "She's running a fever."

Sophie's pulse immediately spiked. "Oh no. What is it?"

"Some kind of flu. A bit of a cough, too. Alika took us to the doctor already; they think it's a virus going around." Armita yawned, and made a patting gesture with her hand. "Momi will be fine. We have the situation in hand. You said you were going to San Francisco?"

"Yes, I'm here in the city now, for a case." Sophie got up. She paced back and forth in agitation, holding the tablet. "I need to see her. Show her to me, Armita."

"All right." Armita carried her phone into Momi's dimly lit bedroom.

Sophie had always appreciated the lovely downstairs bedroom that belonged to her daughter in Alika's mansion in Princeville. It also had a small adjoining bedroom where she or Armita stayed. He'd decorated the room with a beach theme, and the walls were cleverly painted with scenes from the island—whales and dolphins, beautiful mountains, palms and sky, and the rolling sea.

Momi was asleep, rolled onto her side, the handmade quilt her grandmother Esther had made for her scrunched up in a corner of the crib. Even in a video feed rendered grainy by the dim light, Sophie could see how flushed her daughter's cheeks were. Damp hair was plastered to her head with sweat, and her breathing was harsh and loud. Sophie watched helplessly as Armita's slender hand touched Momi's brow, smoothing black curls off of her face. "You are getting better already, my darling," the nanny crooned. "Sleep well. Rest will aid your healing."

Sophie shut her eyes, swallowing a rush of emotion as Armita carried the phone back into her own bedroom and shut the door. She let that breath out as soon as the door was closed. "I can't do this, Armita. I have to see her. Be with her. My daughter is sick!"

"She is fine, Sophie Malee." Only Armita and her mother, Pim Wat, ever called her that. "Momi has a little flu bug. She is under the care of myself, her father, and a doctor. There is nothing that you could add to this that is meaningful. You just want to be here for yourself."

"That was cruel of you to say," Sophie breathed. Her hands curled tight around the edges of the tablet.

"I'm sorry. I'm tired." Armita shook her head, yawned. "Sometimes the truth hurts, Sophie Malee. Perhaps I could have said it differently. But now, I need rest as well. Call in the morning. I'm sure she will be fine." The tablet went black as Armita cut the connection.

"Daughter of a poxy whore!" Sophie resisted the urge to throw the tablet.

She shut her eyes and breathed deeply.

She was overreacting.

Armita was right; her daughter was in good hands. What she'd said was true: Sophie could add nothing important to the care Momi was getting. *But that didn't stanch the pain of being separated from her child.*

She set the tablet down as the doorbell chimed with her room service meal. Sophie checked first, admitted the delivery, tipped the man, and relocked the door. She carried her tray of food to a small table that overlooked the sparkling lights of Marin County on the other side of the iconic red struts of the Golden Gate Bridge. "Nothing to be done about it in this moment," she said aloud. "I will call in the morning."

If only things had worked out with Jake . . . if only Connor wasn't half a world away, a wanted man . . . if only she'd said yes to Raveaux's dinner invitation and skipped this deeply lonely moment.

Sophie uncovered the pasta and ate, fighting the dark pull of her old demon, depression. Halfway through her dinner, her phone buzzed. She picked it up, eager for some distraction.

Connor.

Her heart picked up speed as she took the call. "Connor. What are you calling me for?"

"Hello to you, too, Sophie." She thought she could hear a hint of the Australian accent he used to use. "I think we got cut off, last time."

"We didn't get cut off. I hung up on you." She sat back and pushed her plate away. "I haven't decided what to do about your company. About any of it."

"You sound upset."

"I am." She stood up, paced, pushed a hand into her dense curls. "My baby is sick on Kaua`i, and I'm in San Francisco. Working."

"Oh no. I'm sorry, darling."

"Don't call me that." She tugged at her hair, welcoming the prickling pain. "I feel fragmented by all of this. Pulled in too many directions. I don't like my life right now."

Silence. Then, "That must be so difficult. I hurt for you." His voice was sincere and quiet.

Her stress began to ebb. *He wasn't trying to talk her out of it, or argue, or deflect, or justify the part he'd played in her current situation.* The emotion in his voice melted the tension knotting her muscles. "I'm so mad at you for not coming back. I thought . . ."

"You thought I'd come back, and that we'd be together."

"I . . . suppose. It helped me get over Jake leaving, to imagine us together."

"But you know that I stayed here in Thailand so you and Jake could be together without my coming between you."

"I do know that. But that's not what happened."

"No. It isn't. And in the end . . . it was better that I completed my training. I've learned so much."

"Better for *you*, maybe." She didn't intend to sound so bitter.

"It is what it is," Connor said imperturbably. "We are where we are."

"I don't like the zen monk act, Connor." Sophie began pacing again. "You're pissing me off again."

"Speaking like a true American now, I see." He chuckled. "I have a proposal for you."

"I'm listening." She paused, pressing her fingers against her eyes.

His words came out in a rush. "Come to Phi Ni. Meet with me. Let's talk over what's happened, what to do about the company, how to . . . be together—if we can be together. I know we can figure something out." He drew a breath, blew it out. "The Master called. He said he is with your mother, that he is working with some healers to restore her mind, body, and spirit. He has hopes that Pim Wat will be healed from this, and from that part of her that was so . . ."

"Evil? Sadistic?" Sophie snorted. "Pim Wat is not like other people. She told me that herself."

"It doesn't matter what you or I think. The Master loves her and is trying to heal her, and I've seen him do incredible things. What we think about what he's doing doesn't matter. What *does* matter is that I told him I wanted time away from the compound to meet with you, and he granted it."

"Connor." Sophie shook her head. "A week on Phi Ni is not a solution."

"But it's something. Please. Just say you will meet with me. I will make sure you don't regret it." His voice was silky seduction, melting her defenses. "Give me a weekend, at least. We'll walk on that beach below my house. You loved that beach."

Ah, that half-moon of silky white sand fringed with palms, the turquoise water of the bay, the tall cliffs crowned by his gorgeous house . . . Her lady bits woke up and cast a vote—*say yes!* She'd done nothing but work and be a mother for the last two years. "I'll think about it."

"Good. I'll arrange to be there in a week. Goodbye, Sophie."

CHAPTER TWENTY-EIGHT

Raveaux: Day Six

THE DINER where Detective Pellman had asked them to meet him for breakfast was almost a cliché: battered red plastic booths, checked tablecloths, paper napkins in silver holders, and greasy laminated menus. They'd arrived early, having discovered that the diner was only a few blocks away from their hotel.

Raveaux sneaked a glance at Sophie, seated across from him. She looked like she hadn't slept well; strain showed in the tightness of her mouth and smudges under her eyes. She had not bothered, as others might have, to hide those signs of stress with makeup or extra grooming.

He appreciated the truthfulness of how she presented herself. Sophie had a mask, an inscrutable blankness of expression, but he could always see beyond that to the emotion of the moment. She carried secrets, and though he'd never know what they were, the weight of them was apparent. Her transparency felt refreshing after knowing his wife.

Gita had been a mystery he never quite unraveled. She would never have appeared in public with no makeup on and circles under her eyes from sleeplessness; her hair would have been shiny and sleek, her manner exactly how she chose to present herself at any given moment.

The glimpses Gita had allowed him of her inner soul, made those moments all the sweeter for their rarity.

Detective Pellman arrived, shoving open the door with a tinkle of its bell. He was sensibly dressed for the chill and damp in a heavy waterproof coat, gloves, and a black wool beanie. He slid into the booth next to Raveaux, before the other man could get out to greet him.

"Detective Pellman." He extended a hand to Sophie. The man's eyes were rheumy, with a quarter-inch of white visible above damp-looking lower lids, giving him the visage of a sad hound dog. That impression was reinforced by pouches of saggy flesh beneath his chin, and long fleshy ears.

Sophie shook his gloved hand, smiling warmly. "Sophie Smithson. Thank you for meeting us, and working with us on this case."

The men greeted each other, and Pellman turned back to Sophie. "Was pleased to get the call from Raveaux. Frankly, I'm glad to have a chance to have another look at the case." The older man shrugged out of his padded slicker and flagged down the waitress. "Hey, Alice. Mind hanging this up for me?"

"No problem, Deke." The sixty-ish woman, packed tightly into a flowered polyester knit uniform, took the coat from Pellman. "Can I get anyone coffee?"

They ordered. Raveaux waited to hear what Sophie would disclose about her discovery of Bell's address, but when the waitress returned with coffee and Sophie's hot water, his partner merely dunked the cheap teabag in the thick white mug, a pucker of distaste on her mouth.

"We have some new information since I talked to you last night," Raveaux told Pellman. "We've found a connection at the Lambert Building to our main suspect. You know of her since she did the assessment portion of your case, too. Her name is Mel Samson."

"I remember the videos of Samson. Weird headdress." He patted his beanie.

"She was sick. Terminal cancer. That was her motive to steal—to get money for her treatment," Sophie said. "She committed suicide a couple of days ago."

"A shame," Pellman said. "Was her suicide connected to the case?"

"Most definitely. Finding out we were onto her triggered her suicide," Sophie said. "Samson was the actual thief in both cases we've studied closely. But she said she'd been working with someone else, someone who set up the theft, doctored the surveillance video, and disposed of the gems once Samson turned them over. We've been calling that unsub the master thief." Sophie gave up the teabag dunking and took a sip of the pale brew. "I must remember to bring my own teabags when traveling."

Pellman's gaze turned to Raveaux. "You said there was a connection to the Lambert Building."

"Yes. Sophie discovered that Samson's heir, Elisa Bell, lives in the building," Raveaux said. "We'd like to get in and meet her. Notify her of Samson's death, if no one else has, and see what her response is."

Their breakfast arrived. Raveaux eyed his runny eggs Benedict with dismay. Sophie, across from him, pointed with her fork to her own scrambled eggs and bacon. "Sometimes you have to manage your expectations, Raveaux."

"Just like you enjoyed your tea?" He raised his brows.

She laughed. "You have a point."

Pellman took a bite of his eggs and coughed, which turned into a fit. Raveaux pounded the man's bony back and he hacked into a wad of paper napkins Sophie handed him. "You seem unwell. You should get that checked out."

Pellman laughed, and it sounded as hopeless as his cough. "I did have it checked out, and it's killing me. Don't ever smoke."

"I'm sorry." Raveaux looked down at his coffee, wishing it was something stronger. He was surprised to see Sophie's slender hand reach out to squeeze the older detective's arm.

"I hope you are making plans to enjoy your life as much as you can."

Pellman gave that harsh, painful chuckle again. "Closing cases fulfills my life, such as it is." The man placed his gnarled fingers over Sophie's hand and patted it. "But if my cancer gets me a smile and a touch on the arm from a pretty girl, I'll still take it."

Raveaux scraped the dubious sauce off of his eggs, and ate them plain.

The detective's cancer didn't seem to inhibit his appetite, and the man shoveled in his breakfast vigorously. Sophie, however, ate sparingly and pushed her plate away half finished. She picked up the thread of their conversation, holding her mug. "When I discovered Samson's will, Elisa Bell was named in it as her heir. Bell is thirty-seven, single, and a graphic designer. There must be some relationship to Samson, but I have not been able to identify exactly what it is."

"I think that should be enough for us to get in, introduce ourselves, and see where it goes," Pellman said. "I'll flash my badge and that'll do it with the building super."

Soon they were on their way to the Lambert Building, riding in style in Detective Pellman's vintage Chevrolet Impala. Raveaux sank into the rich leather upholstery of the wide bench seat as he slid in beside Pellman in front. Sophie, in the back, laughed aloud in delight as she bounced on the roomy back seat of the late 1950's-era vehicle with fins on the rear. "Where do you park a vehicle of this size in the city? This is not the usual ride for a place like San Francisco."

"Got this old girl from my grandma. She drove it about three times in her entire life, so it's in good shape, and I was lucky enough to inherit her house with a garage, too." Pellman stroked the large, gleaming steering wheel.

The Impala navigated the city just fine, floating over the steep streets in style. They soon pulled up in front of the Lambert Building, where Pellman skillfully maneuvered the boat of a car into a handicap space and hung a placard from his rearview mirror. "Let's do this."

At the door, Pellman rang for the building's manager. A tinny voice inquired their business through a grille. "This is Detective Pellman of the San Francisco Police. We are here to interview one of your residents." Pellman spoke with authority, succumbing to a fit of coughing as soon as the building supervisor buzzed them into a small foyer. A steep set of stairs switchbacked upward, leading to interior landings on each floor. "I'm not going up those stairs. There must be an elevator," Pellman rasped.

Sophie pointed to a small, narrow contraption with a brass door hidden behind the potted palm. "I'll take the stairs. Elisa's apartment is 4B. I'll meet you two there." She headed up the stairs, taking them two at a time. Raveaux and Pellman watched her until she was out of sight as the elevator rumbled down slowly. "She's a looker," the older man mused.

"I hadn't noticed," Raveaux said, and Pellman coughed a feeble laugh.

Sophie was standing outside of the apartment when they got off the elevator, frowning. "I knocked. No one is answering."

"Let me try." Pellman used the side of his fist to pound on the glossy black wood of the apartment door. "Open up! San Francisco Police!"

No answer.

No sound of a barking dog or rustle of footsteps.

Raveaux applied his eye to the spy hole, but there was no shadow of movement on the other side of it.

Pellman bent to slide his card under the door. Sophie stopped him, snatching it from his fingers. "No. Not yet. I want to see if she's heard the news that she is Samson's heir, and see what she says. I'm willing to bet that her lawyer has not yet contacted her. In effect, we can be doing the death notification. And I'm eager to see what her reaction is. I still haven't found a connection between the two women, and I want to know if Samson's legacy comes as a surprise or not."

Raveaux nodded. "Let's find out from the super what her habits are, then intercept her in person."

"Catch her off guard, you mean," Pellman said. "I like it." He tapped the door lightly with his knuckles. "Knock wood."

RAVEAUX SHOOK his contact's hand, slipping a thousand dollars in tightly rolled hundreds into the man's palm as he did so. "Appreciate this, Hoo."

Kim Hoo was a short tubby man dressed in motorcycle leathers marked with the bold insignia of a San Francisco club. They'd ridden across Europe many years ago, and Hoo had been a valuable confidential informant of Raveaux's for those many years.

Hoo bounced his brows suggestively at Raveaux as he slid his hand into his pocket, disappearing the cash. "Anything for you, Raveaux. This guy is cagey, so I'm glad you dressed the part. Did you leave your weapon at the hotel?"

"I did." Raveaux patted his chest reflexively. Hoo had insisted that he leave his Sig and any ID at the hotel in case the fence searched him, and it left him feeling naked. He missed the weight of his ankle piece, and the Sig's weight in his shoulder holster was familiar from his police days. Posing as a buyer, Raveaux had dressed in a tailored bespoke suit Gita had commissioned for him in Paris years ago. It hung on him a bit, but that wasn't entirely a bad thing— he had plenty of room to move, should he need to. "Lead on, Kim."

Hoo checked that his Harley was secured, and touched the gleaming handlebars as if for luck as they headed out. "We won't be long, I hope."

He set off, Raveaux following, and they walked down the sidewalk of the fairly decent street. Raveaux was prepared to go down some dark alley, but instead, after a couple of blocks Hoo stopped in front of a well-lit, well-maintained office building. He pressed an apartment building number on the call box, and the entry gate buzzed open for them.

Raveaux shifted his messenger bag to his other hand. He glanced down at the leather bag, picturing the interior of the main compartment, where his investigation equipment had been cleaned out and packs of cut paper with cash rubber banded on each side filled the bottom. Not fancy, just enough to pass a cursory inspection to verify he was able to pay. But he didn't intend any transactions to go further than that.

They couldn't, or he'd been in trouble.

The three of them had parted ways after Pellman left them off at their hotel. Sophie had excused herself after the visit to the Lambert Building, telling him that she needed to dig deeper into Elisa Bell's background, and planned to work at her computer. He and Sophie had arranged to reconnect over dinner in the evening to compare notes from the day—but he hadn't told her his agenda.

He'd had the feeling that she could hardly wait to be alone; that she had some plan up her sleeve. *Was she meeting someone?* But he was hardly one to question her; he'd neither told her what he was doing nor invited her, and there was a reason for that: *these people could be dangerous.*

They entered a narrow, shiny brass elevator in the building's lobby. Hoo glanced over at Raveaux. "Something on your mind?"

Raveaux, conscious of an overhead camera on them as they rose toward the third floor, shook his head. *He needed to focus.* It didn't matter what Sophie was doing; he had a challenging situation right here, right now, to handle.

The office door they stopped in front of, with its discreet gold plaque marked *Acquisitions*, looked like every other door leading away into the distance down a luxurious hallway.

Raveaux tugged his jacket down and straightened his tie as Hoo rang the doorbell. He'd survived hundreds of these kinds of meetings. There was no reason to be nervous—but as he glanced around, something just didn't feel right about the heavy silence of the hallway, the oppressive sense of emptiness of the entire floor.

The hair rose on the back of his neck.

That feeling was confirmed when the door swung open, framing a huge, muscular man the color of black licorice, dressed in a tank top and fatigues. The soldier cradled an AK-47 and was draped in bandoliers of ammo. A second mercenary loomed behind him, even taller than the first, and just as strapped.

Congolese.

He'd recognize the look of those bandits anywhere—he'd dealt with them in France. What were they doing in San Francisco?

Dealing in stolen diamonds, obviously.

"Excusez-moi. I do not need your diamonds that much." Staying in character, his French accent heavy, Raveaux stepped back from the doorway with his hands up.

Hoo shouted past the guards. "Kramer! Is this how you greet your guests?"

The guards stepped back, parting on either side of the door. A man who must be Kramer, six foot six in height and built narrow, dressed in shiny, embroidered robes, gestured from within. Overhead light gleamed on the blue-black skin of a shiny shaved head; he looked like a djinn out of a fable. Lucie would have loved the sight of him. "You Americans. So sensitive."

"I am not American," Raveaux snarled. "And neither are you, Monsieur."

Hoo made a settling gesture with his hands. "Well, I *am* American, and I think we're getting off on the wrong foot here. Kramer, if you need to pat us down, do what you gotta do, but we're not armed and don't appreciate the firepower. I for one am here to do business. I was actually hoping for some of that really strong coffee you like to serve."

Kramer gestured with his head. The guards, working in tandem, stepped forward and frisked Hoo and Raveaux efficiently. Raveaux was now glad he had left his weapon at the hotel.

Kramer visibly relaxed once the guards had verified the two men were neither carrying, nor wearing wires. "Can never be too careful. This city is a den of iniquity." He clapped his hands and called out over his shoulder. "Coffee! And something to eat." He waved to a seating area of luxe black leather couches. "Make yourselves comfortable."

Raveaux approached the seating area, assessing. It was never good to sink too deep into a couch in a potentially dangerous situation, and he wanted to keep an eye on as much of the room as he could. He chose an armchair at the far end of the large coffee table, leaving the other chair for the diamond dealer, and the couch to Hoo. He perched on the chair's edge, holding the briefcase on his knees. "I don't need coffee. I just want to see the diamonds."

Kramer chuckled, a surprisingly fat, rich sound coming from such a tall, thin man. "There is a protocol. This kind of business takes place only between friends, and friends break bread together."

Hoo sat down on the couch, and as Raveaux had feared he would, sank deep into it with a grunt. "We're all friends here, Kramer. You know that."

Yet another musclebound guard came out of the kitchen, but along with his bandoliers, this one carried a tray loaded with a small Turkish coffee pot, three espresso cups on saucers, and a plate of biscuits. The guard poured thick black coffee into each of their cups and set a fancy biscuit on one side of each saucer.

Kramer gestured to the array of chocolate-coated tinned cookies on a plate accompanying the coffee. "I have these specially sent to me wherever I am in the world. Enjoy."

Raveaux picked up his cup. The last thing he wanted to do was partake of this man's food and drink, but there was no choice.

Hoo leaned forward and shoveled several spoonfuls of sugar into his coffee and stirred it with a loud tinkling sound. "My favorite thing about visiting you, Kramer. This stuff is rocket fuel."

"I hope our business makes it pleasant, as well." Kramer chuckled that fat laugh.

Raveaux waited until both Kramer and Hoo had taken sips of coffee to sample his. The taste was smoky and dark, almost oily on his tongue. He took a bite of a chocolate biscuit as well. "Delicious." The niceties observed, he set down his cup and saucer. "Please. I am a busy man. May I see the merchandise?"

Kramer caught the eye of the guard who had brought in the coffee tray, and gave a nod. The soldier disappeared into a back room, and returned with a large black metal case. He set the case on the table and cleared away the tray of refreshments.

Kramer reached into an interior pocket in his golden robe, and removed a key. He unlocked the case.

Diamonds sparkled inside stacked trays that telescoped out as Kramer opened the lid. Sorted by size and shape, they glittered cold fire from velvet-lined niches. The expanding tiered construction allowed Kramer to lift the top tray, revealing four more trays nested below it, each tray holding diamonds in singles and clusters. Colored diamonds rested on white velvet, clear ones on black.

Raveaux scanned the trays. "As I told you, I am in the market for blue diamonds. I have a buyer who appreciates the rare. I don't see any here."

"I have just the thing." Kramer lifted out the bottom tray to reveal a series of small, color-coded velvet pouches filling the bottom of the box. Kramer removed a royal blue pouch and emptied its contents onto a white velvet tray. Several dazzling, dark blue gems rolled out of the pouch and winked up at Raveaux from their snowy resting place.

Raveaux mentally reconstructed the Finewell's necklace in his mind.

The color of these stones was right: a captivating blue somewhere between navy and sky. The shapes were right: a series of graduated teardrops. Not the most common cut, and a rare color: *these were some of the missing Finewell's stones.*

Kramer handed Raveaux a loupe. Raveaux picked up the largest diamond, likely the centerpiece of the necklace he remembered seeing. He held the gem up and looked at it through the magnifying viewer.

The stone was flawless. Looking into the blue of the stone felt like gazing into infinity. He couldn't see anything. And then, in the upper left quadrant, the ghost of an inclusion, a shape like a tiny feather.

Raveaux hadn't just memorized what the diamonds looked like. He had memorized an interior map of each stone, and he immediately recognized this one.

Confirmation. This stone was definitely part of the set that had been stolen from Finewell's.

Raveaux set the diamond back on the white velvet tray. "I like this one."

He removed his phone and thumbed to the photo app—but before he could take the picture, he felt the cold steel of a gun muzzle, resting in the notch at the back of his head.

"No photos. Put that phone away," Kramer growled, no hint of the jovial host in his voice.

"I always take a reference photo of the goods I buy," Raveaux said. "I was not aware that was against your policy." The hand holding the phone, still pointed at the diamond, trembled realistically. Raveaux didn't have to try hard to fake that.

Hoo heaved forward, trying to dig himself out of the couch. "Hey! My bad. I should have told my colleague that no one gets to use their phones in here. Sorry, I forgot to give him the memo."

"May I put my phone away?" Raveaux asked. *If only someone, anyone, knew where he was . . .* The round bore of the weapon pressed harder into the back of his head, forcing him to bend over, his chest touching his knees.

"I don't like the smell of you. I don't think I'll sell you my diamonds after all," Kramer growled.

"I meant no offense." Raveaux moved his hand down, very

slowly, sliding his phone into his pocket and raising both hands. "But I don't think I want to buy your diamonds, after all, either."

The gun was abruptly removed from his head. The man standing behind him yanked upward on the back of Raveaux's jacket, tugging him upright. The rending of the fine fabric as it ripped under one of his arms sounded almost obscene—until the boom of a door cannon obliterated every other sound.

The portal flew open so hard it smashed into the wall, and a familiar voice shouted: "San Francisco Police!"

Detective Pellman had tracked him, and was walking into a nest of vipers.

"Gun!" Raveaux screamed in warning, and dove for the floor.

CHAPTER TWENTY-NINE

Sophie: Day Six, Afternoon

SOPHIE SHUT her laptop with a click. She'd just finished digging further into Elisa Bell's background.

The woman had been adopted, but she'd had an uneventful childhood and both of her parents were middle class professionals. She met her parents at holidays, according to her scanty social media posts, and they seemed to be on cordial terms. Bell had been a good student, according to records, and was a talented artist, a standout star at Pearson School of Design during her college years. Her career appeared to be successful; her website featured many product marketing designs, from labels to ads, and she had a nice portfolio of original wall art, too.

Why hadn't the woman married? Why hadn't she had children? There was no sign of any romantic involvements with either a male or a female partner, either. Bell was attractive, with a well-shaped figure and riveting blue eyes—and yet she did not seem to have had any major relationships with anyone. Friends were also absent from any postings, which struck Sophie as odd.

Bell had her own business, and her tax returns showed a solid upper-middle-class income. She owned her apartment; she carried a small balance on one credit card which she used to accumulate travel miles. She was in good health, and owned a decent life insurance policy whose main function was to guarantee she had income if she was ever disabled.

In short, Sophie wasn't able to find any critical need or motivator that would tie her to Samson, or anything to do with their case.

Why was Bell spying on Samson with the keylogger program?

Sophie got up, did a quick set of yoga stretches to limber up her body, and buckled on a fanny pack. She strapped on her shoulder holster next, and shrugged her light jacket on over it, wishing she had brought a sensible coat like Raveaux's. She left the hotel room, calling for a rideshare on her phone as she rode down to the lobby in the elevator.

Where *was* Raveaux, and what was he doing?

Whatever his activity this afternoon was, he hadn't volunteered it. She remembered the closed expression on his face as he lifted his hand in a brief goodbye to her at the door of the hotel . . . maybe he was running through the city for exercise, or reading his book while sampling some gourmet afternoon snack. Wistfulness to join him for either of those activities was an unfamiliar curl of feeling in her chest.

Likeliest of all, Raveaux was meeting some of his old contacts for the case, and didn't want to tell her what he was up to. *That was fine.* She hadn't wanted him to get in her way, either, because she was on her way to do a little breaking and entering.

NOW THAT HER bona fides have been established by Pellman, the building super buzzed Sophie into the Lambert Building without question. She took the stairs once more, and at Bell's apartment, knocked on the door.

Sophie had been away from the location no more than a couple of hours, so she wasn't surprised when no one answered.

She knocked again, for form's sake.

No answer.

Sophie unzipped her waist pack and removed a pair of latex gloves, glancing down the empty hall. She'd already verified that there were no visible video surveillance nodes. She snapped on the gloves and took out her lockpicks, zipping the pack shut.

Two minutes later, she turned the knob and pushed the door gently inward.

The apartment was dimly lit: the blinds were down and closed, but a graceful reading lamp on a brass arm, shone onto the corner of a sensuously shaped, ruby velvet couch. A drift of prints of designs covered the surface of the coffee table in front of the couch.

Sophie started at a twitch of movement in the doorway leading out of the living area, her hand coming up automatically to land on her weapon.

A large Persian, the fluffy gray of a San Francisco dawn, stood in the doorway. The cat blinked huge green eyes. "Meerow."

"Well hello, kitty." The cat trotted toward Sophie, huge soft tail quirking from one side to the other like a feather boa in motion. Sophie squatted and stroked the cat's head. "Aren't you a pretty thing."

"Don't move a muscle." A woman's voice, hoarse with strain, came from the doorway across the room.

Sophie looked up to meet Elisa Bell's intense blue gaze. The woman held a police issue Taser, the type that shot prongs, aimed at Sophie.

Sophie lifted her hands slowly away from the cat, holding them up in a surrender gesture, but she was in a deep squat with little ability to move. She'd been tased by one of these weapons before, and it had been extremely unpleasant. The weapon would put her out of commission for at least fifteen minutes, probably longer. "I mean you no harm."

"Who are you? And what are you doing, breaking into my place?" Bell came forward a step. The cat wound around Sophie's legs, purring.

"I apologize. I'm a private investigator, working on a case. Truly, I mean you no harm. I came by earlier today, with the police . . ."

"That doesn't answer why you broke into my place!" Bell gestured with the weapon. "Stand up."

Sophie stood, slowly, her hands still high. "Can I get my ID out?"

"Show me."

Sophie slid a hand into her pocket and pulled out the laminated, clip-on Fidelity Mutual insurance ID. "Can I toss this to you?"

Bell nodded. Sophie tossed the ID to Bell's feet, and the woman squatted to pick it up, her eyes and weapon never leaving Sophie. "Okay. You're with an insurance company. That doesn't answer why you're here."

"The truth?"

"Of course, I want the truth." Bell's voice rose. The cat sensed trouble and bolted for the bedroom.

"We came by today to give you some news. You have an inheritance," Sophie said.

"If I had a nickel . . . and why would you break in to tell me that?"

"This is real." Sophie gestured with her head toward the couch. "Can we sit down? Keep the Taser on me if you need to. I promise I just want to talk." She infused her voice with sincerity.

"Keep your hands up where I can see them." Bell gestured with the Taser. "No funny business." The line sounded like something out of an old movie, and Sophie almost smiled as she turned, making her way around the coffee table and sitting down carefully on the red couch, her knees together and hands up.

"You still haven't told me why you broke into my place." Bell sat in a high-backed armchair and faced Sophie across the coffee table.

"Like I said, you have an inheritance. My partner and I, along with an SFPD detective, came to give you the news earlier."

Bell's eyes were remarkable, large and long lashed, aqua flecked with green and navy. She made a "go on" gesture with the weapon, and Sophie sighed. "I'm investigating the death of the woman who left you that inheritance. I have no good explanation for why I broke in, except that I was curious about you." Sophie held the woman's gaze. "I wanted to find out more about you. I was curious what your connection to her might be."

Of course, the truth was, Sophie had wanted to see if there was something on Bell's computer that gave an answer to the keylogger question. She carried a write blocker mechanism that could make a complete, mirror copy of Bell's hard drive in her waist pack. "Are you going to call the police? Because if so, ask for Detective Pellman. He can back up my story."

"He'll back you up on breaking in here?" Bell shook her head. "I don't think so."

"That was all my idea. I apologize."

"I admit, you've piqued my interest in spite of myself. Who is this person I have an inheritance from?"

"I would be much more comfortable telling you those answers if you would put the weapon down," Sophie said.

"I bet you would." The Taser still pointed at Sophie's midsection.

"Do you know a woman named Mel Samson?"

"No idea who that is." A flicker of Bell's eyes, the slightest glance to the left. *Bell was lying.*

"Well. Mel Samson knows you. And she died last week under suspicious circumstances."

"I don't know what that has to do with me."

"I don't either, quite frankly. I've been searching for a link between the two of you, and I haven't been able to come up with one. But clearly, there's something there if Samson left you all her worldly possessions, including a considerable life insurance policy."

Bell lowered the Taser. Following her lead, Sophie dropped her hands, resting them, palms down, on her thighs.

"I should call the police," Bell said.

"You probably should. Please do, in fact. Ask for Detective Pellman." Sophie kept a calm mask in place.

"Why is an insurance investigator involved with my inheritance, and what does that have to do with me?"

"Once again, I apologize, but I'm not authorized to discuss the case with you, Ms. Bell. Would you be willing to come with me to the SFPD station and talk to Detective Pellman? Or would you just like to tell me what your relationship is to Mel Samson?"

They locked eyes for a long moment; Bell had a good poker face, but she sighed suddenly, setting the Taser on the coffee table. "Mel Samson is my mother. She gave me up for adoption at birth."

A rush of excitement energized Sophie. She'd hoped for something like this, and hadn't been able to find it anywhere online. "Tell me more."

"I went looking for my mother when I turned thirty. I found Mel, and we've been in touch ever since. I've only met her in person one time."

"No one could find any trace of a relationship between you two. Why did you keep it secret?"

"She wanted it that way." Bell pushed a hand through short black hair in agitation, disrupting an artfully-styled crest at the front in an endearing gesture. "I'm so . . . upset to hear she's dead. I didn't know."

"How often did you communicate?"

"Once a month or so."

"Did you know about her cancer?"

"Cancer?" Bell's eyes widened. "What cancer?"

"Mel Samson had terminal cancer. And she was involved with something illegal. In the end it resulted in her death. That's why there's an investigation. I can't tell you anything more, though. Detective Pellman will want to talk to you."

Bell's face crumpled, and she covered it with her hands. "I can't take this in." She stood up abruptly. Her eyes were dry and stark when she dropped her hands. "I just found out my mother died. You need to leave."

Sophie stood too. "I'm so sorry for your loss. I met Ms. Samson, and she was an impressive woman." She took the business card Detective Pellman had given her out of her waist pack. "Please call the detective and set up a time to meet him and talk, or I promise he will be calling you."

Bell did not move to take the card. She seemed frozen, a pillar of salt, her thoughts turned inward and invisible, her face white.

"Again, I'm sorry for your loss." Sophie set the card on the coffee table. "I'll let myself out."

CHAPTER THIRTY

Raveaux: Day Six, Afternoon

GUNFIRE ROARED OVERHEAD as Raveaux pitched forward off his chair, diving under the coffee table. The six-foot slab of teak tipped up to accommodate him as it scraped along his backbone, knocking over the remaining cups and saucers. The coffee items crashed to the floor—but that minor sound was obliterated in the thunderous stuttering of automatic weapons fire.

"Merde!" Raveaux covered his ears, pressing his face into the nap of the expensive Turkish carpet, his face turned to one side. *What a time to be unarmed...* His ears rang so loudly it was hard to differentiate the sounds. He crawled deeper under the table, pressed instinctively as flat as he could, but braced for the impact of a bullet.

Shouts.

Screams.

More gunfire.

Raveaux shut his eyes, pressing his hands even tighter over his ringing ears.

What was his next move? His best move?

He was an unarmed man in the middle of a gunfight.

His best move was not to get shot.

A thump on his right. Something had just hit the floor beside him.

Raveaux opened his eyes. He was staring into Kim Hoo's face. His former colleague's eyes and mouth were open in an expression of surprise, but the man was quite dead already. Blood from too many holes to count poured out of the corpse. It oozed toward Raveaux across the carpet in a spreading pool.

Raveaux belly-crawled to the far end of the coffee table using his elbows, thankful that the piece of furniture was large and heavy. *He might still get out of this alive . . .*

He peered out from under, around the corner of the couch, as soon as the gunfire paused.

"Put your weapons down! San Francisco Police!" A new voice, young, strong and unfamiliar, reverberated in the room.

Silence. The room had gone still. *Was everyone dead already?*

Raveaux raised his hands from under the end of the coffee table. "I'm a friendly! Private investigator Pierre Raveaux," he called out.

"Raveaux. We know who you are." Pellman's voice gurgled weakly from near the doorway.

Raveaux spotted the older man slumped against the wall, a long smear of blood decorating the stucco surface behind him.

Another cop, the one who'd called out, dropped into Raveaux's line of sight, yelling emergency codes into his cell phone even as his gaze darted around the room, looking for threats—but the dead diamond dealer's soldiers were sprawled around the room, motionless.

The young detective got up, ignoring Raveaux, and ran forward to kick the weapons away from the fallen mercenaries.

Pellman's hand, resting on the floor, crooked a finger toward Raveaux. The older detective's lips moved as though he wanted to speak.

Raveaux crawled out from under the table and made his way through the carnage to kneel beside the older man, glancing around as he went.

Kramer was sprawled face down at his end of the coffee table, brains and blood splattered across the shiny wood. Gore dripped off the edge, splattering Kim Hoo's astonished face. The mercenary who'd brought their coffee was draped over the back of the sofa. The other two were also down, sprawled in the graceless poses of the unexpectedly dead. Pellman's partner was still yelling into his phone as he checked the bodies for signs of life.

Raveaux turned his attention to Pellman. The detective moved his lips feebly. His eyelids fluttered. His hands trembled and curled with nerve spasms.

"Just relax. Focus on breathing." Raveaux squeezed Pellman's shoulder.

"I made you a copy of the case folder." Pellman gasped out. He grabbed Raveaux's hand. "Left it for you at the hotel."

"Don't worry about that." Raveaux squeezed his hand. "Help is on the way."

"Won't be in time. It's okay. I was dying anyway." Pellman tried to smile, but as he did, a gush of blood bubbled from his lips and rolled down his chin. His eyes were already filming over and his skin had gone the clammy shade of a mushroom.

"Do you have anything you want to say to a loved one? Any messages I can pass on?"

"Don't have any loved ones. Only the job." Pellman gasped. His hand clenched Raveaux's reflexively, and then relaxed as he slumped, a puppet with cut strings.

His partner, seeing this, screamed into his phone. "Get those ambulances here, stat!"

"Too late," Raveaux said. "He's gone." He passed a hand lightly over Pellman's face, and closed the man's eyes.

※

RAVEAUX CALLED Sophie from the police station after the hubbub of the crime scene had died down, and Fremont, Pellman's partner, had taken his recorded statement. A migraine played colored lights across the back of Raveaux's retinas as he thumbed his phone open to her number in his Favorites.

Sophie answered brusquely. "Where are you? I have news."

"I have news, also. You need to come down to the Mission Street San Francisco Police Station. We are now working with a Detective Fremont on the case." Raveaux blew out a breath, rubbing sore, gritty eyes. He could scarcely focus. "I'm down here after making a statement. I was involved in a shootout, and Detective Pellman is dead."

He waited for Sophie to protest, exclaim, to barrage him with questions. She only asked one. "Are you injured?"

"No."

"I'm on my way." And she ended the call.

Raveaux rested his sore head on his crossed arms on the metal table of the interview room. Fremont had not released him. He understood. He would not have released him, either. The whole situation stank to high heaven and had gone deadly so fast . . .

Scenes from the firefight played across the back of his aching eyeballs.

Perhaps he fell asleep.

Maybe an hour later, the door opened and Sophie stood framed in the doorway. "I've spoken with Fremont. You're free to go."

Raveaux stood up, feeling every day of his almost forty years, and a few decades more. He staggered a little, and shut his eyes. "Migraine," he said. "Got to get somewhere to rest."

Sophie hurried over, lifting one of his arms over her shoulder and sliding an arm around his waist to support him. She was three inches shorter, just the right height for him to lean on, and he felt her sturdy strength as they made their way out and into a hall lit with flickering fluorescent bulbs that made Raveaux cover his eyes with his free hand, groaning.

She squeezed his side, almost a hug, and he felt her curves and the firmness of her hip and waist. If he hadn't been crippled by the migraine, he would have enjoyed it.

They got a rideshare back to the hotel, and Sophie didn't try to talk to him. She unlocked his room, helped him past the king-sized bed and seating area, and pushed him into the bathroom. "Take a shower. Where is your medication?"

Raveaux pointed to a plastic bottle on the table next to his bed. She headed toward it as he went into the bathroom.

Once inside, he stripped off his suit jacket, filthy and reeking of gunshot residue and blood. Raveaux tugged his dress shirt out of his trousers, unbuttoning it. Suddenly repulsed by the blood spatter ruining the crisp white fabric, he ripped the shirt off and tossed it into the corner. He stripped the shoes and socks off his feet and wadded them up, throwing them after the shirt, each movement explosive. He dropped his trousers, kicking them away.

He could feel tears, dried now to just a crust of salt, in the creases of his eyes. He didn't remember crying. Must have been when Pellman died. *Poor bastard . . .*

Sophie entered, holding two of the migraine pills in her hand and a glass of water.

Raveaux straightened to his full height, tightening his abs, and met her eyes.

She seemed oblivious to his state of undress, that he stood before her in nothing but his boxers. In spite of the fog of migraine pain and post-traumatic stress, he felt a twinge of disappointment. What would it take to get her to look at him? *Really* look at him?

But she *was* looking at him. Her warm brown eyes on his were compassionate. Kind. "Here. Take these." She held out the pills.

Good enough. *Kindness was all he could handle, anyway.*

Raveaux took the pills and threw them back with a gulp of water. He drained the liquid and handed her the glass. "Thank you."

He turned away and dropped his boxers. He walked forward into the frosted glass shower stall without looking back, and turned on the water.

CHAPTER THIRTY-ONE

Sophie: Day Six, Night

SOPHIE SAT on Raveaux's bed in the lotus position and stared at the bathroom door, listening to the sound of water running.

Raveaux was in rough shape. Hopefully the shower, medication, and some rest would help.

Detective Fremont, Pellman's young partner, had cynical dark eyes and an energetic manner. The young black man had grilled her thoroughly on who she was and all she knew about the case. She had seen no purpose in holding anything back, so had shared all she knew about the diamond heist and their mission in San Francisco. "Raveaux is my partner and works for Security Solutions. He didn't tell me about today's meeting, only that he had a contact he was going to reach out to." She'd showed her ID and shared her business and case information, and then had to wait while he verified everything.

It had seemed like forever, sitting at Pellman's cluttered desk, looking at his messy files and a few personal knickknacks, until Fremont and another detective verified her information and finally gave Sophie permission to take Raveaux home.

Sophie still had little idea of the precipitating incident that had killed Pellman and the diamond traffickers, and how events had come about—Fremont was good at asking her questions, but much less fair in providing her any intel in return. From what she could put together, Pellman had tracked Raveaux with a GPS after he deduced what Raveaux was doing, called Fremont for back up, and the two had walked into a meeting that was about to turn into a bloodbath.

She couldn't wait to give Raveaux a tongue-lashing for leaving her out of such a vital meeting—*not even telling her where he was going or what he was doing!*—but she didn't really have any justification for leaving him out of her trip to Bell's. She had broken into the apartment, and Bell had held her hostage with a Taser. Her field trip could well have devolved into bodily injury, too.

Who knew that pursuing a set of missing diamonds would prove so deadly?

The shower stopped.

Sophie tried not to imagine Raveaux's chiseled form as he stepped out of the shower, the water droplets rolling down his olive-tan skin.

It had taken all her willpower not to let him see that she noticed his body—but once he turned away and dropped his boxers, she'd enjoyed the view.

Raveaux had little body hair. Every muscle on his graceful frame was well-defined. His buttocks flexed like a pair of clenched fists as he walked. He was a human rapier, flexible, honed, and sharp.

And those haunted dark eyes! *The weariness, the pain* . . . She just wanted to pull him close. Make him forget.

Images of how to do that made her cheeks burn and her insides heat.

Raveaux opened the bathroom door, and started at the sight of her. He'd wrapped a fluffy white towel around his narrow hips. Clearly, he had not expected her to still be in the room.

Sophie kept her eyes firmly on his face. "Feeling any better? We need to talk."

"I know." He raised a hand to rub his eyes, grimacing. "Mind if I just put on a robe? I need to lie down. This medication is kicking my ass; it's strong stuff."

"Of course."

He went back into the bathroom. Sophie walked over to the wet bar in the corner of the room. "I'm in need of a glass of wine," she called. She rummaged in the little refrigerator. "There's some apple juice in here. Probably would be good for you to get a little bump in your blood sugar."

Raveaux had walked over to sit on the bed, wrapped in one of the hotel's robes. "Sounds good." His olive skin looked waxy against the bright white terry cloth. His eyes were both bright and too dark, his pupils tiny.

Sophie unscrewed the cap on the bottle of apple juice and held it out to him. "Drink it all. I'm calling for some food, too. You shouldn't take that kind of medicine on an empty stomach."

He nodded, then tipped back his head to drain the bottle of juice. She watched the flexing of his powerful throat, then turned away to peruse the menu on the side table. She picked up the phone and ordered room service, making her best choices for what she thought he'd like. She hung up the phone. "You'll have to take what you can get with the hotel food, Raveaux."

He sat, leaned forward, elbows on knees, a hand shading his eyes. He grunted. "I'm sure it's fine. Thanks for ordering. I can't think right now."

Sophie returned to the wet bar and opened one of the mini-bottles of white wine stocked in the refrigerator. She poured the beverage into a plastic glass, and returned to sit beside Raveaux on the bed. "Start talking."

She stiffened in surprise as Raveaux tipped over slowly until his head rested on her thigh. He drew his legs up on the bed beside her, his body curled and eloquent with silent pain. "Pellman died."

"I know." Sophie set the wine down on the side table. Her hand dropped to stroke the damp, dark curls away from his face. His eyes were closed, thick black lashes resting on high cheekbones, but his mouth was still tight. Sophie stroked the silver at his temples, enjoying the silky feel of his hair. Gradually, Raveaux's mouth relaxed, falling open. His breath came easier.

Finally, he spoke. "I asked him if he had any last words for anyone. Any messages that he wanted me to pass on. He said he had nothing but the job."

"That's terribly sad." She smoothed the feathered black line of Raveaux's brow. "I liked Pellman."

She didn't know what else to say. *Such a strange case.* Somehow, in the course of it, they'd encountered two lonely, single older people dying with no meaningful connections to anyone. Clearly, that had affected Raveaux—and if she were truthful, it haunted her too.

"I didn't know Pellman had planted a GPS in my messenger bag, and was tracking me. His partner pulled the bug out later and showed it to me... I was looking for the diamonds through my friend Kim Hoo, and we found them with Kramer, the fence."

Raveaux's story came out haltingly: he had met his contact, a confidential informant he had worked with many times over the years. Hoo had taken him to Kramer's apartment. Raveaux had positively identified one of the blue diamonds from the Finewell's heist. Things had been progressing with some bumps when Pellman and his partner's surprise arrival had precipitated the gunfight. "Pellman should have known better. He should have come with SWAT," Raveaux said.

"He couldn't have known he'd walk in on a group of heavily armed African diamond dealers," Sophie said. "Who would expect that in San Francisco?"

"Still. Pellman should have talked to me." Raveaux's mouth tightened, regret digging deep lines beside his lips. "Not just tagged and tracked me like that. I would have let him in on the meeting."

"No, you wouldn't have. You would have implicated your CI if you'd done so."

Raveaux stayed silent. A muscle ticked in his jaw. His eyelids twitched.

"You didn't expect it to be what it was." Sophie's fingers smoothed down Raveaux's cheek, stroking that corded muscle in his jaw. "It's no one's fault. These things happen when dealing with dangerous people. Besides, that raid may have cost Pellman his life, but those two cops took out four heavily armed men who likely did more crime than just deal in stolen diamonds. Not a bad way for Pellman to end his career." She moved her hand away from the tempting danger zone of Raveaux's mouth—*how she wanted to touch his lips! See them soften, feel their stern but sensuous shape . . .* she slid her fingers back into his hair, instead. "Perhaps Pellman died the way he wanted to—a hero, doing the job he loved. Not alone, in a hospital bed, from cancer."

Raveaux turned, his face pressing deep into her pelvis. His downward-facing arm came around, hugging her buttocks, as his topmost arm encircled her waist. He rubbed his face back and forth against her thigh, a deliberate, sensual gesture.

Sophie felt the heat of his touch, his need, all the way to her core.

She bent and kissed his head, filled with tenderness and arousal as Raveaux squeezed and caressed her, his arms powerful and his grip tight. She stroked his shoulder, tracing the hard round of his deltoid through the robe, caressing the line of his spine and over his abs.

He felt so good. It had been so long . . .

Raveaux made a sound, deep and half-swallowed, that expressed her feelings perfectly.

She needed this too.

The doorbell rang, a rude buzzing.

Sophie sprang up, dislodging Raveaux. "That must be room service. Let me go see."

"Saved by the bell," her friend Marcella's voice said in her mind, as Sophie hurried across the room. She checked through the peephole and verified the room service delivery. Sophie admitted the waiter pushing the white-covered cart, loaded with domed plates. She signed the room number to the check and tugged the cart further inside, dismissing the waiter.

She turned back, pulling the cart into the room. Her cheeks and chest still felt flushed with what had almost happened. She glanced over at the bed.

Raveaux had not moved—he lay face down in the rumpled bedclothes, his arms open, encircling the place where she'd been sitting.

Sophie left the cart and hurried over, a surge of alarm making her dizzy. "Pierre?" She had never said his first name before.

Breath puffed gently between his parted lips. His eyelids fluttered.

He was deeply asleep.

Sophie pushed Raveaux over onto his back. She slid a pillow under his head and tugged the comforter up and over him, tucking him in. "Guess it's not meant to be," she whispered, kissing his cheek. "Sleep well."

Sophie took her covered dish off the cart and sat down with it at the little table near the window. She ate, and she drank her wine, and she watched the man asleep in the bed.

Raveaux was getting to her.

It was a good thing she was going to see Connor on Phi Ni. She definitely needed to go; she needed to see the Ghost before things got any more complicated with her new partner.

CHAPTER THIRTY-TWO

Raveaux: Day Seven

DETECTIVE FREMONT CURLED his large brown hands around a thick china mug of coffee. The young detective had seated himself in the booth across from Sophie and Raveaux, and he took a sip of black brew. "I took your statement down at the station. Now I just want to have more of a discussion about this case, where it's going, and what you two plan to do next."

Raveaux had woken that morning to his phone ringing insistently —Fremont summoning him and Sophie to a meeting at Pellman's favorite coffee shop on the corner closest to their hotel. Getting up, he found himself clothed in a robe, wrapped in the comforter of his bed, with a single room service meal congealing on the cart and a used set of dishes left behind on the little table.

Sophie had been there, eaten, and left. He didn't remember much about any of it, except an impression of her in his arms.

Had something happened between them? A man could dream . . . and now, Raveaux wished he wasn't so conscious of the brush of Sophie's elbow against his in the booth. He rubbed his eyes, trying to clear them of the last of the effects of the migraine.

"We're happy to help any way we can," Sophie said. "What happened was a tragedy."

"Yes, it was. My partner's dead."

Raveaux looked up, and met Fremont's deep brown eyes. Grief and anger hid in the tightness at the corners.

Sophie moved, inching away from touching Raveaux. *Did she find him so repulsive?* He dimly remembered dropping his boxers and getting into the shower in front of her . . . He'd been so lost in headache pain his nakedness hadn't mattered . . . But upon waking up, he'd had the sense that some line had been crossed, and *damn*, he wished he could remember what exactly that line had been.

"I was working an angle yesterday that might or might not be related to the case," Sophie said. "While you gentlemen were caught up in that shootout, I was visiting a suspect—Elisa Bell, Samson's heir. Mel Samson, if you recall, is the woman who actually stole the gems from both Finewell's sites that we investigated. What you walked in on was the fence aspect of things, and unfortunately, all of those perps are dead now and no longer able answer any questions."

Fremont's eyes kindled with anger. His words fired like bullets. "Do you think I wanted my partner to die for some insurance company's useless rocks?" His hand was so large it engulfed his mug, his skin white at the knuckles with pressure as he squeezed. "Do you think Pellman would've walked into that mess if he'd had any idea what your partner was leading him into?"

"Excusez-moi." Raveaux lifted his hands in a surrender gesture. "I didn't mean to lead anyone anywhere. I was doing my own reconnaissance with my own confidential informant. I didn't even tell Sophie who I was with or where I was going, and that was because I didn't want anyone to be in danger besides myself. I was confident of my CI, Kim Hoo. We'd been in many a tough spot before, and he was a good talker." Raveaux shook his head. "But once I got a look at Kramer and his thugs, saw that the meet could easily go sideways, all I was focused on was getting evidence that those diamonds were from the heist, and getting out of there alive." Raveaux blew out a breath, remembering the feel of the gun muzzle at the back of his neck. "Pellman chose to plant a GPS on me and follow me to the meet after I carelessly let slip that I had a contact that might be able to track the diamonds' fence. That's on him."

The three were staring at each other in a strange sort of standoff when the waitress returned with her notepad—the same waitress that had waited on them the other morning, with Pellman. Her penciled brows rose. "Hey, Fremont. Where's Deke?"

Pellman's first name. Raveaux's gut hollowed as Fremont shook his head. "He's no longer with us, Alice."

The woman's doughy face drained of color, and she covered her mouth with a hand. "I need a minute," she whispered, and her shoes squeaked as she walked rapidly away.

Raveaux met Fremont's eyes squarely. "Detective Fremont, however the debacle came about, we are both very sorry about what happened to Pellman. He was a good man."

Fremont tipped his head, as if assessing the sincerity of Raveaux's words. "He was. I've had a little time to think about it since yesterday, and truthfully, it's how he would've wanted to go."

Raveaux glanced at Sophie, and she nodded. *He seemed to remember talking about it with her . . .* They must have discussed that last night.

Fremont looked down into his coffee cup. "What's done is done, but I need some direction to move forward with on this case. I'd like to solve it in his memory. Pellman was a bird-dog that way; he hated to give up on anything. I knew about that diamond heist at Finewell's, but Pellman never brought me in on it. Frankly, we had more serious fish to fry, and the loss had been covered by insurance. I was as surprised as anyone when he told me he had a fresh lead and that we were going after a possible fence."

"We intend to wrap up this case," Sophie said, leaning forward. "I have an angle that I mentioned to Pellman yesterday. As I told you, we'd identified Mel Samson, an assessor and curator for Finewell's, as the actual jewel thief. She died last week of an apparent suicide. I couldn't find a connection between Samson and Elisa Bell, but on my visit yesterday, Bell admitted that she was Samson's daughter, given up for adoption. She said she had sought out and found her mother seven years ago and they'd been in touch ever since."

Raveaux shot Sophie a glance—*she hadn't told him any of this!*

Sophie met Raveaux's narrowed gaze with earnest brown eyes. "Pierre, I didn't have time to catch you up with what I was doing while you were getting shot at, and then you were pretty out of it when I picked you up at the station, what with that migraine coming on."

She'd used his first name. Raveaux gave a brief nod—he remembered her picking him up, and that he'd been too far gone for further information to register.

Sophie turned back to address Fremont. "Elisa Bell claims to know little about her birth mother, though they were in touch monthly. She says she only met Samson in person once. That part of her story doesn't add up, because she was spying on Samson." Sophie took a sip of her tea, and continued. "I discovered Bell's existence and the Lambert Building in the first place, because she had a keylogger spyware program deployed on Sampson's computer, and was monitoring every keystroke that Samson made."

Fremont's brows rose in surprise. "Why?"

"We don't know that yet," Sophie said.

Raveaux picked up the thread. "Samson had claimed she worked with an unknown partner. She received instructions from this master thief. Someone told her what gems to steal, how to pull off the theft, and where to leave the stones for the fence to pick up. That same person also doctored the video surveillance to hide Samson's activities."

Fremont's gaze seemed to sharpen. "And you think this Bell woman is the master thief?"

"I wish it were that easy," Sophie said. "So far, I've found no evidence of that. I've studied Bell's background thoroughly, and nothing in her history indicates those types of skills. But she was, for some reason, monitoring Samson. We also have an email address that Samson supposedly used to communicate with the architect of the thefts, even though a tracker I planted on an email led us to Samson's address and her body. Because of that, we initially considered that Samson was operating alone, that the email address was something to slow us down or throw us off. And maybe that's all it was. But when I dug deeper into Samson's computer, I found the keylogger program. That led us to the Lambert building, and Samson's will led us to Bell. And Bell had a lot to gain by Samson's death."

"Sounds like we should pay Bell a visit," Fremont rumbled. "If we can ever get some breakfast." He looked around. "The waitress was a friend of Deke's. She seems to have abandoned us."

Sophie was obviously still thinking as she rubbed the scar on her cheek thoughtfully, gazing into the distance. "I left Bell with Detective Pellman's card," she said. "I told her someone from the SFPD needed to speak with her. She will be expecting some sort of visit."

"Just to play devil's advocate here, it's still possible that Samson stole the gems on her own," Raveaux said. "We uncovered motive for the thefts. Samson needed money for her cancer treatments, and the thefts began right around the time of her diagnosis."

Sophie nodded. "Bell denied knowing she was Samson's heir, but perhaps she did know something, and was monitoring Samson for her own reasons."

"Let's go pay Elisa Bell a visit," Fremont repeated. "I want to get eyes on this girl.".

A different waitress appeared, holding her notepad and pen ready. "Alice needed to take a break. I'm here to take your order. What can I get you?"

Fremont looked across at Raveaux first, then Sophie. "I don't know about you, but I've lost my appetite."

Sophie nodded. "I'm not hungry."

Raveaux took a ten-dollar bill out of his wallet and handed it to the waitress. "For your trouble and our use of the table. We have to be somewhere else."

CHAPTER THIRTY-THREE

Sophie: Day Seven

SOPHIE HAD TRIED the phone number Fremont had located for Bell to no avail. Now she stood in front of the door to the woman's apartment in the Lambert Building with Raveaux to her left, and Fremont to her right. She raised her hand and knocked.

No answer.

She knocked again.

Still no answer.

"She didn't answer the door when I was here last, either," Sophie said.

Raveaux shot her a look from under dark brows. "Then how did you end up meeting with her?"

Sophie was saved from having to answer by Fremont pounding on the door. Fremont's deep voice boomed in the hallway along with the thud of his fist. "Elisa Bell! Open up! This is Detective Fremont from the San Francisco Police!"

Still no response.

Fremont cupped his ear in an exaggerated way. "I think I hear someone calling for help from inside. We need to go in and render assistance." He stepped back and cocked his leg to kick the door in, but Sophie held up a hand.

"Let's not add insult to injury by ruining her door." Sophie dug in her waist pack and lifted out her lockpicks. "She's probably hiding inside, like yesterday."

Raveaux's lips tightened in that almost-smile. "Ah, now we know how you two ended up meeting."

Sophie soon had the door open. She gave it a gentle push.

The entry area looked just as before: the lamp was lit next to the ruby-red couch. The door to the bathroom was ajar, and the light was on inside. Sophie stepped through the doorway, the men behind her. "Elisa? It's Sophie Smithson. From the insurance company. You met with me yesterday. We thought we heard you call out for help."

No answer.

Sophie turned to look over her shoulder at Raveaux. "Close the door. She has a cat."

Raveaux did so. Fremont passed Sophie, prowling the room. "Total chick apartment."

"Since Bell's not here, we can just take a look around and leave," Sophie said. "And you can pretend you didn't see me make a copy of her computer's hard drive, which I'm going to do. I guess I don't need to tell you both not to touch anything."

Sophie walked into the bedroom, and stopped with a little gasp. "Gentlemen? I think she's on the run."

The closet door hung open, a light on inside shining down on empty hangers dangling awry. A pile of discarded clothing and books lay on the floor. A dresser drawer hung open like an empty mouth, an abandoned pink nightgown hanging out like a tongue.

Fremont's brow creased. "Why would she run? Maybe she's just visiting a relative or something."

Sophie put her hands on her hips. "Occam's razor. The simplest explanation is usually the right one. She fled because she had something to hide."

"But she just learned her mother died. Perhaps she went to visit someone . . ." Raveaux swiveled, looking into the bathroom. "She emptied her cabinet here, too."

"Does this look like what you do when you go for a short jaunt?" Sophie gestured to the piles of clothes, the emptied desk. "This looks to me like what you do when you activate your go bag."

"Go bag?" Raveaux's brow knit.

"Means you grab your fake passport and pre-packed essentials, and head for the hills," Fremont said.

"Something about your visit definitely spooked her," Raveaux said.

"Or, she's grief stricken and grabbed a few things to go visit a friend, or a villa in Cancun," Fremont insisted. "I'm not sold on this woman as anything but a bystander."

Sophie bit her lip on any further arguments. "My instinct is saying different, but let's just try to find her first. If she had a laptop, look for it. If she had an extra phone, or a safe, let me know. I'm going to milk this computer she left behind for anything it's got." Sophie hooked up her write blocker and enabled it as the two men prowled through the apartment, paper towels on their hands to avoid leaving fingerprints.

"No sign of an extra phone or laptop, and the wall safe, located behind the painting in the living room, was left open. It's empty," Raveaux reported, a few minutes later.

"She didn't try to hide that she left in a hurry," Fremont said. "I want a list of all her known contacts. Friends, relatives, colleagues from work . . ."

"We are not your deputies," Raveaux said. "We have a client we answer to. Finewell's may, or may not, be interested in Bell and where she went. We have to call them and let them know that we have confirmation that the diamonds were fenced, and that some of them are now in evidence as part of a murder case. It might well be enough for them that the breach to their firm has been blocked, with the death of Samson."

Sophie looked up from the data extraction she had underway, catching Fremont's eye. "I already did a lot of legwork on Bell's background. I'm happy to share that information with you, limited as it is. I will send it over on email. I had already noticed that Bell appeared to have lived a very isolated life, so I'm not sure how helpful it will be. In fact . . . I suspect if we dig far enough, we might find that Bell isn't her real name."

Both men turned to stare at her.

Sophie shrugged. "I would have told you if I had found anything more definitive than a suspicion. I have not. Bell's identity held up to the closer inspection I already gave it. But like I said, there's a good chance this isn't her only identity. If she is the master thief, then she may have more than one." An idea bloomed in Sophie's mind. "Perhaps I can lure her out."

Fremont closed the drawer he'd been peeking into. "Why don't we go our separate ways. You go back to your hotel and round up that information, send me that email, and I'll call in a BOLO for Bell, get her picture circulating at all the public transpo, including airports. And if you find a way to flush her out, give me a call."

SOPHIE SETTLED into a chair at the desk, sipping from her tea flask as she got down to business with Bell's copied hard drive. She had dismissed Raveaux to find them some takeaway food; she wanted to dig into that computer immediately and see what she could find.

An attempt had been made to erase the drive; some kind of random fragmentation program had been run on the machine. Sophie reeled back the clock on the drive, downloading a program that could rescue a previous version. Sure enough, an earlier backup had been saved only a week ago, and Bell hadn't taken time to make sure that all of her backups had been deleted.

Sophie shunted the older drive into DAVID and ran a search on

Bell's name and all the business and personal keywords she'd already uncovered, including her birthday, first jobs and hobbies, and school graduations. As the information began to scroll down, filling one of DAVID's "caches," Sophie gasped.

What she knew about Bell was only the beginning.

CHAPTER THIRTY-FOUR

Sophie: Day Nine

SOPHIE GLANCED around the very public venue Elisa Bell had chosen for their meeting: the Music Concourse in San Francisco's Golden Gate Park. She sat on a stone bench facing the large central fountain and the Academy of Arts building; directly behind her, the famous de Young Museum trumpeted its latest art exhibit.

Laid out in a cross shape, four concrete entrance paths led to the central fountain area. A stone-flagged performance bandshell anchored one end, and statuary and trees filled the interior of the segments laid out around the fountain.

The plane and Scotch elm trees of the Concourse stood rock-steady, their heavily-pruned and pollarded branches held aloft like gnarled arms; but their leaves, in shades of scarlet, ochre, yellow and brown, trembled and released from their moorings on a brisk gust of wind, and swirled around Sophie's legs.

She'd dressed carefully for her part as the insurance investigation agent for a major company, wearing comfortable black stretch pants, a sweater in an amber color that brought out the color of her eyes, and carrying her faithful calfskin briefcase. She tugged her thin jacket tighter, grateful for the neck protection of a fall-toned scarf she'd bought to brighten up her outfit.

Elisa Bell approached from the south end of the park. Her short, angled black bob gleamed in the sunshine peeking through last of the morning's fog. Bell wore a short skirt with boots that came to her knees over tights, and a large, multicolored shawl draped artfully around her shoulders. A pair of wraparound sunglasses obscured her eyes and a slash of red lipstick brightened her mouth. She could have been any elegantly dressed San Francisco sophisticate, here at the Concourse to browse the Park on her lunch break from some high-powered job.

But she was here, now, in response to Sophie's carefully-worded email.

Sophie moved a little further to the right, making room as Bell eyed the bench she sat on. "I don't bite," Sophie said, patting the slatted wood, making sure both hands were visible.

Bell perched on the bench, one arm clamped over a bulging black Coach bag, the other concealed beneath her shawl. "You said you had knowledge of an additional inheritance from my mother."

"I did say that, didn't I?" Sophie smiled. "Yes. My company contacted me about an additional life insurance policy you stand to benefit from. Your mother, Melanie Samson, who we spoke of before, made you the beneficiary."

"You didn't mention it when you broke into my apartment last time."

"I didn't because I didn't know at that time." Sophie lifted her briefcase onto her knees. "Fidelity Mutual has updated me since. We just need you to sign some forms to submit your claim. It's lucky for you I was still in town when I got the memo; sometimes these things take months." Sophie fussed with the briefcase's brass clasps. "Did that detective ever talk with you?"

"No." Bell frowned. "I went out of town. The news of my mother's death hit me hard."

"I don't believe you." Sophie drew her weapon from within the case and shut it with a snap. She held her own police-issue Taser on Bell. "About Mel Samson's death hitting you hard."

Bell stood up, clutching her bulky Coach purse like a life preserver. "You're an insurance agent. Insurance agents don't tase people."

Sophie smiled, but it held little warmth. "I am no more an insurance agent than you are Mel Samson's daughter." The abandoned computer had been a gold mine for Sophie. "You used the publicly recorded death of Samson's daughter as a starting point, and Samson was just one of your marks. You reached out to her, impersonating her child, of course never telling her that her real child had died. You appeared in her life at just the right time and preyed on her guilt, getting her to steal to pay for treatment, and yet planning to inherit everything from her in the end. You're a grifter, a con artist." Sophie spat on Bell's shiny, high-heeled black boots. "Shame on you, preying on a dying woman's hopes and dreams."

"Bitch," Bell snarled. She whirled to run, but Raveaux stepped out from behind one of the trees, blocking her path, his arms spread.

"Pardon, Mademoiselle. Stay with us, please."

Bell bolted in the other direction, and slammed into Fremont's sturdy chest. "I'll take this, thank you." He grabbed for the bag. "I'm sure it contains a few missing diamonds."

"No!" Bell kicked Fremont in the shin with her pointy-toed boot. Fremont howled but kept hold of the bag. Bell tossed off her wrap and brought up the hand she'd kept concealed, and shot Fremont with her Taser. The man fell, twitching. She wrested the bag from the cop's nerveless fingers and fled.

Sophie leaped after Bell. She brought up her own Taser, and shot the woman from behind. The prongs nailed Bell between the shoulder blades and she slammed to the ground, spasming on the concrete not far from Fremont.

Raveaux put his hands on his hips. "You knew Bell had that Taser under her shawl, and you didn't want to get shot with it. Nice move, Sophie." Raveaux was smiling, and damn if that man didn't have a set of dimples.

She'd made Raveaux smile at last.

Sophie savored the sight of his grin, smiling right back. "Fremont will get credit for Bell's capture, and he will have earned it." She leaned over and detached the prongs of Bell's weapon from the detective's shirt front. "He'll be fine. Grab his cuffs and restrain her. I'll check the bag and see if she's carrying any of the stolen gems."

Sophie upended the purse on the bench as Raveaux put the restraints on a still unconscious Bell.

The bag contained, along with sunglasses, lipstick, tissues, a bottle of pain reliever, and other contents common to women's purses, a bulky Ziploc bag of rubber banded cash and several passports.

No diamonds.

Bell had to have kept some. She seemed like the type . . . Sophie flipped the bag to and fro, turned it inside out, stroking the seams. She felt a nubbin of something, an odd shape in the lining. She picked at the handsewn seam, and found a small locker key as Fremont moaned, curling onto his side and holding his head as he sat up. Sophie palmed the key and slipped it into her pocket.

She replaced Bell's items in the bag and set it in Fremont's lap as the man continued to groan. "Here. This ought to make you feel better. All you need to put Bell away is right here."

CHAPTER THIRTY-FIVE

Sophie: Day Ten

Sᴏᴘʜɪᴇ ᴡᴀʟᴋᴇᴅ into the exclusive women-only gym dressed for the occasion in spandex workout shorts and a black Lycra running bra, her zip front nylon parka open to expose her tight abs. She'd told Raveaux she was going to a gym, blowing off steam from their take-down and the lengthy police station interviews that had taken up the rest of that day . . . but instead, she was tracking down the key's origin.

Sophie strode confidently to the fitness center's reception desk, the key a tiny weight in one pocket of her parka. "Hi. I called an hour ago about trying your gym out for a membership?"

The blonde, ponytailed receptionist swept Sophie's physique with a glance and met her eyes with a welcoming smile. "Oh yes, Ms. Smithson. I'm happy to give you a quick tour of the facilities and let you use them for a complimentary workout."

Half an hour later, Sophie stood in the locker room, hands on her hips, and looked for Bell's locker. She'd scanned the key, then hacked into a proprietary FBI database of key types and manufacturers. From there, it had been a simple matter to match the key's type to a membership Bell had at the posh gym.

Sophie checked that the room was empty, and approached Bell's locker. She slid the key into the lock, turned it, and opened it.

A red canvas bag hung from the hook at the top. Bell's gym shoes rested on the floor of the locker with a deodorizer sachet in each. Sophie took out the bag, carried it to one of the bathroom stalls, and searched it quickly as other women came and went.

Nothing but a clean towel, a change of clothes, and some toiletries. The seams of the bag held no further hidden treasure.

Sophie waited for the locker room to clear once more, then searched the inside of the metal locker for any irregularities. *Nothing.*

That left the shoes.

Sophie took out the cloth sachets and felt inside, pulling up the insole, exploring the toes. *Nothing.*

Sophie palpated the sachets as she slid them back into the toes of the shoes, and felt several hard lumps inside. Rather than search now, she slid the sachets into her pocket and re-locked the locker. She walked over to her own locker assigned for the day, took off the parka, and hung it up inside, locking it securely.

She might as well get that free workout since she was here. She headed for the weight room.

BACK AT HER HOTEL ROOM, Sophie dumped the scented sawdust filling from the sachets out onto a clean white hotel towel. She smiled, smoothing the dust away from several large, glittering diamonds. *One from each heist, most likely.*

She plucked the stones out and rinsed them under the tap. They glittered from her palm, each of them several carats in weight, the blue one from the San Francisco job an exquisite teardrop the color of a peacock's breast.

She had ruined the chain of evidence by taking the key and tracking down these diamonds, but Fremont wouldn't need the stones to make his case against Bell—he had plenty else to work with. Not only that, Finewell's would never miss them—they'd already been compensated by insurance for their loss.

She had hunted down these stones to right a different wrong.

Sophie wrapped the diamonds in tissue and slid them back into the cloth sachet bag she'd found them in. She inserted that into a padded postal mailer. She printed a note from her computer onto plain white paper via the hotel's office station:

This donation of genuine diamonds is made anonymously to the American Cancer Society in memory of Melanie Samson and Detective Deke Pellman. Please sell them, and use the funds to further research into the treatment of cancer."

Sophie sealed the envelope, zipped up her parka for modesty, and rode down in the elevator. She left the mailer, with a ten-dollar tip, at the front desk to go out with that day's post.

Sophie took the stairs on her way back up. She and Raveaux were planning to meet for a quick meal on the way to the airport, and she still had to shower, change and pack.

The Ghost wasn't the only one who could mete out a little justice.

CHAPTER THIRTY-SIX

Raveaux: Day Eleven

SEATED in the corporate conference room back on Oahu, Kendall Bix was well-dressed by Hawaii standards in khakis and a short sleeved linen button-down. His dark hair was short and gelled; he was freshly shaven. Bix was the one who had hired Raveaux, and the man's careful grooming had been a contributing factor in Raveaux's decision to work for Security Solutions. An operations director who cared enough to pay attention to his appearance would also pay attention to workplace protocols. So far that had been true.

"I have your final reports, and I'm submitting billing to Finewell's," Bix said to Raveaux and Sophie, seated on either side of him at the company's long koa wood conference table. "The client expanded from just Mr. Childer to the corporation of Finewell's, as you two connected the dots on their breaches. They seemed very pleased with your work, and they're a good client to have." He made a hand gesture that encompassed both Sophie and Raveaux. "You two make a good team."

Sophie inclined her head. She wore her usual simple, elegant black, and her dense, shoulder-length curls were swirled into a knot atop her head. Pearls the size of cherries dangled on their tiny chains from her ears, and red lipstick emphasized the lush curves of her mouth. "I spoke with the Executive Vice President in charge of the San Francisco branch of Finewell's. He was pleased with our discretion, and with the fact that we were able to plug the leak permanently without any further information reaching the public. I hope they will use us for jobs in the future." She indicated Raveaux. "Your background and connections proved most helpful . . . even if a little complicated by that shootout."

"I regret the death of my confidential informant, and the fact that none of the diamond dealer's men survived long enough to be interviewed," Raveaux said. "But I have other contacts in the high-end art and antiques market that we can tap should we have need in the future."

"You both will have to be available for more questioning regarding the investigation into Kramer's operation," Bix said. "Since that connects to their investigation, I can do a supplemental billing to Finewell's to cover any expenses that would ensue."

"I'm taking a week off, Bix. I'm going to Thailand," Sophie said. "You may give my private number to any detectives who follow up and need to speak with me."

Raveaux felt a pang—*he'd hoped to ask her to dinner again*. He caught her eye. "Seeing family?"

"You could say that." She addressed Bix. "When I get back, I want to discuss a slight reorganization of the company's management structure. I'd like to take a more active role in investigations, and hand off more of the administration duties to you. I'm sure a job title change and a raise will be involved."

Bix's brows lifted. "What brought this on?"

"Even though I initiated proceedings to have Sheldon Hamilton declared dead, I kept hoping he would return. I was keeping things going for him." Sophie shook her head in a gesture that was both thoughtful and sad. She raised warm brown eyes to meet Raveaux's gaze. "But I know Sheldon's not coming back, and life is short. We met people on this investigation that reminded us of that."

Raveaux nodded. "Yes. Sometimes the most important things you learn on a case are not written in the report."

Bix glanced back and forth between them. "Like what?"

"Like, if you have a chance at love, you should take it." Sophie stood. "Well, gentlemen, if that's all, I have to pack."

Bix gathered his things and took his leave. Raveaux lingered in the doorway, waiting for Sophie to close up her laptop and join him.

"I enjoyed working with you." A tightness in his chest and throat closed off Raveaux's ability to ask her for a date. He cleared his throat, trying to get his vocal cords to work.

Sophie's smile infused her beautiful face with vivacity. "We will do it again. Soon, I hope."

Raveaux inhaled the faint scent of coconut oil infused with jasmine as she passed him, and he shut his eyes to savor it.

CHAPTER THIRTY-SEVEN

Sophie: Day Thirteen

SOPHIE WALKED down the short flight of steps off of the corporate jet where it had landed on the short runway that paved Connor's private island of Phi Ni. She paused on the tarmac to take in the waving palms and the peaceful turquoise Andaman Sea, lapping gently against the white sand beach that rimmed the island. The light breeze that kept the island cool was calming with approaching evening, and she enjoyed the sight of the dazzling clouds reflected on the water's surface.

She stifled a stab of guilt that Momi was still on Kaua`i. Her daughter had long since recovered from her flu bug, and she would be here soon enough. Sophie had made arrangements for Armita and Momi to be flown out in a couple of days . . . *after she had met with Connor.*

They deserved privacy for this meeting.

He had texted that he was arriving a few hours after Sophie was, by boat, and her pulse picked up at the thought.

Nam, Connor's faithful houseman, drove up to meet her in the estate's pick-up truck. Nam inclined his head in that dignified way he had, a smile lifting his seamed cheeks, his dark eyes bright. He spoke to her in Thai, and the sound of her native language caressed her ears. "Welcome, Mistress Sophie. Yindī t̂xnrạb nāy Sofī."

"So good to see you as well, Nam," she replied in the same language, as she set her tightly packed tote into the truck bed and got into the cab with its familiar smell of clove cigarettes.

"When is Little Bean coming?" Momi's nickname persisted with those close to them.

"In a few days. You will find my child much changed when she arrives with Armita. She will make you old before your time, like she's doing to us."

"I could never be anything but pleased to see my Little Bean." Nam put the truck in gear, and they trundled off the airstrip. Glancing at him, Sophie couldn't help being reminded of another favorite retainer of Connor's—Thom Tang. Thom had been Connor's driver, pilot, and also a friend.

Thom was one of the men massacred by her mother. *She would always miss him, and feel responsible for his death . . .*

"The master arrives soon, but we are ready for both of you," Nam said. They turned onto the crushed coral road, leaving the jet already wheeling around to return to Hawaii. "We have been looking forward to your visit for a long time."

"It *has* been too long since I've come. Thank you." Sophie didn't try to converse further with the generally quiet houseman. Instead, she feasted her eyes on the details of an island that had come to feel like a long-lost home: groves of coconut trees, grown in some previous owner's agricultural attempt, surrounded a sheltered aquamarine bay containing the island's boathouse. The drive they followed, its crushed, white coral surface gleaming brightly in the sun, wound through rock outcroppings and heat tolerant palms, bushes, and grasses toward the rise at one end of the island where Connor's mansion had been built.

Nam parked, and Sophie got out of the truck and walked around a large utilitarian storage barn past gracious tropical plantings. She ascended wide stone steps leading up onto the house's veranda. The building, a perfect blend of east and west, clung to the edge of a bluff overlooking the sea, and she looked forward to the views she'd see out of its huge double-paned glass windows.

"It feels good to be back." Sophie rubbed the head of one of a pair of bronze lions guarding the entry. Nam preceded her, opening the large double doors for her to enter.

He held her bag aloft and cleared his throat delicately. "Would you like me to put this in the master's suite?"

Sophie's eyes widened. "No. The guest area will be fine. Where I usually stay." *What had Connor told Nam, that he'd think they might be sleeping together?* Her heart raced, and it was as much apprehension as excitement.

Sophie settled into her familiar guest suite, and made a quick call to Armita. A video of Momi taking a nap and a detailed description of the day's activities satisfied her maternal cravings. "I'll see you both very soon. I can't wait."

She unpacked and, nervous about meeting Connor, primped a little. She rubbed her favorite scented coconut oil into her skin, enjoying the way her pores had opened in the heat and humidity. Her whole being seemed to be softening in the tropics, a relief from chilly San Francisco. She changed into a lightweight silk wrap dress and a pair of sandals.

She drove the truck back down the hill and past the palm orchard's stately rows, toward the boathouse. She kept the vehicle's windows down, enjoying the warm breeze and the liquid song of native shama thrushes in the underbrush, as the long shadows of evening deepened the rich colors of the island.

She pulled up at the large covered building that had been the site of much drama the last time she'd been on Phi Ni. The door of the boathouse was unlocked, and swung wide easily on oiled hinges. She stepped into the cool dim of the boathouse.

The Chris-Craft she'd become intimately familiar with two years ago rocked gently at its mooring, fine woodwork squeaking against the rubber edge of the dock. Nam had retrieved the beautiful motor launch from the tiny atoll where she had left it after her adventure to the Thai mainland. He'd kept the boat stored up out of the water until recently—he'd reviewed workers' bills via email for the restoration of the hulls and brass, and given it a thorough cleaning in anticipation of her and Connor's visit.

The island, the house, the boat—everything was hers now, but Sophie continued to feel as if she were just holding it in trust.

As if she had conjured his return, she heard the thrum of an approaching boat engine. *Connor was here.*

Sophie hit the big red button controlling the automatic door facing the ocean. The aluminum barrier rose, rattling, from its setting several feet above the level of the sea, rotating upward into the roof of the boathouse like a giant garage door.

What kind of craft would he be piloting? Would he be surrounded by ninjas, or would he be alone?

And most of all . . . would he still want her? Did she still want him?

Connor came into view, driving a fishing boat. He stood alone behind the wheel, wearing a woven bamboo hat and simple fisherman's clothes. The skin visible beneath the shade of the hat and at his wrists was so tanned that he could pass as a Thai, but she'd recognize the set of his shoulders anywhere.

Sophie stood quietly, observing, as he piloted the boat into the cavernous space and cut the motor. "Hey, Sophie," he said, as casual as if he'd just seen her last week.

"Connor. You're here at last." She caught the rope he tossed her and snuggled the nose of the weathered aluminum craft against the dock, directly across from the magnificent Chris-Craft. She gestured to the motor launch. "Quite a step down from what you left behind."

"Doesn't matter." Connor leapt onto the dock with a movement so fluid that he seemed to float from inside the fishing boat to land on the balls of his feet on the dock, with hardly a sound or a vibration. He walked toward her, lifting the coolie-style hat off and drop-

228

ping it to dangle from a cord around his neck. His sea-blue eyes seemed to glow in his tan face. He grasped her shoulders and pulled her into a tight hug. "You're what matters." His voice was husky with emotion.

Sophie stood stiffly. His unfamiliarity, her long celibacy, just the fact that it had been so long since she'd been touched at all, stiffened her spine and set up alarms.

He released her and took a step back. "I'm sorry. I didn't mean to scare you."

"You don't scare me." And he didn't—but that quick invasion of her space still did. *Damn Assan Ang . . .* Sometimes months went by when she didn't even remember her sadistic ex.

Connor stood perfectly still, his gaze on her face as she took him in. She lifted a hand, reaching out to cup the chiseled corner of his jaw. The bone felt warm and solid under her hand, and she caressed his cheek with her thumb. His skin was smooth, freshly shaven. His eyes, up close, held secrets and depths, as well as all the colors of the ocean.

"You've changed." Her tone was accusing, and she tried to modify it. "I thought I knew you. Now I'm not sure any more."

"You've changed too. Motherhood agrees with you, Sophie."

His voice felt like a caress, but still . . . she felt disembodied, unable to reach him.

She stepped closer. "Kiss me."

He made no move, so she slid her hand from his jaw around to the back of his neck, feeling the shorn velvet of his short blond hair, stroking it with her fingers. She drew him closer, into her space, tipped her head up and finally, closed her eyes.

Their mouths touched, held. Opened and tasted. Their arms curled around each other, stroking and touching.

Sophie waited for the magic. For the *zing*, for the surge of unstoppable passion she remembered with Jake.

She waited for that hot coiling in her lower belly, for that sense of crackling fire searing up her spine and along her veins, for that wild urge to lose herself in someone else—for the passion locked inside her to rise and take over.

But nothing happened.

She floated above the scene, looking down at two physically beautiful people kissing and embracing . . . And she felt nothing.

Sophie let it go on a while, and then she stepped back, sliding her hands down his arms to squeeze his hands. They felt as hard and strong as carved wood, completely unfamiliar. She turned them over, recognizing only their general shape in the mass of nicks, scars, callouses and sun damage altering their appearance. *All those hours with weapons each day . . .*

Connor had remade himself into someone she no longer recognized.

"You're not feeling it." Connor's voice was cool, detached. "Very interesting. Neither am I."

They stared at each other for another long moment.

"I want this to work." Tears filled Sophie's eyes and she squeezed his hands as hard as she could, desperate for him to feel her urgency, her sincerity. "Maybe we just need more time. Time to get used to each other, to get to know each other again . . ." Grief constricted her chest. *Was this really her life?* A single mother who had had a chance with three wonderful men, and now had no one?

She flung herself on Connor, desperate to break through the deadness between them. She kissed him feverishly, her hands sliding over his taut, hard body, her mouth tearing at his until she tasted blood mixed with the salt of tears pouring out of her eyes.

He stood, his arms at his sides, and let her batter at him.

She gave up and dropped her face to his shoulder. She let the tears come, sobbing freely. Only then did his arms come up around her, stroking her spine, squeezing her gently.

"Too much has happened, and you love another," he said in her ear. "As for me, you're the only woman I've ever cared for, but we've both changed. Moved on. And it's all right. We will always be friends, and partners as much as you want to be in the pursuit of justice."

Sophie sobbed harder, letting go of a dream that had sustained her through the grief of losing Jake. "I didn't know I loved him this much," she sobbed. "I don't want to love him so much. I want to love *you*."

He gave a little snort of laughter that almost sounded like the old Connor. "Sorry, babe, that's not how it works. Come on, let's go up to the house. I'm ready to get drunk and have Nam wait on my every wish. The Yām Khûmkạn compound is not exactly vacationland, you know."

CHAPTER THIRTY-EIGHT

Sophie: Day Twenty

CONNOR OPENED the door of Sophie's suite, entering with Momi in his wake. "Mama!" Momi yelled with her usual loud enthusiasm, and ran in to embrace Sophie's legs.

Sophie and Armita had been packing, and Sophie swept the toddler up into her arms, blowing a raspberry onto her daughter's tender, sweet-smelling neck. Momi giggled, her sturdy little body arching back in Sophie's arms. Armita bustled in the background, continuing to pack for the trio's return to Hawaii.

"She ate a good breakfast and gave the dogs some heck already," Connor reported. "Didn't you, sweetie?"

"We go walk, Unco!" Momi bellowed. She called all adult males "uncle" and women "auntie" in the way of Hawaiian children.

"We sure did." Connor grinned, his hands on his hips. "I'm going to miss you, Bean." Even Connor still used Momi's pet nickname.

Momi and Armita had arrived as scheduled for their visit with the two dogs in tow, and the five of them had spent a blissful time on Phi Ni, playing in the ocean, walking the beach and making sandcastles, and eating delicious, fresh food made by Nam and his wife.

Connor had been with them much more than Sophie expected, spending little time in his computer cave, and they had fallen into the rhythm of their old friendship. There would always be something deeper between them, but in spite of continued proximity and even a few more attempts at physical intimacy, the spark was gone.

"I'll get the rest of our laundry," Armita said, and left the room.

Connor stepped up to Sophie, still holding Momi, and embraced both of them. Momi laughed, grabbing his ear, and Sophie leaned into their threesome, chuckling too as she enjoyed the strength of his arms around them.

"In a way, this simplifies things," Connor told her. "We can just get together for vacations out here, or if we're working a case together."

Sophie set Momi down and the toddler ran to the open suitcase holding her toys, and began taking them out. "As we discussed earlier, I'm going to be handing the CEO role off to Bix and taking a more active role doing investigations. But I don't know how you mean for us to work cases together, with you a wanted man."

"I didn't mean cases that were on the books," Connor said, and she flicked her gaze to meet his inscrutable one.

"You plan to go back to that . . . online thing you did?" She didn't want to speak aloud of his Ghost vigilante activities, even just in front of a toddler.

"Already on it. Now that I have access to the computer lab at the compound, I'm assuming the reins for that organization's online presence. There will definitely be situations for us to pursue together. I hope you will want to take that step and be my United States contact."

Sophie tightened her mouth. "I'll think about it."

Growing bored with her toy unpacking, Momi ran back to Connor and slammed into his leg so hard he grunted. "Unco Connor! Up, up!"

Connor tossed Momi effortlessly up into the air, so high she almost touched the ceiling, then caught her under the armpits. Momi shrieked with delight, but Sophie's heart stuttered. As many times as he did that, and as addicted as Momi was to his active play, Sophie still gasped—though in the time they'd shared at the house, he'd shown her some of his physical mastery. He seemed able to bend physical space to his will.

More worrisome to Sophie than Connor's extraordinary abilities was how Momi seemed to be developing into an adrenaline junkie. Fearless and impulsive, the toddler loved nothing more than climbing and launching off of anything raised, and Connor, Sophie, Armita, and even the dogs were constantly trying to keep her away from the cliff's edge. Nam had spent the week overseeing the building of a fence to ensure her safety, and to combat a fear of Momi drowning they'd begun teaching the toddler to swim.

Soon they'd finished the whirlwind of packing. Nam drove the pickup with their baggage and the dogs, loaded in their carriers, in back of it, while Connor drove the women in his rugged SUV down to the airstrip.

The Security Solutions jet already awaited them, and Connor pulled a billed sports cap down, avoiding contact with the pilot and crew. He and Nam helped them with the luggage and the dogs, and with settling in on board. Amid Momi's desolate shrieks as Connor said goodbye, Sophie followed him back down the jet's steps and over into the shadow cast by his SUV to say goodbye. "Thank you for coming all this way to visit. I needed this," he said, hugging her close. "When can you come again?"

"I don't know. Got a lot of changes to implement. But it won't be long. Nam's cooking is already on my mind," Sophie said.

"Mine too." Connor kissed her on the nose. "Wish something else had happened here."

"Me too." She leaned her head on his chest for a moment, sighing.

"Something will work out for you," he said.

"And for you?" She raised her head to look into his sea-colored eyes.

"Probably not. I'm married to my work, and she's a brutal mistress."

She punched his shoulder. "Glad I don't have to compete with her, then."

"Travel safe. I'll be in touch." He hopped into the SUV, and she waved as he and Nam pulled away in their vehicles. She hurried up the steps of the jet as the engines warmed up, and settled into her seat next to Momi, with Armita on the other side.

"Where Unco Connor?" Momi piped, straining to see around Sophie toward the doorway. "I want Unco Connor!"

"Uncle Connor will meet us here again," Sophie said, tucking her blanket around her daughter. "We'll be back to see him and Uncle Nam soon."

Tired from her tantrum and busy antics of the morning, Momi soon fell asleep. Armita extended her seat into a lounger and took a well-deserved nap, and Sophie unpacked her laptop. She booted up her neglected email and weeded through various profit and loss reports, and finally slept.

MOMI WAS fussy and the dogs were rambunctious when they finally arrived mid-morning in Hawaii and got home to the Pendragon Arches apartment. "Take the dogs and Momi for a run," Armita told Sophie. "I need some peace and quiet to unpack and get us some fresh food."

"Yes, ma'am," Sophie said. "We know who the boss is around here." That made Armita smile, and Sophie was glad to see it as she put Momi into the jogging stroller and the dogs on their leashes.

She'd signed Ginger up for extra training at the boarding kennel she'd been at while Sophie worked the case in San Francisco, and Connor had helped work with the energetic Labrador while they were on the island. Ginger, though wagging her thick tail excessively, no longer pulled and tugged at the leash, and Sophie was able to manage both dogs and the stroller getting onto the elevator with only a little maneuvering.

Outside the building, jogging down the sidewalk in the sunshine with Anubis on one side and Ginger on the other, Sophie felt her spirits rise as she approached the ocean. She'd worn her bathing suit under her running clothes, and packed Momi's pink swimwear in the backpack that held their beach essentials.

She might be alone, but she didn't have time to be lonely. Her life was full, and rich, and really rather wonderful.

Once they'd swum in the ocean, she tied the dogs loosely to a tree, and they flopped in the shade. Sophie and Momi rinsed off in the park showers. Sophie rolled out her towel, and settled on it to read on her phone, with Momi playing in the sand nearby with a pail and shovel.

The phone buzzed in her hand with an incoming call, and Sophie blinked in surprise at the sight of the caller's name. "Jake?"

"Hey, Sophie." His voice was low, hoarse.

Sophie gripped the edge of her towel. Her heart rate leaped into overdrive. She rolled onto her side to keep Momi in visual range. "What's up?"

"I need to see you."

Her spine tingled with alarm. "What's going on? Is someone hurt?"

"No, no." Jake made a sound that was almost a laugh. "Sorry if I scared you. I just . . . I don't know how to make this call."

"I don't understand." Sophie massaged her throat, trying to calm her galloping heart, trying to strengthen her voice. "Is it . . . Ginger? I assure you, she's fine. She's adjusting well. She and Anubis love being together. I don't want to give her back."

"No, it's not Ginger. Damn it. I'm making a hash of this." He blew out a breath. "I need to talk to you. For personal reasons."

Sophie's pulse pounded. She reached out a hand to stroke her daughter's warm, soft black curls, grounding herself. Momi muttered some internal narrative and flung a spadeful of sand gleefully toward the dogs, then jumped up and ran toward them, spade aloft in one fat fist.

Sophie sat up on her towel and put her free hand over the left side of her chest and massaged, willing her heart to settle into a regular rhythm. "Please, Jake. Just tell me. What's this about?"

"I have to tell you in person."

A tiny flare of something Sophie couldn't name burst into heat under her sternum. Her voice was satisfyingly cool even if her skin felt on fire. "Well, then, I guess we have to meet."

"That's all I'm asking for. Just a little of your time."

"I'm not sure what purpose that would serve, honestly. Unless this is about work. Bix told me you were doing some contract work for us again." She felt herself stiffening, her voice going wooden and flat, her old defense mechanisms kicking into place. *Stop it, Sophie. You just realized you still love him. He's reaching out. Just see where it goes.* "But since you insist . . ."

"I'm here in Honolulu. Want to meet tonight at that noodle place you used to like?"

Sophie remembered the tiny hole-in-the-wall restaurant near Waikiki. She used to eat there all the time; now it had been years. "Yes, of course. Momi will be down by seven, so I'll meet you there at seven thirty." She ended the call with a punch of her thumb—*she had to keep the upper hand, somehow!*

She glanced over at her sandy toddler. Momi had climbed up onto Ginger's prone body, and now was dumping sand onto the Lab with her shovel. "Momi! No!"

As she hurried over to rescue the Lab, she was glad she'd be too busy to obsess on what he wanted to talk about until she finally got her daughter into bed.

SOPHIE DRESSED for dinner with Jake in her usual black work outfit after getting Momi down to sleep fifteen minutes early. She didn't want to seem overeager, so she left makeup off, too, except for a bit of red lip stain.

"I'm off for my meeting. She's down," she told Armita as she passed through the living room, where her nanny was doing yoga while watching the news. "I'll be back in a couple of hours."

"Take all the time you need." Armita waved, and Sophie wiggled her fingers back as she shut the door of the apartment.

It wasn't so much that Armita disapproved of Sophie dating; it was more that she didn't understand Sophie's desire to even try to have a relationship. Romantic entanglements were an irrelevant distraction, and men were overgrown children. "You already have a toddler, Sophie," she'd said the last time Sophie went on a date. "Why would you want another?"

It was easier just to tell her nothing, and Armita didn't expect anything more, anyway.

The Waikiki noodle house looked exactly the same as the last time Sophie had been there. She stepped inside the restaurant to the familiar rattle of the row of beads across the glass door. The deep single room with its long, battered wooden counter and barstools along one wall and row of booths on the other, filled her with a sense of homecoming—as did the rich scent of savory broth, the clash of utensils, and chatter in a plethora of languages.

Sophie was ensconced at a corner booth with her back against the wall, nursing a cup of green tea, when Jake walked in.

She vividly remembered the day she'd brought him here to meet her friend Marcella for the first time: the way he'd entered and so effortlessly dominated the room, the way he seemed to radiate heat and light, his own self-contained sun.

That sun was dimmed in the man walking toward her now.

His eyes were the color of ash. Dark shadows hung beneath them; his thick shoulders sagged in wrinkled clothing. Comb tracks in his short dark hair and the familiar smell of his lemony aftershave told her he'd cleaned up, likely from the gym if his pumped-up fore-arms were anything to go by.

Jake slid into the booth opposite her. "This place hasn't changed a bit."

"There's something comforting in that. I get tired of everything changing all the time." Sophie sipped her tea. "I ordered saimin with everything on it for you."

"That sounds good."

They stared at each other for a long moment. Jake rested his big hands on the table's surface, flexing them restlessly. He dropped his eyes, and she missed seeing them.

"You asked for this meeting," Sophie said.

"You look beautiful." He shook his head. "But then, you always do."

"And you look tired, Jake. What's going on?"

He sighed. "California isn't working. Felicia and I aren't working."

Sophie set the small, handleless teacup down so he wouldn't see her hand tremble. "What do you mean?"

"She dumped me. Said I wasn't . . . there for her."

"I'm hardly the person to give you relationship advice." The arrival of their large, steaming bowls of noodles provided a welcome distraction.

Silence reigned for a stretch of time, filled only with the sounds involved with eating a lot of slippery noodles in a fragrant broth redolent with meat and vegetables. Jake finished first, pushing his bowl away with a muffled belch, patting his belly. "That was just what the doctor ordered."

Sophie smiled at him over the rim of her large plastic spoon. "You always did like noodles as a comfort food." She poured more tea into her small cup, and picked it up to occupy her hands. "It's time you came to the point about why you asked to talk with me."

"Felicia thinks I'm still in love with you." Jake's eyes heated to the color of warm steel as they met hers. "She said she's not wasting any more of her best reproductive years on a guy who can't commit because he's hung up on someone else."

"Felicia is a smart woman. I always liked her." Sophie's heart beat with slow, heavy thuds that seemed to echo in her ears. "But how is this my problem? *You* dumped *me* two years ago."

She set down the teacup, and Jake reached across the table and took one of her hands. "I'm sorry. For being such a total dick. I wouldn't listen to you. I was wrong."

"That you were." A smile tugged at Sophie's mouth. "A huge dick. With purple pustules on it, *you big hairy son of a yak.*"

"Hey. Keep the insults in English, please, so I can continue to grovel properly."

"You dumped me, and you stole our office manager and ran off with her and started your own company and you . . . broke my heart." Sophie's eyes filled. "I was so alone." She pulled her hand away, clutching a napkin, dabbing her eyes.

"No, not the crying. No fair." He whisked a tear from her cheek with the ball of his thumb. "And you weren't alone! In fact, I couldn't get a minute of your time even before Momi was born. After you got her back, you had your baby, and that battle-axe ninja nanny of yours, and don't forget Alika, whisking you all away to his mansion. I felt like . . . what did I have to give you? I was broken by what happened in the compound. I thought Connor was my friend . . . and I thought you were with him behind my back." Jake shook his head. "It's taken me all this time to realize it wasn't all about me. Felicia was the one to help me see that."

"Like I said. Felicia's a smart woman. You should try to win her back." The tears wouldn't stop coming. "She's good for you. I'm not."

"Bullshit on that last part. Are you dating anyone?"

The part of her that was terrified of opening herself to more pain wanted to say yes, and Raveaux's face flickered briefly across her mind's eye. *She'd have dated him if he'd asked . . .* "No. Though I'm not without possibilities."

"Of course, you have possibilities." Jake picked up her hand again, and stroked his thumb across the callus at the base of her fingers. That *zing* that she'd been unable to spark with Connor zipped up her spine and back down, lighting her nerve endings along the way. "I suspect you always will have possibilities, and that I won't always know what they are or who they are. I couldn't live with that before." He lifted her hand and kissed the tips of her fingers, then held it in both of his. His heat and strength warmed her. "I've . . . matured, I guess you could say. At least, I hope so." He sighed, shook his head a little. "My sister Patty tried to tell me this years ago, and I wish I'd listened. Could have saved us all a world of hurt. Here's the thing: sometimes, things are a mixed bag. Not all evasions are lies . . . and some lies are necessary. Like who Connor is."

"He refuses to lie about himself anymore," Sophie said. "He can never leave the shelter of the Yām Khûmkạn, now that you outed him to the authorities."

"Then you two are in touch," Jake said carefully.

"We met on Phi Ni for a week. I just got back." Sophie tightened her grip on his hands as he tried to withdraw them. "Connor and I aren't together. We're just friends." She met his gaze, and drew a breath for courage. "You're not the only one still in love with someone else."

The waiter returned to clear away their bowls. The moment the man was gone, Jake tugged on her hands. "Come here. Next to me."

Sophie tightened her lips, shook her head. "No. I'm afraid . . ."

"Fine." He stood up and maneuvered to her side of the booth, sliding in and looping an arm around her. He shifted her up onto his lap and wrapped his arms around her as if she were dainty and small, not a well-muscled woman of five foot nine.

"This." He sighed against her nape, relaxing into her even as she sagged into him. "I've missed this. You." He nuzzled her neck.

"I've missed you, too," Sophie whispered. She shut her eyes to close out the embarrassment of such a public display in a booth not built to accommodate it, even as she smiled. This wasn't the first time Jake had manhandled her onto his lap in a booth in a restaurant.

She hadn't been this warm in more than two years.

It felt so good to be surrounded by his arms, his familiar strength, and to feel his breath stirring the hairs on her neck, his heart thumping against her back.

Jake felt like home.

Where did they go from here? How? What came next? Were they a couple now?

She didn't need to know the answers. It was enough just to be in this moment with him, and that was the truth.

Turn the page for a sneak peek of, *Wired Ghost*, Paradise Crime Thrillers book 11.

SNEAK PEEK
WIRED GHOST, PARADISE CRIME THRILLERS BOOK 11

Sophie
Day one, two weeks after the end of Wired Truth

LOOKING for a runaway teen living with meth cookers, especially during a massive volcanic eruption, was probably not a good idea.

But it was too late now. They were committed.

Sophie Smithson grabbed the sissy strap to stabilize herself as the Security Solutions SUV, driven by her partner, Jake Dunn, bumped across a black rock plain on the Big Island. Their client, Ki Ayabe, an import business owner, had hired Security Solutions to locate and retrieve his seventeen-year-old daughter Lia, who'd supposedly run off with a meth cooker named Finn O'Brien "to shame and anger me," Ayabe had declared. Sophie hadn't liked the pompous, sharp-tempered Japanese man, but his tale of an out-of-control teen being taken advantage of by an older drug dealer was compelling.

"Weird set of directions," Jake frowned, peering through the windshield to scan the empty black plain, made mysterious by a heavy mist of volcanic emissions. "Not much out here."

Sophie tapped the navigation app on her phone. "There are no road signs to the *kipuka* where the meth lab is located. Natural formations and GPS coordinates were the best our informant could do. Thankfully, there's a track we can follow." *Kipukas,* small, raised "islands" of old growth trees, bushes, and wildlife, surrounded by fields of raw, new lava, were a phenomenon unique to the Big Island.

Jake flexed his large hands on the wheel. "We've got a big chuckhole ahead."

The white Ford Escape wasn't really built for the terrain of their current route, and Sophie clung to the dash, as well as the strap, as the vehicle bucked through the stony rut. She glanced at Jake. "You sure you aren't missing your easy California life installing alarm systems?"

"You know I hated that," Jake grinned, a flash of white teeth. "Thanks for getting me back on the Security Solutions payroll. It was a relief to let Felicia buy me out of the business." Jake had recently gone through a breakup with his girlfriend/business partner, and relocated to Oahu to be with Sophie. They were taking it slow, just beginning to date again, and this was their first job together in more than two years.

"The case looked interesting. A chance to get away from Oahu with my boyfriend." They hit a particularly deep hole, and Sophie yelped as her head banged the door frame, swearing in Thai. *"Daughter of a rabid jackal!"*

"Sorry." Jake wrestled the wheel, slowing them further. "This is a bit rugged, but it's an adventure. And the end of your month with Momi is always a good time to be distracted."

"Exactly what I was thinking." Sophie stabilized herself with a hand on the dash. "Ginger and Anubis love all the socialization they'll get with other dogs at the boarding kennel while we're gone. And I always try to fill my schedule when I have to send Momi back to Kaua`i." Sophie's two-year-old daughter was currently with her biological father, Alika Wolcott, and nanny, Armita, in their unusual custody arrangement of one month on, one month off. While always a hard adjustment for Sophie when Momi and Armita left, the situation gave her time to work active cases in the field. When her daughter and Armita were with her, Sophie did administrative tasks in the office. Her child seemed to take the changes of venue in stride, with the consistency of care that Armita maintained by accompanying Momi back and forth between homes.

Jake slowed the SUV further and crawled the vehicle over a mound of rock. "I don't like the seismic reports we've been seeing the last few days for Kilauea Volcano."

"There *have* been a lot of micro-earthquakes reported lately. But the eruption at Kilauea has been steady since the 1980's. There is no reason to assume there's going to be any new lava flows in this area," Sophie said. "The main danger we have to watch out for is the emissions. The gases can be quite toxic, but they're only present around the areas with fresh activity. According to my source, this *kipuka* is where the meth lab is hidden. I had to call in a favor to get this intel, but hopefully it's here, and saves us a lot of time."

"Still. It's too bad the wind is coming from the south and pushing in all this vog," Jake said. "Visibility is so much better when it's blowing out to sea."

The vog blanketed the plain in a soft, gray shroud. The sun glared acid yellow through the particulate gases and hurt Sophie's eyes, adding to a spooky feeling as they moved through the rough terrain. She slid on a pair of mirrored sunglasses as they reached a flat area marked by several rusted out vehicles.

"I think this is the end of the road," Sophie said.

Jake already had his hand on his weapon as he guided the SUV into a turn. "I'm positioning us for a quick getaway."

"Good idea." Sophie jumped out of the Ford and covered them visually with her Glock, as Jake maneuvered the vehicle into position pointed back the way they'd come. She saw no one, but that didn't mean they weren't being watched.

Jake checked his weapon, ejecting the magazine and then ramming it back into the grip. Sophie had gotten used to her Glock 19 police issue pistol during her FBI years. They both wore body armor under camo fatigues done in a gray, brownish-black and slate blue pattern that Sophie hoped would help blend with the surroundings.

Sophie headed for a rough path visible between the junked cars and checked her GPS again. "This track is heading in the direction of the coordinates. We're on the right path."

They moved out, Sophie in front, Jake at her back.

"What's the plan? Arrive, guns blazing, grab the girl, and haul her back to her father, tucked under my arm?" Jake asked.

"Like I told you back at the office, I don't really know. You're the extraction specialist." Sophie slanted a glance over her shoulder at Jake. "I still remember that from your business card when I first met you."

"And I remember being sandbagged by how gorgeous you were in that skimpy red top when you first met me at your door," Jake said.

"That was my sleep outfit. I wasn't expecting you."

"All the more unforgettable."

Sophie smiled, but kept scanning the barren lava for hostiles.

Yes, she and Jake were reconnecting and taking it slow, but that didn't mean they didn't have a history—an intense one that had been blossoming until Momi's kidnapping as a newborn, when the circumstances around that devastating event had torn them apart.

Sophie continued to watch carefully as they trekked through the vog along the stony, uneven trail worn onto the raw lava surface. "All we really know about the case is that Lia is supposed to be with this guy Finn O'Brien. He's an undocumented Irishman who supposedly came to the Big Island on vacation, and outstayed his visa. The man found a way to make an illegal living out here, and has gathered a close team of scoundrels and rogues to help him with that."

"Scoundrels and rogues?"

"If the adjective fits . . ."

"I think we should be prepared for resistance, beginning with our target. Lia's a minor, but she's not likely to want to come back to daddy because, although Ayabe won't admit it, she basically ran away. O'Brien's a meth cooker and dealer with a record and not much to lose. Let's recon their camp first, then pull back and figure out a plan. We might need reinforcements."

"Just what I was going to suggest." Sophie flashed her smile at him. The last wisps of her depression, easily activated when her daughter was gone, had been dispelled by the upcoming action.

"Would you mind if I moved out in front?" Jake raised his brows, steel-gray eyes serious.

"Not at all. I was wondering how long you'd be able to hang back," Sophie said. "I wasn't joking when I said I relied on your Special Ops background in situations like this."

"Thanks." He kissed her as he passed by, a quick touch on the lips that lit her nerve endings.

Yes, she had a boyfriend in Jake—but the jury was still out on whether they would make it. So much had happened between them, and others. . . *like Connor*. Now the de facto leader of a clandestine spy organization with its roots in guarding Thailand's royal family, her former lover known as the Ghost continued to practice his unique brand of cyber justice, and through that organization he now commanded an army of ninjas. He wanted her to help him with his "mission," and though Sophie had dabbled in equalizing the scales of justice, she wasn't ready to commit to anything more.

Maybe this time with Jake would show her a new direction—and meanwhile, his rear view wasn't hard to look at. She suppressed a grin.

They reached a fork in the trail. Jake stopped. "You've got the GPS. Which way do we go?"

Continue reading *Wired Ghost*: tobyneal.net/WGwb

ACKNOWLEDGMENTS

Dear Readers!

Mahalo for joining me on Sophie's latest adventure!

I confess, these characters continue to surprise and challenge me. I really, truly thought we were done with Jake! I had a whole other plan, and I said goodbye to him in the last book and put the period on it when he returned Ginger at the beginning of this one.

But as the book went on, though I love Raveaux (and I hope you do too, and he's going to be around complicating things) and though I love Connor (and I hope you do too, and he also has a major role in coming events), Sophie just wasn't going along with my new plan for her romantic life. She pined, and rebelled, and truth to tell (since this book is all about truth) I missed Jake on the page. His fiery passion, his bigger than life boldness, his impulsivity and courage, his black and white thinking . . . he brought energy and random twists to the story. He brought a SPARK, that *zing,* even if I didn't always like who he was—and in the end, sensible Felicia dumped his ass, as she should have.

He is just in love with Sophie, and she with him, come what may for both of them—and who am I to fight the kind of chemistry they have?

The truth is, I don't always like these characters. What they do. Who they are. Pim Wat, for instance. I love to hate her as much as you do, and the fact that the Master has had some grand scheme for her and is executing it? Well, my plan was to leave her in Guantánamo to rot, but he had other plans, and talk about a twisted and intense love . . . that's what Pim Wat and the Master got goin' on, and I guess we're in for some more adventures with them down the road.

Here's the thing: when you're a writer, you think, "this is the one tiny bit of the universe I can control. I can play God here: kill people, make them fall in love, orchestrate seasons and wars and time . . ." but that's not actually true, if you want to have any fun at all with this mysterious calling. Stephen King says that stories pre-exist, and we writers just uncover them "like fossils." Psychologist Carl Jung agrees. In his explanation of the mind, he posits that we collectively create "leitmotifs" which are heroic stories of the human experience that transcend cultures and are universal.

Sometimes, when I'm writing, I completely believe that.

Other times, I'm sure I know what's best for my characters and story.

But the truth is, I'm happiest when I trust the people on the page, let them reveal what they've come to show us, and get out of the way.

I hope you'll join me again for *Wired Ghost*, Paradise Crime Thriller #11, as Sophie's story continues! But before that happens... I'm working on a new Lei book, *Razor Rocks*!

Yeah, I know, the Paradise Crime Mystery series had a perfect ending with *Bitter Feast*, book 12, and I was done with them, yada yada.

But didn't I just get done telling you some stories are bigger than our plans, and some characters have a life and mind of their own? Lei, Stevens, Pono and their families wanted back into the world, so I'm hard at work on *Razor Rocks*, Paradise Crime Mysteries #13. You can read a sneak peek of the new book, a killer mystery involving PIRATES!

If you're not familiar with the Paradise Crime Mysteries, you're in for a treat! Get started with #1, *Blood Orchids*, and discover Lei Texeira and her dog Keiki, the amazing pair that brought Sophie to life in book 4 of their series. Happy reading!

And if you enjoyed *Wired Truth*, **please leave a review**. They mean more than you will ever know, and are the best gift a writer can receive.

Much aloha,

Toby Neal

FREE BOOKS

Join my mystery and romance lists and receive free, full-length, award-winning ebooks of *Torch Ginger & Somewhere on St. Thomas* as welcome gifts: tobyneal.net/TNNews

TOBY'S BOOKSHELF

PARADISE CRIME SERIES

Paradise Crime Mysteries
Blood Orchids

Torch Ginger

Black Jasmine

Broken Ferns

Twisted Vine

Shattered Palms

Dark Lava

Fire Beach

Rip Tides

Bone Hook

Red Rain

Bitter Feast

Razor Rocks

Wrong Turn

Shark Cove

Coming 2021

Paradise Crime Mysteries Novella
Clipped Wings

Paradise Crime Mystery
Special Agent Marcella Scott
Stolen in Paradise

Paradise Crime Suspense Mysteries
Unsound

Paradise Crime Thrillers
Wired In
Wired Rogue
Wired Hard
Wired Dark
Wired Dawn
Wired Justice
Wired Secret
Wired Fear
Wired Courage
Wired Truth
Wired Ghost
Wired Strong
Wired Revenge
Coming 2021

ROMANCES
Toby Jane

The Somewhere Series
Somewhere on St. Thomas
Somewhere in the City
Somewhere in California

The Somewhere Series
Secret Billionaire Romance

Somewhere in Wine Country
Somewhere in Montana
Date TBA
Somewhere in San Francisco
Date TBA

A Second Chance Hawaii Romance

Somewhere on Maui

Co-Authored Romance Thrillers
The Scorch Series

Scorch Road
Cinder Road
Smoke Road
Burnt Road
Flame Road
Smolder Road

YOUNG ADULT

Standalone

Island Fire

NONFICTION
TW Neal

Memoir

Freckled
Open Road

ABOUT THE AUTHOR

Kirkus Reviews calls Neal's writing, *"persistently riveting. Masterly."*

Award-winning, USA Today bestselling social worker turned author Toby Neal grew up on the island of Kaua`i in Hawaii. Neal is a mental health therapist, a career that has informed the depth and complexity of the characters in her stories. Neal's mysteries and thrillers explore the crimes and issues of Hawaii from the bottom of the ocean to the top of volcanoes. Fans call her stories, *"Immersive, addicting, and the next best thing to being there."*

Neal also pens romance, romantic thrillers, and writes memoir/non-fiction under TW Neal.

Visit tobyneal.net for more ways to stay in touch!
or
Join my Facebook readers group, *Friends Who Like Toby Neal Books,* for special giveaways and perks.

Made in the USA
Las Vegas, NV
19 April 2022

47717199R00156